Marked By Forever

Beller Ties Book 4

Lee Dawna

LeeDawna Books, Inc.

First edition

Cover design by Premade Ebook Cover Shop

www.premadeebookcovershop.com

ISBN 978-1-949192-14-8 (paperback)

ISBN 978-1-949192-13-1 (ebook)

ISBN 978-1-949192-15-5 (audiobook)

Published by LeeDawna Books

https://leedawnabooks.com

leedawnabooks@gmail.com

~

This book is dedicated to Jill——and her alter ego Angela.

~

~|~

To this day, I don't recall the whole of what happened that night. All I ever remember with clarity is copper-brown hair framing emerald eyes, and plump pink lips dangerously close to mine. One second, Lily was leaning over my shoulder to examine the file of the patient I'd seen outside the clinic earlier in the day. In the very next instant, her fingers were trailing along my arm, her scent flowing over me like a heady fog. I turned toward the heavenly aroma, the hair on my body standing on end as the sixteen-year-old locked eyes with me, desire burning between us with an intensity that begged me to devour her.

I stayed in that tidal wave of desire for too long. Drowning as it crashed over me, suffocating beneath the swell until the agonizing truth of what I was doing broke through the tempest. I was a twenty-eight-year-old man *desperate* to claim the mouth of a too-young girl. One I'd known her entire life.

The day Lily Beller was born, I was twelve, a gangly boy sitting on the edge of her parents' bed as her daddy's big hands lifted a tiny red-faced bundle from the birthing pool. Before that day, I'd already known that I would follow in my father's footsteps and become a doctor. Being part of Lily's remarkable birth solidified my decision to also work in the medical practice Dad spent his whole life building. Few doctors get to experience the range of circumstances that come with being a concierge who caters to the whims of the wealthy, and fewer still get to do that while also operating a clinic that serves the general public.

I worked hard to earn the right to be Dad's partner at Mansfield Clinic. Then, in moments that stopped time itself, I looked into eyes as green as spring grass and watched all of my ambition go up in smoke.

My fall from being a near replica of the father I idolized to being an in-house doctor at a hospital that's too big to put patient care above money, was five years ago. And I'm no more capable of controlling myself around Lily now than I was back then. A debilitating truth that surged through my chest like debris stuck in a tornado when she walked into Pemberton Medical last week and straight up to my med-surg floor. At twenty-one, Lily is even more beautiful than the memory I've spent every day of the last five years trying to forget.

"Doc, we hittin' up the gym later?" Jeremy asks as he passes by on his way to draw blood from one of my patients.

I peel my eyes from the nurses' station where I've been glaring at Lily and her perfect little button nose. I don't need her in my physical proximity to know how that nose sits perfectly above the curve of her lips. My brain has played her face on a loop, tugging on every rotten place inside me, every day of the last five years. "Sure, Jeremy. If you're not going to wimp out halfway through the workout again."

"I didn't wimp out," he scoffs. "I got tired of hearing you complain about the lovely Nurse Beller. So what if she left a coffee cup sitting on the desk? Jill caught it and tossed it out before anything got spilled."

I shove my pen into the pocket of my jacket. Even at Lily's now *legal* age, as the daughter of Dad's wealthiest clients, she remains forbidden fruit. Not that she'd want me even if she wasn't. I'll always be twelve years older than her and there's nothing either of us can do about that. But I *can* make her life miserable until she goes back to the rehab center she's been working at. After all, leaving is the least she can do for me since the last time someone ran away, it was me. "Rules are in place for a reason, and no nurse should have to clean up after another just because one of them is carelessly leaving *open* containers sitting out where they're not supposed to have *any* food or drink."

Jeremy smacks his lips, eyes flashing like a strobe as he looks past me to where Lily is. "I'm not even single and *I'm* forgiving her for *anything* she does."

I follow his gaze to where Lily is bending over to retrieve a pen that rolled off the cart next to her, her copper hair falling over her shoulder like a curtain of thick silk. I take hold of the pen from my own pocket again, as if touching the exact same type of thing that Lily is touching somehow connects us.

Grinding my teeth, I stuff the pen back into my pocket, ripping a hole through the center of the fabric and letting loose a curse I'm not proud of. Jeremy cocks a brow. "You okay, Darren?"

No. I'm not remotely okay. Of all the clinics and hospitals in this world, why does Lily have to keep showing up in mine? The girl doesn't even need to work. Yet every member of her family does, and Lily is particularly gifted in her chosen profession because she not only could memorize entire books at the ripe old age of four, but as a teen she interned with my dad, being his shadow the way I was once his shadow.

I was a little surprised when she settled on becoming a registered nurse instead of going to medical school. She would have made it through as easily as I did. Or made it look so easy I'd feel like more of a chump than I already do. My only saving grace in this situation is that she works a late shift and I work days, so our paths only cross for a matter of hours. "Doc?" Jeremy nudges me.

I blink my eyes away from where Lily is placing the pen back onto the pushcart that everyone refers to as a *cow*. "Lily is an adult."

He chuckles. "So are you. I think. But you might have a little something right..."

He reaches for the corner of my mouth and I bat his hand away. "I'm saying that Lily is old enough to be responsible for her actions and trained enough to know that actions have consequences. If she wants to flit about being irresponsible, she needs to pick a profession outside of the medical field."

His voice deepens an octave, trying to imitate mine. "So her million-watt smile isn't enough to melt the ice from around the Terminator's cold heart? That's a shame, because the attitude you copped when that beautiful creature strolled down this hall for the first time seemed like something you needed to lie on a couch to talk about. Or at her feet. Either would probably work."

Frustration claws at my gut. I met Jeremy the first day I started at Pemberton, back when I already had a good amount of muscle on my body. He was much the same and we started working out together. But the only reason I now look like an overgrown ape and he doesn't is *Lily*. These last five years have been brutal and the only thing that silences the call of desires I *shouldn't* feel is exhausting my physical body until it forces my mind to shut down. "Jeremy, just go get me that bloodwork."

He nods toward where I know Lily is, but I force myself to keep my focus trained on him. He wiggles his brows. "Pemberton might *strongly* discourage dating co-workers, but there aren't any actual rules against it."

I fold my oversized arms across my chest, tense muscles threatening the seams of my shirt. "Lily Beller is too young for both of us, and you're married. Bloodwork. Now."

He shrugs. "I was just saying––"

"Bloodwork!"

"Fine," he grumbles, walking away mumbling about *Dr. Terminator* being in a mood.

"Mansfield," I correct. "That's Dr. Mansfield to you, Jeremy."

I haven't shared any of my struggles with him because I'd prefer not to go to prison. I may be at the end of the statute of limitations but if Lily's family found out that I was physical with her when she was sixteen, laws wouldn't save me. I'd be in jail...or dead. And I'd prefer the latter because in admitting to taking advantage of one teenager, I'd destroy what's left of my career. In the process, I break what's left of my dad's heart––having already let him down when I broke all the promises I ever made to him and left Mansfield Clinic.

I couldn't tell him the real reason—that I was fleeing from the presence of his too-young mentee so neither of them would be robbed of that experience simply because I was a lust-filled monster. It was Lily who put her lips on mine first, but I was the adult, so I accepted the consequences and gave up on every dream I ever had. A choice that came easily when I nearly wrapped Lily's body around me three days after I'd untangled from it the first time. All it took was her standing next to me, fingers trailing softly over my bicep again. So while Pemberton Medical might not be remotely fulfilling, it's what I have. Lily doesn't get to come into this hospital and turn me into a sick little drooling puppy who can't see what lines he's crossing because he's blinded by the shine coming off of her copper hair. Lily is leaving Pemberton. Even if I have to force her out.

Jeremy dips into a patient's room and I turn in the opposite direction, making my way to the nurses' station, or the *fishbowl* as the nurses call it. It's round and in the center of an open space halfway down the main hallway. Jill, one of the registered nurses who started on this floor a couple of years ago, looks up with a bright smile. I give her a nod, the toe of my shoe slamming against the outside of the desk when Lily pops up from the floor behind Jill, another pen in her hand. "How many pens are you going to drop today?" I grumble to cover how startled I am by her sudden appearance.

Lily gives the pen to Jill. "I've dropped zero. But I've picked up quite a few. Why? Are we supposed to leave dropped pens on the floor in your hospital?"

Her nippy tone stokes my anger. I didn't see her leave the cup of coffee on the desk but after Kassidy told me about it, I confronted Lily. She's been snotty ever since. "If you have a problem following rules, maybe you should find another job. I'm sure the rehabilitation center you were working for hasn't filled your position yet, you might be able to get your old job back."

She reaches across the top of the counter and tugs my pen through the rip in my pocket. "My shift is ending so you're going to want to watch out for all the pens on the floor. But if they trip you up, don't worry, I'll put in a good word for you at the rehabilitation center. I'm pretty sure my old job will suit you."

Jill shoots up from her stool, eyes wide and cheeks flushed. "Lily is so funny, isn't she? But enough of that. Did you need something, Doctor?"

I force my eyes from Lily's challenging gaze. It makes me want to rip this counter from between us and make her regret looking at me that way. In a thousand indecent ways.

I grind my focus into Jill's striking blue eyes. They're set in satin skin and framed by diamond-blonde waves. She's a bombshell, and the opposite of Lily in every possible way. "Yes, Jill," I answer her honestly. "I do need something. You. Will you have dinner with me tonight?"

~2~

Thanks to excessive parkour and calisthenics training, I can practically leap small buildings in a single bound. But I can't sever the connection my body insists on having to Lily. She's a virus written into my genetic material and short of having a lobotomy, I'm doomed to keep having knee-jerk reactions every time my eyes land on her ethereal face. Yes, Jill is an age-appropriate and beautiful woman, but I have absolutely no interest in taking her on a date. Yet in the presence of Lily Beller, the invitation to Jill rolled off my tongue with disturbing ease.

I've told myself that I asked Jill out to prove to *Jeremy* that I'm not attracted to Lily, but the truth is that I did it in hopes that it would bother Lily. As if she cares about me. In the days following the ruinous night in my office at Mansfield Clinic, she only spoke to me once, her touch as soft as my name whispered from her lips. I refused to even look at her and afterward, she acted as if nothing had happened. As if nothing had changed between us when for me, every single cell in my body had morphed. I haven't been the same person since.

My identity was tied to the plan I'd discussed with my dad from the time I was a small boy. I wanted so badly to mold myself in his likeness, to become a husband, father, and doctor with the same compassion he modeled for me every day. But I'll never be a man as great as him. I'm no longer his shadow, his partner, his protégé... I'm no one. Certainly not a predator. Before or since Lily, I've never had an attraction to anyone underage. Honestly, I was never much attracted to women before the night Lily obliterated my impulse control. I was always too driven, my aspirations keeping me too occupied to date. Since *that* night, it's only been Lily. Always Lily.

I run a hand down my face and knock on the door of the Tudor-style house Jill shares with her fraternal twin. Emelia Alice designs jewelry, and I recall overhearing Jill telling some of the other nurses about how the entire upper level of the home belongs to her sister, mainly serving as a studio and workshop space for the jewelry business, with a bedroom suite off to one side. I've met Emelia Alice a few times when she's stopped by the hospital to see Jill, so I recognize her as the rustic door opens. "Good to see you again, Emelia Alice. Is Jill ready?"

Emelia Alice sweeps her hand across the threshold, inviting me in with amusement tinging her voice. "She's almost ready. Even though you asked her out without planning where you were going to take her *out* to."

I move past Emelia Alice and off to the side, not really wanting to sit down in the living room while I wait because *asking* Jill on this date was much easier than actually going through with it. It didn't even occur to me that I didn't make a dinner reservation until an hour ago when Jill messaged to ask where we were going so she could *dress appropriately*. "Yeah, I put the cart before the horse with this one, so thanks for making the reservation for us."

Emelia Alice runs her hand over my bicep, an annoyance I'm unfortunately used to. Women are always trying to get their fingers all the way around it even though it's apparent that it's a lost cause, even with two hands. I shift away from her, trying to politely let her know that it's rude to feel a man up just because you think his muscles are a challenge for your fingers.

She grins at me. "I booked you two at the new brewery in town. I hear it's fantastic. And lucky for you, they had a table available on short notice."

I nod, feeling more awkward than I did that time in junior high when Mom forced me to go to a school dance with the daughter of a friend of hers. "Thanks, I really do appreciate you taking care of that for me."

Emelia Alice sashays to the couch, sitting and crossing her legs, her eyes watching me expectantly. "What would you have done if I couldn't find you a nice place to take my sister? Junk food from some drive-through? Or did you plan to offer to cook for her at *your* place?"

I give her a lighthearted smile, careful not to let her push this conversation past the already uncomfortable bounds. "All I really know how to cook are protein shakes and sides of beef, so you'll never hear me offer to host dinner at my place."

She laughs, hair swaying as her head shakes. Her hair is longer than Jill's and two shades darker. She's also a little shorter and rail-thin, but she has the same piercing blue eyes and light skin. Every time I've seen her, she's been poised and polished, not a hair out of place or a nail chipped. Tonight is no exception. But it's my age-appropriate date who is stealing the show. Jill emerges from a room on my left, stunning in a silver dress that hits slightly above her knee and dips a little below her collarbone. Everything in between is sleek and trim. She smiles at me. "I bet I could show you how to open a jar of spaghetti sauce and boil some noodles. *If* we ever find ourselves without a reservation again."

Emelia Alice makes a clicking noise with her tongue. "Since I'm the one who showed *you* how to boil noodles, I think it's only fair if you invite me along."

Jill rolls her eyes. "Ignore my sister, she goes through men as if they grow on trees in the front yard."

Emelia Alice winks at me. "Only because I didn't know the tree himself was available."

I resist the urge to run. The tinge of red creeping up Jill's neck says she wants to get out of here, too. I open the door for her. "You are much too lovely for jarred spaghetti sauce, so let's get going before we miss our reservation."

~

Jill and I take our seats and order drinks, mine being water with lemon. We're at a brewery but I don't typically drink, and I'm driving tonight, so I'll err on the side of caution and only have water.

"You've been at Pemberton for a couple of years now, right?" I ask her, making more small talk because that's all we seem to be accomplishing, though it feels like we should know each other better.

She nods, dark lashes framing her spectacular eyes. "Eighteen months. That's why I was so shocked when Angela offered me the night supervisor position."

"Supervisor?" I whistle. "For the med-surg floor?"

Jill tucks a carefully styled curl of hair behind her ear. "Primarily. I'll be on our floor but I'm the only floor supervisor working nights, so I'll be on call for the other floors if they need help."

"Night shift," I hear myself mutter, thinking of Lily's familiar face and the knife slicing me open, sternum to navel, every time she shows up in my mind.

Jill's breath comes out in a rush. "I know. I considered what my shift change would do to us now that we're finally acting on our feelings for one another, but when Angela offered me the job, she also *congratulated* us. I think she realizes that us being on different shifts will keep us from being too handsy at work. And I'm sure we'll be able to figure out how to see each other on our days off, if nothing else."

Jill's hand slides across the table toward mine and I replay what little I heard of her words. *Us?* I pretend I don't see the move she's making and busy my hands with placing a napkin in my lap. Then I give them some silverware to occupy them while I cut into the loaf of dark bread that's part of our appetizer.

If Angela, our hospital administrator, *congratulated* Jill on this date, it was definitely done snarkily. Angela's job is to make the hospital money. Mine is to make people feel better. Those two purposes don't always coexist easily and when push comes to shove, I'm adept at pushing. In a way that feels a lot like being shoved off a cliff. So Angela isn't going to send any good wishes my way, and I don't care to offer her any either. "Did you tell Angela we had a date planned for tonight? Or is the hospital's rumor mill broadcasting the news?"

Jill picks up her knife and spreads butter over the warm slice of bread I placed on her plate. "I'm not sure who told her. She asked me to stop by her office before I left and our date was the first thing she brought up."

Then Angela overheard the news. I only hope Jeremy keeps his mouth shut on his theory about my recent attitude problem being a product of unrequited feelings for Lily because I don't need Angela to *also* overhear that news. It was hard enough to drag myself through the torture of every challenge in my home gym until I collapsed in a pool of sweat, punishment for having succumbed to the idiocy that beckons me whenever I'm in the presence of Lily. I don't need the added layer of being seen as a two-timer. By Angela, of all people.

"Angela knowing we're having dinner together isn't a big deal," I say for Jill's benefit as much as my own. I obviously didn't consider what Jill might think when a man asks her out, because I never intended to be having dinner with her. "I hope you told Angela that us sharing a solitary meal wasn't an event in need of congratulations."

Silence snakes its way across the table. I meet Jill's eyes, wishing I didn't see sadness crawling out of them. I was moderately flirty when I asked her to come to dinner with me, but I've never before given her a reason to think I was interested. And I for darn sure haven't implied that I want to get *handsy* with her at work. "Did Angela say anything more about this meal between coworkers?"

Jill's eyes drop to her plate. "No, she just offered me the supervisor role and I took it because I need the money. I was hoping you wouldn't be mad." She meets my eyes again. "I know we can navigate our way through working different shifts."

I balance the silverware on the edge of my plate. "I'm not mad. Why would I be? We're having *one* date, that doesn't give me the clout to factor into your life decisions. I'm glad you got a promotion, and I'm glad you took the job based on your own needs and goals."

Her silver bracelets scratch over the table, her fingers circling the mug of beer she ordered. "I know this is our first date. I'm not trying to jump ahead and put expectations on you. But I feel like we've gotten to know each other pretty well over the last eighteen months and at the very least, I consider you a dear friend. One I don't want to lose just because I took a different position at work."

The only person I consider a friend is Jeremy, but my definition of what constitutes friendship is severe. I tend to place everyone into the acquaintance box. "Nothing at all is at stake, Jill. So let's chat and have a good time because you're a lot better looking than my usual date. Dad is getting on in years and he eats so early I normally end up raiding the refrigerator in the middle of the night after having dinner with him."

The tension falls out of her shoulders and I search her relieved eyes, wishing I could find a spark in them that would ignite something inside me. But all I see in Jill's depths is her own desire. I break the contact and let my eyes drift over her head. Behind Jill and to the right, on the other side of the restaurant, is a champagne-colored dress allowing for a show of entirely too much thigh. The lanky redhead next to Lily is enjoying every inch of that exposed skin. His palm wraps over her knee, fingers splayed up her thigh and moving higher. My body ignites, the sting of a thousand hornets lighting me up from the inside out. I bolt up out of my seat, bumping into a server carrying a flight of beer to a nearby table. I bite down and curse under my breath, grabbing the man's beer paddle and placing it on my own table, fingers curling tightly around the first glass in the flight. I throw it back, letting the amber liquid crash down my throat without hitting a tastebud. I slam the empty glass onto the paddle and grab the next, repeating the process.

Jill laughs. "I see you changed your mind about having a drink."

I throw back two more and then set my sights on her. She might not carry the flame I want, but I need her to extinguish my urge to break every bone in that redhead's body. "Do you want to get out of here?"

~3~

I'm swimming in turbulent waters with no land in sight. I can't think about where I'm driving to or how under the influence I may be. I can't focus on it being *Jill* who is draped over my console, her lips attacking my neck. Because if I kick myself out of this unthinking autopilot, I'm going to turn this vehicle around and head straight back to the brewery.

I'm supposed to be a doctor, a *healer*, not a destroyer. But right now, all I want to do is rip this planet right out of orbit and smash it into the sun.

Jill's teeth scrape against my skin. I take one hand from the wheel, fisting my fingers in her hair. I want to feel this. I want to be with a woman again, one who is real and solid beneath me. One who is my age and who could be a wife and mother. I want the life I dreamed of. The one that's a carbon copy of the life my dad has lived. I want back what Lily stole from me five years ago.

I swing into Jill's driveway in a haze of rage and seduction, the alcohol dampening my senses until I don't care *who* I'm kissing. Her mouth is on mine and the more she gives, the more I take. I cup her bottom and pull her onto my lap, hands already opening the car door. I lift her up and out, staying attached to her mouth.

We crash through her front door in a tangle of limbs, stumbling backward until she's underneath me on the couch, my hand trapped behind her as it fights with the zipper on the back of her dress. I *need* this off of her. I want to see her. Feel her. Touch her. I want to taste her until nothing else lives inside me except the sweet bliss of a woman who *isn't* Lily Beller.

"Oh!" A gasp comes from my right. I look up, panting against swollen lips. Emelia Alice is redder than the hair on the punk kid who was with Lily tonight. *Lily.* No matter what I do, my every thought is about her.

I sit up and tug the straps of Jill's dress back over her shoulders. She's blushing just as much as her sister is. Emelia Alice laughs, pulling a plate from the microwave but keeping her eyes trained on us. "It's okay, my sister doesn't have anything I haven't seen before. But you, you beautiful beast of a man, are still clothed. So carry on and let me have a little peep."

I move to the edge of the couch, leaning my elbows onto my knees, dropping my head into my hands and cursing like a sailor inside it. Jill scoots next to me, taking an icy tone with her twin. "Em, leave him alone. This is just as embarrassing for you as it is for us."

"You think?" Emelia Alice titters. "I'm all for naked men in the living room, but a little warning would be nice next time."

Jill rubs my back, Emelia Alice's retreating footfalls growing softer as she reaches the stairs and heads back up to her room. "Let's move this into my bedroom before my sister returns and starts filming us."

I climb to my feet. "I'm sorry, Jill, but I don't normally do anything like this and I didn't...I *don't* want this to happen." I throw a hand toward the door. "I'm also sorry I endangered your life. I've never driven after having even one drink, so what I just did is...inconceivable."

She stands, smoothing down her rumpled dress. "Well, I don't think you drank enough to be over the limit. And..." Her cheeks turn red again. "I'm still up for finding out just how much of a beast you really are."

I swallow. "I can't, Jill. I'm really sorry for even making it seem like I could."

~

I stare at the ceiling in the doctors' lounge. After my behavior this weekend, I'm reluctant to face Jill. Even more so to come face-to-face with Lily. Who knows what I'll do when I see her again? I'm liable to propose to Angela. And considering she already despises me, in addition to being thirty years older and married already, it would be best if I didn't go rocking that boat.

I'm not sure how I turned out to be an utter failure of a human being, but if there were any doubts left about the integrity of my moral compass after what I did with a sixteen-year-old Lily, what I did to Jill clarifies my depravity. The fact that I can't even remember the color of the dress that I nearly removed from her body but feel like I know every thread of that damnable champagne-colored minidress wrapped around a green-eyed girl who filled it out in a way that proved beyond all of my wildest dreams that Lily Beller *is* a fully grown woman now, dissolves all remaining illusions about the man I've tried to convince myself that I am.

"Here you are," Angela pierces me with a glare. I can feel it. No need to look at her for confirmation.

"Here I am." I groan, pushing my chair forward and giving her the respect of eye contact. Because I'm real respectable these days. "What can I do for you?"

Her shoulders press up into the outdated shoulder pads of her jacket. "Your job, for starters."

I tap the tablet in front of me. "I am doing my job. I'm in the doctors' lounge working on patient notes. What are you doing in the doctors' lounge?"

She glances at the table, my login screen displayed so she knows I haven't been sitting here working on notes. "You haven't started doing your rounds this morning, and I distinctly remember you *insisting* that you had to do that first thing *every* morning, so I came to make sure you were feeling okay. Do I need to find a replacement for you? Because it wouldn't be that hard, I already have a list of candidates."

"So you keep telling me." I give her a resolute smile. "Just like I keep telling you that taking care of patients tops doing *any* press relations that you cook up for the start of every day. Now that we've settled that, again, care to explain why I'm *really* getting your special attention this morning?"

She shoves her proud nose skyward to look down on me because even seated, I'm nearly as tall as her. "I just told you the real reason. I was on this floor checking in with my new nurse and found your absence notable."

I rest my forearms on the table. "The nurse you just put into a floor supervisor role? Or the one who is about five foot six and has a whole lot of dollar signs attached to her name?"

Angela's dark brows draw over her even darker eyes. "I *personally* sought out Ms. Beller for a position here, and you got *your* job because of who your father is. Keep that in mind the next time you decide to bully one of my nurses."

The vein at my temple throbs. "If one of your nurses filed a formal complaint against me, we'll take it through the proper channels. But just because you're gluing yourself to Lily Beller in hopes that you'll get a new hospital wing paid for doesn't mean she's above following protocol, and I'm not above making sure she does just that. So don't ever threaten my job again because that girl and her money mean nothing to me."

Angela flattens both of her palms onto the table and bends toward me. "Good, Darren. Because *none* of our nurses should mean anything to you, even the pretty blonde ones."

I don't respond. She pushes herself back to her full height, nose jutting a little higher this time. She sweeps out of the room as if she just put me in my place. Not even close. She may see an opportunity in having Lily here, but all I see is destruction. I've sacrificed, given up everything, and punished myself until I bled, with none of it mattering to any god I've prayed to. They've led Lily right back to my doorstep. And now, the object of a desire I don't want is complaining to Angela about me? Well, if Lily doesn't like me being a thorn in her side, she can take her pretty little self right back out of Pemberton's door.

I check the time. Lily's shift doesn't end for fifteen minutes. I abandon the safety of my chair and follow the path Angela took, exiting the lounge with long strides. Lily isn't in the fishbowl so I turn down the righthand corridor, finding her around the next bend. She's outside Mr. Vass's room, chumming it up with Jeremy, the fluorescent hallway light that makes everyone else look sallow dancing off her copper hair, casting an aura around her head like she's adorned by the glow of a halo. My already sour mood curdles even further.

I invade their space, eyes trained on Lily in reckless courage. "Everything okay with my patient this morning, Nurse Beller? Or have you not found time to do your job in between flirting with married men."

"Whoa," Jeremy throws up his hands. "The only person doing any flirting around here is your patient, and Lily's dealing with the old man like a champ, so wipe the piss out of your mouth and give her a medal."

I glance into the room. Mr. Vass is asleep, his thin gray hair mussed and his wrinkled skin nearly translucent. "He's harmless."

Lily snorts. "Says a man."

I narrow my eyes at her. "Says a *doctor*. Mr. Vass is still recovering from pneumonia, so he doesn't have the strength to do much of anything."

Jeremy rests a protective hand on Lily's shoulder. "Vass has the muscle to flap his jaws, and he's been doing plenty of that."

My pulse rises, counting the seconds that Jeremy leaves his hand on Lily's shoulder. I'm not mad that he's touching her. I'm furious that I *care* that he's touching her. "Vass isn't the only one with a loose tongue. I need to speak to Nurse Beller. Privately."

Lily bristles. Jeremy glances at her, then back to me. "If this is about coffee that *didn't* spill——"

I remove his hand from her shoulder, shoving it toward him. "I don't want to talk to her about coffee that *could* have spilled. I need to discuss another matter with her, and she doesn't need you guarding her. She's a big girl, and she already has a daddy."

His jaw tics, bewilderment tracing deep in his eyes. He opens his mouth but I shake my head, silencing him before I take all my frustration out on him. "Don't you have somewhere to be, Jeremy? Maybe calling your *wife*."

Lily presses a hand to his arm. "It's fine, Jer. I'm sure Dr. Mansfield has a non-petty issue to discuss with me."

The shortened pet name is acid in my veins. He sees it, shaking his head right back at me as he walks away. I resist the urge to yell. In all the years I've known Lily, she's never called me anything endearing. She rarely even uses my first name. I'm only just realizing how odd that is.

Lily has always been older than her years, someone I could speak to like any other adult and though she never talked much, our conversations were always engaging. She doesn't simply read books, she memorizes them, and I was continually intrigued by the concept of her being a walking library. Prior to *that* night, had I been forced to define my relationship with her, I would have most definitely called her a friend. But the way she just treated Jeremy is how she treats her friends, and I've never been the recipient of that type of familiarity.

Tongue suddenly heavy in my mouth, I look away from her inquisitive eyes. "I just spoke to Angela. Is there anything you'd like to say to my face?"

"No," she answers flatly.

I force myself to look back at her, but find I can only stare at her lips. "Twelve years isn't that big of an age difference."

Her lips part, close, then move slowly. "Excuse me? Are you talking about the age gap between us?"

I flex my hands, breaking my eyes away so I can breathe again. "I'm talking about you running off to Angela like a tattletale. I remember being twenty-one, since it wasn't that long ago, and by then I'd grown out of the stage where I needed to get someone else in trouble to make myself feel better."

She pats my shoulder, two solid thumps. "Good for you. I never went through that stage but I'm glad you finally found some confidence. Anything else? If not, I need to finish my shift."

My jaw clenches. "This isn't a game, Lily. You went to the hospital administrator to complain about how I'm treating you when it was *you* who treated this entire hospital with disregard when you left an *open* container sitting in the fishbowl. And I'm not the only one who was bothered by that. I wouldn't have even known it happened if one of your fellow nurses hadn't told me about it."

She nods. "I messed up. I not only admit it, but I've apologized for it and can give my solemn swear that I won't make the same mistake again. I can also swear to you that I did *not* go to Angela about *anything*. So maybe you should stop being so high-minded with me, and instead go confront whoever it is that has a chip on their shoulder as big as yours.

I bet it was *them* who told Angela that I left coffee sitting out and that you've made it your life mission to remind me of the error *every single day*."

She moves to go past me but I thrust out my arm, blocking her. I lower my mouth to her ear. "Angela brought you here because she wants your family's money. I say you keep the money and go find a job where you won't have to worry about spilling your coffee, *angel*, because that halo of yours has a champagne-colored crack in it."

Lily still smells exactly the same. Tangerines and orange blossoms, dusted with a hint of vanilla. This woman is nectar straight from the gods and I hate them for placing her in my life. Almost as much as I hate myself for making her beautiful eyes dull with sorrow.

"Lily, wait," I beg as I fall in beside her, an image of that scrap of champagne fabric pulsing beneath my eyelids. "What I just said...I..." Can't speak to her about her clothing without losing my mind. "If Angela recruited you, it was because of your money. So you really should find a different job, one where people will appreciate that you're an excellently trained nurse. Any medical facility would be lucky to have you. Just not this one."

She slides into the fishbowl. "*Pemberton* is lucky to have me."

I move around the front of the desk, keeping myself in line with her. Jill is on the opposite side of us, throwing glances my way. I lower my voice. "Lily, I learned more at Dad's side than I ever did in medical school and you had the same benefit, so don't tie yourself down to this place. Go to a facility where you'll be valued for more than your money."

Her movements are sharp, a fierceness in their origins. She taps Jill on the shoulder. "Dr. Mansfield is worried about the well-being of the nurses. Could you address his concerns? I'm sure he mostly wants to make sure *you're* okay, since he and Mr. Vass have *both* marked you as their favorite."

"Lily," I growl.

She ignores the sound. "I don't have time to ease his mind because my shift is ending and I need to go make sure I didn't leave any open containers anywhere."

She exits the fishbowl with deliberate movements. I want to chase after her but ultimately, this is the best outcome. She's angry, and I haven't proposed to anyone, asked random women on dates, or fell prostrate at Lily's feet. If there's any hope of ever deleting her from my brain, this is how I get there. I only wish insulting her, and being insulted by her, didn't hurt this much.

Jill moves in my periphery. After the disgusting way in which I used her as an outlet for my despondency, I can't leave her standing here to chase after Lily. Even if I thought chasing Lily *was* the right thing to do. Instead, I flick my wrist like there's nothing happening. "You're busy and I don't need anything, I was just trying to clear up some misinformation, and Lily is the one who needs to do that for me."

Jill moves forward, the tension rolling off of her matching my own. "Emelia Alice feels terrible about interrupting us the other night."

I scratch the back of my neck. "I'm sure you told her it was good that she did. I'd feel even worse than I already do if we'd...gone further."

She picks at the counter. "I told her, which makes her sulking worse. She wishes she waited a couple more minutes so she could have had the view of you she's been dreaming about." Jill makes a face. "I did mention we're only fraternal twins, right?"

I chuckle, changing the topic. "What kind of trouble is Mr. Vass giving you?"

Jill leans against the counter with an exaggerated sigh. "He's doing nothing that I haven't encountered from male patients before. Some of them have nurse fantasies, and some of the *nurses* are happy to feed those fantasies." She looks at me pointedly. "Maybe so *said* nurse can make a fuss about how they're being treated."

I cock a brow. "Are you telling me *Lily* is encouraging Mr. Vass to be crude?"

Jill tightly crosses her arms. "I'm saying you should start paying more attention to what's going on around here because it isn't hard to figure out who all the drama surrounds. And speaking of *Lily*, will you come to the party I'm hosting for her next Saturday night?"

"No." The word slings out of my mouth with the tact of a derailed freight train.

Disappointment skitters across Jill's face. "It's just a small get-together to welcome Em's and my new roommate to the fold."

A chill as cold as the frost covering my windshield this morning snakes up my spine. "New *roommate*? As in Lily Beller is your *roommate*?"

Jill frowns. "I should have asked you about her before I rented her my spare room. You knew her before she started working here, right?"

My pulse thuds in my ears. "I know Lily very well and there's no reason under the sun that she would need to rent a *room* in *your* house."

Jill's nostrils flare. "I'm aware that Lily comes from money, but it isn't like I'm living in squalor. Em and I put all we had into that house and it's really nice. You know, you saw it."

I pinch my temples and drag my fingers across my closed eyelids. Jill's neighborhood isn't the greatest but her home *is* updated, unlike mine. "Your house being nice or not isn't the point. Lily could buy your entire neighborhood without tapping a line of credit, so I don't understand why she's renting a *room*. Where has she been living?"

Jill slams her hands onto her hips. "I have no idea where Lily was living, I only know that she's moving into my house *today*, and when I showed her the place *yesterday*, she didn't stick her nose up about how much money she has. She said the room was nice and that she'd take it."

I ignore Jill's ire because my words being twisted into insults isn't important. Lily infiltrating my life is the urgent matter. There's only one reason I can think of that would make her rent a room in Jill's house: *me*. I asked Jill out in front of Lily, so now Lily is going to move into Jill's house to...spy on me? Sabotage the relationship she thinks I'm trying to have with Jill? "When did all this nonsense with Lily renting a room come about? I was just at your house and no one mentioned anything about renting a room."

Jill's gaze narrows. "Emelia Alice has been working on getting the room rented. She delivered some jewelry to the hospital's gift shop recently and happened to meet Lily. Lily then hooked Em up with a couple of new vendors——some of Lily's family, I think. Now the two of them are like best friends."

"Lily hasn't worked here long enough to be anyone's friend, let alone be a *best* one."

All traces of amiability splinter and fall from Jill's face. "They're close enough that when Emelia Alice mentioned appreciating the new distributors because then maybe we wouldn't have to take on a renter, Lily asked if *she* could rent the room. Em was ecstatic, and still is."

I stare at Jill but she's out of focus. "Is Lily the person who told Emelia Alice that the brewery would be a good place to eat?"

"Yeah, Lily made the suggestion. Why?"

It wasn't happenchance that put Lily in the brewery. She sat in my line of sight intentionally, which means she knows *exactly* what she's doing to me. If she knows it now, then she wasn't innocent that night in my office. She wasn't misguided. She baited me. She picked a scent made for seduction and then leaned over me so I had no choice but to get my fill of her. All the times I thought her lips landed on mine by accident, that I'd unwittingly been the one to move forward instead of her, were lies. She did this to me on purpose. And while I've spent these last five years trying to get over her, she's spent them mapping out a new plan of seduction. That's why I smelled the same scent on her today. That's why she's moving into the home of a woman she thinks I'm interested in. It's why she came to Pemberton to begin with.

But what's her end game? Does Lily Beller have a plan to ruin me? Because she didn't do the job thoroughly enough the first time?

"...for the games this weekend?" Jill's voice slices into my thoughts.

I frown. "I'm not playing games."

Her breath rushes out. "You already signed up! And I put you down as a lead volunteer, you'll be in charge of the youth day's obstacle course again."

I rub my face. "Right. Youth day. I forgot that was this weekend. Yeah, I'll be here to help out."

"You better be," she grumbles. "The obstacles are the same as last year and I heard the kids loved you, so this year, I expect to hear more of the same. And you'll be happy to know your buddy Jeremy volunteered to assist you." She points at me. "And he's bringing Lily with him. So ask *her* why she's lowering herself to live in my spare room."

~5~

Lily was one of those kids who was reading full books by the age of three and when I'd tag along with Dad and we'd visit her family's home, she'd tug on my pants leg and I'd end up sitting with her, letting her recite whole chapters to me. I never really wanted to, preferring to be with Dad so I could see and hear everything he was doing, but Lily was so muted I felt obligated to indulge her. More than once, I wondered if she ever spoke to anyone if it wasn't for a book recitation.

Maybe she sensed my reluctance and it made her angry. Maybe she mistook my patience and developed an unhealthy attachment that I was completely oblivious to. Or maybe she sensed a darkness inside me that made her grow up wanting to exploit every terrible part of me. After all, her brother and his wife run a private investigation firm that specializes in tracking down child predators so Lily's had exposure to those crimes.

Whatever her reasoning, I feel no vindication in her having intentionally attracted me. I can't even bask in having outsmarted her when I wasn't even trying to. Lily might be living under the same steep-pitched roof as a woman she'll soon find I have no actual interest in, but I'm living in a relic of broken dreams. The lights over my head strobe, and I'm not surprised. I've done nothing to update even the cosmetics of this old house, let alone the wiring. It looks the same today as it did when I was growing up, though devoid of furniture, save for my parents' old bedroom suite, the thick oak dining table, and Dad's old recliner.

The lights pulse again but this time the strobe is accompanied by the smell of smoke. I run through the cramped hallways and into the kitchen, hearing the sizzle and snaps from the microwave before I see the sparks. I hit it full force, metal clanging from the back as I shove the microwave away from the outlet and yank the plug. My leftover bean burrito is aflame.

I take a set of metal tongs from a drawer and pull open the microwave door, smoke billowing out as I use the tongs to scrape the burning food onto my waiting plate and then dump the plate into the sink. I turn on the faucet, soaking the charred remains of my breakfast, and cast my eyes to the ceiling, envisioning the vast sky above it. Dad always told me that I should believe in a higher power. I do. I just wish they were benevolent. "Really? It isn't enough that I have to cope with seeing Lily at the youth event today, so now I have to do it on an empty stomach?"

~

Jill rushes toward me as I enter the registration tent the hospital set up for today's public relations stunt. The event is for ages nine to twelve and is supposed to teach children about living a healthy lifestyle, but there's little learning. As a kid, I would have hated it. I suspect Lily would have, too.

"Darren! Thank goodness, I thought you were standing me up."

I disregard the jab because Jill's face is flushed and her hair is mussed, all the makings of her being flustered before the day even gets started. I cup my hands over her shoulders. "Breathe, Jill. The hospital runs this day camp every year, and the kids are easily entertained so there really isn't anything that can go wrong."

She chews her lip. "That's the problem. The rest of you have done this before and here I am having never even attended, but yet *I'm* in charge of managing all of the volunteers. What if the kids *aren't* entertained? It will blow back on me, and Angela is the one who *suggested* I be in charge of this. She's testing me, not to mention watching my every move. It's like she's waiting for me to fail and if that's the way it is, why did she even give me the supervisory position?"

My eyes float over Jill's head, tracking Lily's movements as she picks up her name tag and presses it to her chest, a sticker identifying her as *Nurse Lily*. So many times, I've questioned what happened with her that night. I thought I was letting my sick brain twist the scenario to place some kind of blame on the teenager because if I could have faulted Lily, I'd somehow be less depraved. But Lily *is* at fault. And because of her manipulation, I've unwittingly put Jill in a vulnerable position.

I can't tell Jill that Angela's behavior is due to Lily's venom leaking off of me and onto her, so I give Jill's shoulders a squeeze and then remove my hands because the less we interact, the better for her. "I promise you that the instant the kids get started with the physical activities, they will be having fun. And if they get bored making their nutritional lunch, the day ends with a huge relay race that will make them forget they even ate lunch."

She holds a folder up to me. "I hope you're right because I have a feeling that if anything goes sideways, Angela will make sure I'm to blame."

I tuck the folder under my arm. "The obstacle course is the kids' favorite station, so I can personally guarantee you that they'll have rave reviews. So don't worry about Angela, and while you're not worrying, put Lily somewhere else. I don't need her on my team. Jeremy and I can handle it."

Jill frowns. "I get that you don't like her, I'm starting to have issues with her myself, not to mention second thoughts about the whole roommate situation. But there has to be a female at every station and all the other women are already assigned."

I widen my stance, trying to be nonchalant. "What's Lily doing to you?"

"She's just...creepy." Jill glances over her shoulder, seeing where Lily is before moving closer to me. "Like this morning, before we came here, I looked up from the bowl of oatmeal I was eating to find her staring at me. She didn't try to hide that she was staring at me either. I asked her if she was hungry, she said no. *Still continuing to stare.* So I asked if she wanted to ride here together, you know, just to say something to make the situation not as weird. But Lily said she was meeting someone afterward. The whole time she never moved or looked away. I don't think she blinked once. So I got up to empty my bowl and she took it from me."

"She took your food?"

Jill shrugs. "I didn't stick around to see if she ate my leftovers. She grabbed the bowl and said she'd wash it because she wouldn't be staying for cleanup after the event today." Jill turns her palms up. "Like washing my bowl negates being responsible for helping out here. But I was already so freaked out that I didn't bother to question her. So believe me, I do feel sorry for you that Jeremy arranged for Lily to work with the two of you today, but there's nothing I can do about it."

I have a feeling that Lily is the one who designed this working trio. She probably smells extra good today, too. She sure as heck looks good, and that simply shouldn't be possible seeing how we're all wearing the same bland t-shirts. Even Jill's beauty is tamed by the event-staff garb. But not Lily's. Everywhere she goes, she's washed in a dazzling beam of light that's straight from the heavens themselves.

My jaw tenses, a stampede of wildebeests trampling across my chest just *thinking* about being near Lily today. I swear I ticked off a god in a former life, and he's punishing me for it now. "Trade places with her, Jill. You've already organized everything and surely Lily won't mess it up. Let her take it from here, and you come be my female."

She raises up onto her toes, eyes sparkling as she places her lips against mine. "I'm yours. Right after we close the curtains on this show, because I am *not* giving Angela a reason to take away my promotion."

Jill turns and strolls away, leaving me grinding my teeth. Per usual, Lily's proximity makes my brain fritz and words fall out of my mouth in ways I don't mean for them to. I glance toward where I last saw her. She's still there. But this time *she's* watching me, and every hair on my body stands erect.

~

Convincing Jeremy that we don't need Lily would be easier if she wasn't standing ten feet away looking like pure ambrosia. She *is* food of the gods, and they sent her to poison me. Knowing she's lethal doesn't make me any less interested in taking a bite. It never has. Because I think the day she was born, a curse was placed on me.

I rip my eyes from her and stare at Jeremy. "I've never had a single kid get hurt on my watch and today won't be an exception."

He folds his arms over his chest, eyes narrowed. "Having Lily on our team isn't about sprained ankles and skinned knees."

"It absolutely is," I defend. "Which is why you'll run the first half of the challenge, bringing the kids across the slackline and up the netted rope climb, and then I'll see them down from there, across the logs, and then have them wait there until three kids can form a team and help each other over the wall."

He thrusts his hands toward the course. "Lily should be at the front with the slackline, and then I can wait at the top of the netting, bring the kids across the logs, and you can help them over the wall."

"No. Lily can sit over there where she is, and if a kid happens to get hurt, which they won't, we can call Lily in to help them."

He drops his chin. "I used to respect you, but lately, I don't even recognize you. What is your problem? Lily is nothing but nice to *everyone* and you treat her like she's a nuisance. I can't imagine how that makes her feel. That's why I invited her out here today. I thought maybe I'd be a go-between for you but straight out of the gate, you're acting like she's worthless. Do you have any humanity left? Or did the demon that got inside of you devour your entire soul?"

I lean my face into his. "Fine, Jeremy. She can help, but she stays on the slackline. You take the net, and I'll do the rest. Have her start the kids two at a time and the next set doesn't start until the ones ahead are on the logs. And *if* one of the larger kids tumbles from the slackline with enough gusto to topple her over, that's on you. All of my demons and I will be busy minding our own business."

I'm disgusted with myself, both for being the soulless man Jeremy accused me of being and for spending the entire day noticing the depth of color in Lily's copper hair. Every time she moved, it caught the light differently, and I had to remind myself that the kids climbing all over me were supposed to be doing something other than using me as a jungle gym.

We spaced the kids out and I positioned myself as far away from Lily as possible, but that didn't stop my eyes from wandering every chance they got. Nor did it block her heavenly aroma from being a heat-seeking missile straight to the nose. I've spent so many years thwarting every possibility of seeing her—going as far as to convert my living room into a home gym, placing obstacles between myself and the breezeway that connects to the clinic to ensure I couldn't make up an excuse to go inside while she was still interning—that the sensation of being physically near her again is overwhelming.

I can't help but to study her. The encounter Jill described is so unlike the Lily I remember. The girl rarely made eye contact because she was always focused, whether it be on a book or a task. But this adult woman is imbued with the radiance of the sun itself, her confident presence as large as her laugh. I've heard the melody so much today that I wish it was my hearing that went up in smoke this morning instead of my burrito. I'm never going to get the sound out of my head.

"Go on, I'll be down soon." I shake off the last two kids and send them running toward the lunch tables set át the base of the hill below the flat where the obstacle course is spread. Giggles erupt from behind me. I swing around. Jeremy is wobbling across the logs while Lily dashes over the ground beside him.

"Cheater," he proclaims with a chuckle as he jumps from the end of the log, still well ahead of Lily, and holds his hand out to her. She takes it, stepping onto his bent knee and latching onto the top of the wall when he gives her a boost up. He pulls himself onto the wall, straddling the top and taking Lily's hand again. My teeth clench. Jeremy pulls her dangling body up to him and then makes her scream when he pretends to push her over. "I'm not going to drop you. Who do you think I am? Darren Mansfield?"

I run for the wall. Jeremy disappears over the side, calling up to her. "Jump, Lily, I'll catch you."

She slides off the edge. I leap, fingers barely scraping the top of the wall as I catapult myself overtop. In one fluid motion, I land directly in front of where she's peeling herself out of his *catching* arms. He whistles. "Dr. T, now I see why you beast out in the gym. If I wasn't already married I'd be out here wanting to show off for all these nurses, too."

I glare at him. He got all of the kids calling me this stupid name because some of them had a hard time saying *Terminator*, and none of them understood the reference. He shortened it and is overly amused when some of them slip up and call me *mister* instead of *doctor*, another television reference they're all too young to get. "So you do remember that you have a wife? Because while you were exploiting Lily's lack of upper body strength, it looked like you forgot all about Camilla."

He turns his hands up, showing Lily his calloused palms. "I carry around my reminder of Camilla. She's in my heart, and she thinks these battle scars I got during my last workout with Dr. T. are sexy. What do you think, Lily?"

She inspects his hands, making a face. "I think I'm less inclined to want lunch now."

He winces. "That's bad news for Doc over there because his callouses have callouses."

Lily's eyes meet mine and I flick my gaze to Jeremy. "If the pads of my *capable* palms being durable is a turn-off for women, *good*. Because I have no interest in *any* of them."

Lily's head tilts, that damnable copper hair catching my eye as it trails over her shoulder. "What about the nurse you were kissing earlier?"

Jeremy's eyes fly wide. "Kissing? Who were you lip-locking? I thought you said Jill was only one date and you were done with that?"

Lily huffs. "They didn't look *done* this morning."

I shove my arms into place across my chest. "My dating life isn't the business of either of you. And if you don't want rumors starting about the two of you not being *done*, I suggest you stop being so handsy."

Jeremy slips an arm around Lily. "Camilla is my one and only, and everybody knows that. So you worry about taking care of your one and only because there's Jill, and it sounds like it's a good thing she was too far away to hear you denying her just now."

They walk toward the lunch tables, his arm sliding from around Lily's shoulders, but not before he tosses me a smug smile. I anchor my feet to the earth. I'll deal with Jeremy when Lily isn't around to give me murderous urges and oral maladies.

Jill sidles up next to me, standing close enough that her shoulder brushes my bicep. "You guys were moving so slow I didn't think the kids were going to get finished in time for lunch."

I adjust away an inch. "We had a system. Slow and steady so all the kids made it through injury-free."

She looks up at me with a grin. "Injury-free and practically yawning, until they got to climb the tree. Once Emelia Alice hears about it, she's going to ask you to set up an obstacle course at our house."

I drop my arms. "At an event full of doctors and nurses, I figured it was better to have the kids going home yawning than going home with sprained ankles. And at an event full of kids, it's probably best to not repeat any colorful commentary you think your sister might say."

Jill links her arm through mine. "Point taken. Now let's go learn how to make *healthy* pizza wraps so these youngsters can move on to the relay races and I can finally be done with this day. Angela better be singing my praises after this."

~

Lily is somewhere in this mass of people, and no matter how hard I fight against every drop of attraction to her, it still beats through my veins. Along with jealousy, resentment, and an ever-increasing sense of foreboding.

I scratch the callouses on my palms, my skin so thick across the pads that I don't normally feel anything. But Lily has a way of making a man feel things he never thought he would, and I have no doubt that my current deep-skinned itch is due to her.

"Are you ready?" Ronald calls into a megaphone from his perch at the front of the crowd where he's organizing the final event of the day. Jill is beside him as he details the series of races. "Each eight-member team will consist of six kids and two adults..." He drones on about the event starting with two members of each team racing to the far end of the field to plant their team's flag at the finish line. Once the flag is in place, two different teammates don sacks and hop through a zigzag course. When they reach the other side, two different teammates place plastic eggs on oversized spoons and navigate the same course. The two remaining teammates then take off on a three-legged race. The first team to complete all the challenges wins.

His voice rises to a shout, drawing my attention back to the makeshift stage. Jill tips a microphone to her mouth. "Grab your teammates, boys and girls!"

Shouts erupt all around me. "Dr. T! Dr. T!"

Shelby, a young girl of ten, runs over and yanks my arm. "You're on my team!"

Her friend Ryan grabs my other arm. "Everyone wants you, but we got here first!"

I allow them to pull me toward their team mat, giving apologetic shrugs to the stragglers who didn't get to me fast enough. "Maybe next year, guys."

Ryan and Shelby pull me toward a red mat to our left. My feet slam to a halt. There among the other teammates is Lily, her long hair now braided and her cheeks flushed. Every part of me is acutely aware of *every* part of her. "Looks like the rest of your team already selected someone else."

Shelby tugs my arm harder, still barely lifting it. "We get two adults. Now come on before someone tries to steal you from us."

Tons of excuses filter through my mind but these kids don't deserve to hear any of them. I summon all of my willpower and force my feet to move. Lily offers me a smile when I join our team on the too-small red mat but I look away, putting my attention on Shelby, who flounces her hands onto her hips and looks between Lily and me. "You two are our clenchers."

She says the words as if everything she says is final, and judging from how Ryan and the others are nodding along with her, I suppose it is. "Y'all are going to *crush* the three-legged race!"

My throat burns. The last thing I need to do is strap myself to Lily Beller. "The final event? That's where all the glory is. You and Ryan should run that one together. Nurse Lily and I will do the spoon race." Where I can dust her and then get the heck away from her.

Shelby gives me a look that can cut glass. "No one will beat you two in *any* of the races, and our best shot at winning is having you at the end so you can make up time if we fall behind. That's the whole point of having a *clencher.*"

As annoying as it is, she's right. Again, I have to be the adult here and put myself out over Lily to ensure no one else suffers. Not that these kids losing this race would be the worst thing. Still, I concede. "I'll run the last race with Nurse Lily."

Shelby turns away from me and finishes organizing the team. I'm not sure if the other kids voted on who would be their team leader or if Shelby just has a natural gift for stepping into that role, but while the teams around us are noisy and shouting, Shelby has our group rapt. Everyone is listening and nodding along while I break out into my first sweat of the day.

The kids position themselves in the pairs they'll be racing in, lining up in the order they'll be starting in. That puts Lily and me last, and side by side. Every time she takes a breath, the soft hair of her arms brushes mine. It's causing friction under my skin, like dragging my feet across a carpet and building up enough electricity to power a city block. Or maybe a whole continent.

The starting horn blows. I fold my arms over my chest as our first teammates leave the mat, watching nervously as they make good time. The flag goes up and our next pair takes off, both of them struggling to keep their feet from twisting up in the sacks. They both get lapped, multiple other teams pulling ahead.

The crowd around me roars but I block it all out, listening only to the irregular beat of my heart. I'm getting ready to connect one of my legs to one of Lily's. That means touching her. *Her* touching *me*. And we've really never had much physical contact before. Not when I would miss out on what Dad was doing so she could show off her memory skills and certainly not since she grew up and blasted a hole through my compass.

I glance at her, the girl who stole my desire and the woman who continues to own it. Her green eyes meet mine. "Are you ready for this?"

I face forward, heart pounding. "No."

She holds up the bands that go around our legs. "Me neither. I told the kids not to pick me because I have zero athletic ability."

"Yet somehow, here you are."

She drops her hand, the movement brushing my arm and sending gooseflesh skittering over my body. "I'm here because the kids insisted."

"Did you give in to them before or *after* you found out that I was the second adult on this team?"

She huffs out a breath. "I didn't know you were on this team until you walked over to the mat. The one I was *already* on. Rest assured that I was just as disappointed to see you as you were to see me."

I yank the bands from her grip and squat down to attach them. "Why did you move in with Jill? And don't tell me it's because you want to eat her leftover oatmeal. Which creeps her out, by the way."

Lily slides closer to me, steadying herself with a hand on my shoulder as I wrap the three straps of Velcro around our legs. "Technically, I moved in with her sister. And yeah, me eating Jill's leftover oatmeal would be creepy. I guess that's why I didn't do it."

"Well, staring at people is also creepy." I make sure the last bit of Velcro is secure, fighting the urge to wrap myself around her legs. Her scent is everywhere, and I want to bury my face in it.

I straighten back to my full height before I do something stupid, like make out with her jean-clad knee. "You're not a kid anymore, Lily, so stop with the tit-for-tat. You moved into Jill's house because of me."

Lily wiggles her leg around, tugging on mine in the process. "When did you hit your head? It must have been quite a blow to leave you delusional enough to think I do *anything* because of you."

I tug my left leg against my right, making her pitch against my side. "The bands are secure, so stop fidgeting. And you know good and well the only thing wrong with my head is *you*."

She drops down, fingers tugging on the thick straps. I lower myself beside her and fix back what she's undoing. "You designed this entire situation, Lily, so you're not getting out of it now."

She glares at me. "I'm sorry the kids didn't pick Jill for you instead of me, but it is *not* my fault. I told those kids that with me on their team they were bound to lose, yet they *insisted*. I didn't have the heart to keep saying no to them. But they aren't here anymore, so take these straps off of my leg and I'll give you what you want, Darren. I'll tag Jill in for you."

~7~

I can practically feel Lily's pulse racing, its frantic beat matching my own. Pain traces through my chest over the emotion she's trying so hard to mask. I stare into her emeralds and see the distress registering deep inside. It's the same look she had after I broke us apart *that* night. A look that's haunted me all these years. I rest my hand along her jaw, whispering. "I'm sorry, Lily. And I don't want Jill. I never have."

Lily bats away my touch and waves a hand to the field in front of us. "Then you better decide who you do want because Shelby's strategy to have her team's adults at the end is solid, but every other team did the same. That means she'll expect you to win and there's no chance of that happening with me as your partner."

"I'm pretty sure having you as my partner is the only way I do win," I mutter, looking away from the view of her too-close profile. Jeremy is two mats away from us. He winks at Lily and blows me a taunting kiss. My chest rumbles. If I was racing kids, I could fight the urge to display my physical prowess like some jacked-up baboon doing tricks for the pretty girl next to him, but I'm too competitive to let *any* of the other men here beat me. Particularly Jeremy. He's never bested me in a single thing, especially a foot race. I practically had to give him mouth-to-mouth the first time I took him on a parkour run through the forest that surrounds my house. We swung from branches, jumped over logs, and skittered across rocky inclines. He'd never done anything so intense because the pace I set is meant to be cruel. Punishing. It's what I deserve for being tempted by Lily, even if she did do everything within her power to make sure I was.

I don't want to fail in front of her again either. I want to show her that my only weakness is her, and that I've grown enough to cope with it. "I saw your lack of athletic ability earlier, Lily, but we're still going to win. I've got this."

She snaps her fingers in my face, breaking the stare-off I'm having with Jeremy. "There's another human you'll be dragging along while you *got this*. I didn't sign up to get mangled just because you men can't stand to lose."

"Then maybe you should have jumped on Jeremy's team," I quip. "I'm sure he would have coddled you."

She crosses her arms, her elbows poking into my ribs. "Trust me, if I was given that choice, I would have."

I bite down against the anger of her dismissal. I can't stop thinking about her for one miserable second while she gets to go about her life making out with redheads and fondling married men. "You do understand that Jeremy is *married*, right?"

She looks up at me. "You do understand that you making comments about Jeremy and me is insulting to his *wife*, right? Not one single time has he been untoward and neither have I."

"That would depend on his wife's definition of *untoward*," I smirk. "You're practically on a date with her husband today."

"And you're on a time limit. Our kids are getting ready to finish their race so if you aren't going to replace me, then take a break from degrading me and find it in your heart not to break my legs while you win this stupid thing."

My throat tightens. I try to hold onto the anger, remembering all the reasons I'm ticked at her. She purposefully seduced me, made me yearn for her in a way that forced me to punish myself with round after round of grueling circuits, and now she has the hospital administrator threatening me. My job is on the line again as if my abandoning my father wasn't enough. Yet I'd willingly forget about all of it, even Jeremy, if doing so would allow me to comfort her.

"I'm sorry I disparaged you. I know Jeremy's wife and I think she'd be uncomfortable with how close he seems to be getting to you, but he's been in my business a lot lately so I know how it feels to have someone constantly judging you. Even when their judgment is correct."

She shrugs. "Correct or not, no one has a right to tell someone else how to live. I'm not doing anything with Jeremy that I'd be uncomfortable doing in front of his wife, and he hasn't indicated that she's anything but amused by our friendship. He sent her a bunch of pictures of us earlier and I could hear her laughing when he called her afterward."

"Then maybe I'm wrong about how she'd react. Either way, my opinion on the matter is merely an opinion. And a biased one at that." I stretch my arm around Lily's shoulders, my palm swallowing the entire upper half of her opposite arm. It's as if she was made to be nestled in my grip, and this feels so right that a swarm of emotions has me confusing the ground beneath my feet with the heavens above my head. I'm barely touching her and already breaking apart.

She tentatively wraps an arm around my back, fingers curling over the muscle at my hip. A shockwave ripples through me, her delicate touch the epicenter. I curse under my breath, but she's so close she hears it. Her hand retreats from off my hip. I grab it, staring down into her eyes. She sinks her teeth into her lip. I swallow. "I made my choice. And everyone has their arms around each other, that's how this race is designed. So you hold onto me, Lily, and don't let go." I press her hand back against my thick muscle, hating how that last part has nothing to do with the race and everything to do with how this angel affects me. I even hate that all the planes of my body are rock hard instead of soft flesh for her to dig her fingers into the way mine are sinking into her. "I will *never* drag you, and there's absolutely no chance of any bones breaking. Just hold onto me, *tight*, and I won't let a hair on your beautiful head get damaged."

Her chest heaves. "There's more to pain than physical hurt and you've already done the internal damage, so it isn't really my hair that I'm concerned with."

My heart thuds low and heavy. I tuck her closer into my side, tightening my grip and lowering my voice. "I never wanted to harm you. Physically or emotionally. So right after the event ends, let's find a quiet place to talk and see if we can get all of this pain between us sorted out."

She inhales a shaky breath, sliding her fingers into my pocket and twisting them inside the fabric. "I have someplace to be right after this. So just go slow. I have seven left feet and I *really* don't want to break any bones today."

Disappointment trickles through me but I give her a smile nonetheless. "Angel, I promise that you're going to make it to the other end of this course in the perfectly pristine condition that you're in now. At least on the outside. We'll work on the inside stuff later."

She twines the fabric of my pocket tighter, her nails scraping along my thigh. Air sucks between my teeth, the touch setting me on fire. A satisfied glint twinkles in her eye, then she looks away. My mouth falls open. She points in front of her. "I think we're supposed to run now."

I look, but can't register the faces of the kids whose team I'm supposed to be racing for. Or the teams of adults who have already left their mats. Every cell in my body is shouting, and not for the right reasons.

Lily moves forward, I use her motion as my signal and dash away from the mat, pent-up emotions setting thunder under my feet. The threat of everything I feel for Lily being unleashed despite her manipulation, makes me default to the only way I know of subduing the attraction. Physical exertion.

I drop my hand from her shoulder and clamp it onto her waist, tipping her further into me so her feet are off the ground and can't bump against it as I run. "Hold on to me," I order, tucking her into the muscle above my thigh as if she's part of it. Her free hand comes around the front of me, her fingers digging into the sinew of my shoulder as her body clings to mine, jostling with the pound of my feet as I pick up speed.

I breathe deeply. Her scent clogs my nose, taking over my lungs and spreading warmth through my limbs. Everywhere her body touches mine, I'm filled with the heat of the sun that is this glorious woman. *Abort!*

I fake a twisted ankle, coming to an abrupt stop and setting Lily on her feet, sliding down to undo the straps in one rushed movement. I step away from her and walk in a circle, pretending to favor my left ankle. Or should it be the right? I can't remember which one I faked hurting.

She hurries toward me, nurse mode shining in her eyes.

"I'll be fine in a second." I wave her off, pulling away again as she tries to lower down to check my ankles. I'm sure she thinks they're both tweaked from how I'm limping around. "Sorry about the race. I'll let the kids know it was my fault."

Her brows knit together. "Your fault that you won? Somehow I don't think they're going to question your participation."

I look behind us and see the kids charging our way, their shouts finally reaching my ears. I don't recall even running the course. I was too focused on the woman in my arms. Lily is soft, and meaty enough that my hands had no problem finding perfect spots to dig my fingers into. And contemplating just how good she felt against me made me overrun the finish line by fifty yards. *What is wrong with me?*

I drag a hand down my face but shouts of "Dr. T!" and "We won!" keep me from having to say anything else to Lily. I've never been happier to have children jumping and screaming in circles around me. The louder they shout, the less chance I have of digging any more holes to bury myself in.

Lily stands aside, smiling as the kids mill around me. Her eyes dart to Jill, the smile remaining, though less brightly. "Your doctor was determined to win, even with being forced to have me as his partner."

Jill laughs. "I saw. He cheated though, because your feet never touched the ground."

Shelby's face scrunches. "The rules didn't say the second person had to run, just that there have to be two legs tied together, and they did that."

Jill leans onto her knees and gives the little girl a sweet smile. "We're going to reprimand Dr. T for showing off, but your team does win. Fair and square."

Shelby's face lights up. "He made everyone else look like they were standing still."

Jill chuckles, straightening and looking at me the way I wish Lily would. "He should have toned down his superhuman ability, but I imagine that's hard to do when you're no mere mortal."

I close my eyes against the compliment. I should have been out here setting a good example of sportsmanship, not letting my feelings run amok. Lips press to mine. My eyes snap open, met with a vision of blue. Not green. I move backward, away from Jill, a wave of loneliness breaking over me as I catch sight of Lily's copper hair moving off across the field with the kids in tow. Jill places a hand on my stomach. "Are you okay? Did you twist your ankle?"

I look down at her, her hollow touch serving as a stark reminder that I died five years ago, with only one hope of ever being resurrected.

I remove Jill's hand, knowing that what I have to say isn't what she wants to hear. "We're not a couple. That means you have to stop kissing me because people are seeing it and they're cranking up the rumor mill. Neither of us needs words about exclusivity being put into our mouths. Especially you. You don't want to be labeled as being my partner only to miss out on someone who is ready to sweep you off your feet right this very minute."

She runs her shoe across grass that won't be green much longer, this late fall day luckily a warm one. "I know you said you're not ready to do this right now, and I understand. It's just that...sometimes it feels like you are ready. And I like those times, Darren. I like the feel of your lips on mine, even if they aren't exclusively on mine."

I stroke her blushing cheek. "You deserve better than that. Better than me. My head is pretty messed up these days and nothing good can come of that for you. So go find your happiness, and let me be jealous about having missed out on you."

It's easy to sugarcoat my words for her. She doesn't possess the power to bend my emotions to her will, send them careening out of control until the whole of me is undone and I'm faking sprained ankles to keep from begging for a kiss. Jill isn't Lily, the angel I need to see about the pain we're both harboring because if she feels anything close to what I do, I need to beg for more than a kiss. I'll have to plead for a chance to carry her over a finish line I gave up on five years ago, when I locked my love in a cage and began punishing it every time it rattles the bars.

Seeing how all the light in the universe likes to reserve itself for only Lily, I know she isn't in the crowd of adults cleaning up from the day's event. I walk through the parking lot, scanning for her coppery braid. I spotted her car when I first arrived. It's the same Alpine white BMW she's been driving since she was sixteen, with the same forest-green frog dangling from the rearview. I recall the frog being a gift from her sister-in-law, some sort of running joke between them, so it isn't curious that she still has it. The car is baffling, though. Lily's family owns a chain of car lots, and I'd think that would make it all too convenient to opt for new rides.

My knees feel like jelly littered with shards of glass as I make a loop around the outside of the lot, dread mingling with anticipation. If Lily isn't gone, I have to follow through with my promise to talk to her. Meaning I'll ask her to go to dinner with me. Or for a walk in a park. I remember she was fond of taking walks on her lunch breaks back when she was interning at Mansfield Clinic.

While I'm interacting with Lily, if I don't look directly at her *or* breathe, I have a shot at being an adult who is simply having a conversation with another adult.

Earlier, Jill said Lily wasn't staying for cleanup and Lily confirmed that she had somewhere to be, but I didn't think that meant she was leaving the second time was called. Apparently, it did. I've walked the entire lot, she didn't move to a new parking spot, her vehicle is gone.

Disappointment makes my feet drag as I trek back the way I came, heading for my own vehicle because I'd rather not be here anymore either. I shouldn't feel this dejected. Talking to Lily is only an invitation to trouble anyway. Still, her absence hits like a rejection and despite the anger that's usually at my fingertips when I think of her and all the terrible things that have happened to me since she came into my life, being refused is disheartening.

I open the door of the silver Subaru I bought three years ago and slide into the seat. I should probably tell Jill I'm leaving, but I'd rather not deal with seeing anyone right now. I shift into gear and pull forward. A pop echoes through the cab. I hit the brake, the high-pitched hiss of rushing air forcing me to shift back into park.

I get back out of the vehicle and circle around to the front passenger tire. It's deflating fast. "Looks like karma is biting you for skipping out early instead of staying for cleanup duty." Jeremy stands at the corner of my bumper, arms crossed over his chest. "Or for being a jerk to Lily. Probably both."

I kneel down and inspect the tire, pulling a wooden-handled object from underneath the carnage. It's a blade of some sort, v-shaped with two sharp edges and a deadly point that's probably what pierced my tire. "What I do and don't do, particularly regarding Lily, is none of your business. Get that through your thick skull." I hand him the object. "Any idea what this is?"

He rolls it over in his hands, running his fingers along the knife-like edges. "Kind of looks like one of the tools the tile guy used when he refloored my entryway recently." He hands it back to me. "I'm no doctor, but my thick skull understands that you're bothered by Lily. What it doesn't know is *why*. Why do you turn into someone I don't recognize every time she's around?"

I open my trunk and take out the bag I keep in the back, pulling out mechanics' gloves and tugging them onto hands that eclipse Jeremy's. "I get that you think you're protecting Lily, but try considering that you're the one who needs protection from her."

He snorts. "Don't start with that junk about me having a thing for her because that's going to get you punched in the mouth. I have a wife and

I know my place. You're the one who's forgetting himself. Even if you have a torch for Lily but can't act on it because apparently, you're hot and heavy with Jill, you have no right to mistreat Lily."

I face him, finding the anger I lacked earlier. Because he's right about how I treat Lily, and it guts me. "Jeremy, if you're dumb enough to throw a punch, go ahead. I'll be happy to put you in the *place* you belong. The one that *isn't* in my business."

~

My friendship with Jeremy will never be the same, if I can even call him a friend at this point. I certainly haven't treated him like one. He can't be my confidant, though. What's inside me needs to stay there because even if Jeremy wouldn't fault me for my past, admitting out loud that I have feelings for Lily would be akin to stabbing myself in the chest. I don't even have a valid reason to desire her as much as I do. She's beautiful, but so are many other women. She's smart, at a level few other people are. She likes to read even more than I do, is in the medical profession same as me, isn't high maintenance as far as I can tell, and has the ambiance of a lazy Sunday afternoon spent curled up with a book and someone you love. She's basically all the things I've ever wanted. And she was all of those things far too young.

I grip my steering wheel, forcing the leather into the palm where the soft curve of Lily's hip is burned. I can still feel the warmth of her against me. It's as if her touch seared a brand straight through my clothing and everywhere our bodies connected, my skin remembers.

I give the clinic a sidelong glance as I drive past, slowing down to make the turn into the driveway that's obscured by a towering row of pines. Dad built the house first, then when he was ready to open his own clinic, he cleared the land by the main road and once the clinic was complete, connected it to the house with a breezeway. It was an easy commute for him and was supposed to be for me, too. When I returned from medical school, my parents gifted me the house. That was back when I still had dreams of raising my own family here.

I lose sight of the clinic once I'm behind the pines, and I'm glad for it. Now that I don't have a reason for the convenience of the location, the building is a weight around my neck. I park next to the mailbox that's as old as the house and stare at the childhood home turned cave of punishment. I had every intention of fixing this place up but the effort seems so pointless now. I'm Lily or bust, and one look around me says I'm bust.

I drag myself from the car, glancing at the only part of the clinic I can see from here——the windowless back where the breezeway juts off to join the house. Having only this view was a problem back when Lily interned here. I couldn't see if her car was out front or not. So once I left my job at Mansfield Clinic, I hung a pull-up bar from the ceiling just before the door on my side of the breezeway, setting a rule that for me to enter the clinic, I had to first do fifty pull-ups. While I did them, I would check my motives and ensure my intentions were pure. *Necessary*. Not excuses to put myself in the same room with Lily.

The pull-ups eventually became too easy so I added box jumps, making them progressively taller as they move toward that blessed clinic entrance. Other machines and obstacles came later, anything and everything to thwart every ill intention on my part.

I walk inside, tossing my keys into the dish sitting on the edge of the linoleum just before the carpet starts. Buying furniture also seems pointless. I don't invite people over. I'm simply going through the motions of life, holding down a mediocre job, and longing for physical fatigue. I want to hurt until the pain grinds down every thought of Lily. Especially ones that have me thinking I should tell her that I'm hopelessly in love with her.

I move through the small halls of a house built in an era when open floor plans didn't exist, bypassing the room I occupied as a child and navigating to the largest bedroom where my parents' old furniture still fills the space. I bought a new mattress and some bedding, but that was the extent of making this room mine.

I strip off my clothes and tug on a pair of cotton shorts, senses still heightened from having been so close to Lily. I smell her as strongly as if she's standing next to me. A problem I'll deal with by sweating until blood is dripping from my pores.

I hurry back through the halls, passing by the living room devoid of furniture save for Dad's old recliner. I kept it so he'd have a place to sit when he came to visit, but he doesn't come here anymore. What I've let the place turn into is embarrassing for both of us. Same as my presence in the clinic. So he doesn't come here and I don't go there.

I took the job at Pemberton and then slowly let my life fade away, never stepping foot in the clinic again, even after Lily left for the rehabilitation center. By then, all of my interactions with Dad were outside of working hours and we had developed unspoken rules about those interactions. I'm an only child so my betrayal in leaving his clinic hurt him deeply. He depended on me, and letting him down hollowed a chasm between us that he attempts to pretend isn't there, but nothing has been the same between us since I left.

I head back out the front door and cross over the gravel drive, slipping between branches until I hit a forest trail. I pick up my pace, looking for the obstacles I know are here, an easy rhythm taking over despite the uphill climb.

Legs pumping, I race up the incline and leap just as the hill falls away from where years of heavy spring rains have left their mark. I sail through the air, hands slamming around a sturdy branch with enough momentum that I swing my legs up and over, jumping from that branch to another. This one is thick. My hands struggle to maintain their grip. I pull up, clinging to the damp bark with all my might. I raise my chin above the branch, gritting my teeth and holding the position even with my hand strength failing.

I lower slowly, fingers aching and forearms burning, steam coiling from my nose like some savage beast. I hang in limbo, digging my grip into the branch until every muscle in my upper body screams in protest. When the pain reaches its height, I let go.

I drop to the forest floor, landing on the balls of my feet and pressing down into a squat. Sweat trickles down my back, my underarms already soaked. It's nearly impossible to burn out my legs but that never stops me from trying. With my upper body spent, the crucible begins for the rest of me.

I push up out of the squat, a prickle starting at the base of my skull and running icily over my neck. I wipe a hand over the spiky hairs and look around. It's rare to encounter another human out here, I can count the number of times it's happened on one hand. Not one of those times have I ever experienced my skin crawling with unease.

I move out of the trees and back onto the trail, scanning the woods around me. Silence surrounds me in every direction, except for the lone woodpecker carving through a dead stump in search of his dinner. I place my hands on my hips and turn in a slow circle, mimicking someone who's tired after a long run.

No one is on the trail, so they must be hiding in the foliage. *Why?*

Leaning into a lunge, I keep my eyes trained on my surroundings, ears open to any sound. There's nothing out of the ordinary and it's unlikely anyone could move out here without snapping a twig. I lunge in the other direction, stretching for the heck of it while I listen to the woodpecker fly off in search of his next meal. I'm not a paranoid person and I can't recall ever being afraid of anyone. Unless I count myself. What I feel for Lily has scared me since the night she imprinted herself on my soul. What's happening now is different. Someone *is* out here with me, and they're being very, very still.

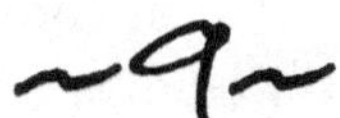

Dusk is setting. I leave the eerie stillness of the forest behind, sweat tinged with blood dripping down my face from the recklessness of busting through the underbrush to spook whoever was watching me. Branches and briars tore at me, but nothing moved. Not even a chipmunk.

With winter upon us, the nights are too cold for anyone to sleep in the forest. So if a human was out there, nerves of steel keeping them motionless as I careened through the woods around them, they'll soon be heading back to wherever they came from.

I don't own the forest so anyone is allowed to be in there, but there aren't many reasons for a person to hide. And none of them are good. Runaway, on the run, lost and hallucinating... I'll check in with the local police to see if anyone in the area is missing. A few of the detectives are Dad's patients.

I walk through my familiar front door, spine stiffening. Just like I *know* someone was in the woods today, I know someone is in my house. Or recently was. The air is different in here, a change in the stale environment as evident as lightning against a dark sky.

I move slowly from the foyer, confident that even in this closed floor plan, no one can catch me by surprise. I know every creak and squeak of every square inch. And I know exactly where the change of atmosphere is coming from. Someone is in the back of the house, at the breezeway door.

Moving by feel through the darkening house, I close in on the source of the disturbance. I circumvent the weight machines and box jumps, stopping outside the wooden door that leads into the breezeway. My pull-up bar hangs low in front of it, but it's wide open.

I don't leave this door ajar, let alone open. Not that I lock it. The key was lost when I was a teen and we never bothered calling a locksmith or even replacing the knob because on the other side of the cubicle-style breezeway is a solid steel door. It's thick and set into the brick walls of the clinic, making entry only possible if you know the keypad code.

The clinic door automatically locks when it's closed, so this simply isn't a viable access point for the clinic. But suppose a person didn't know that. In that case, they might think they could wait for me to leave on one of my routine runs and then slip inside while their lookout in the woods stayed perfectly still in order to alert the would-be thief of my return.

I spin away from the empty breezeway and do a quick scan of the rest of the house, grabbing a towel from the bathroom and running it over my face and chest. No one is in the house now, and I'm not concerned with whether or not they stole anything from me. I doubt there's any value to my parents' old bedroom set, and if someone really wants my rack of dumbbells, they're welcome to them. I need to replace some of them anyway, along with that old bed frame.

I meander back through my maze of gym equipment and enter the code I share with my dad into the keypad of the clinic's steel door, apprehension dripping through me as the deadbolt unlocks. I had no reason to believe Dad would change our code, but no reason to expect him not to either.

I push the door open and move into the hallway of the building that has become as taboo to me as Lily. Using the same code, I press my fingers over the buttons of the alarm pad and wait. The system disarms and I sigh in relief. The fact that it was set and not already blaring is another indicator that the clinic wasn't breached.

I walk with purposefully meticulous steps, checking each room and every closet. Dad always ran a tight ship and it's good to see that he still is. Everything is in its proper place and the pharmaceuticals appear to be in order.

Nostalgia swallows me as I sit down at Dad's desk, the prick of loss hitting me all over again. My mark should be inside of this building, but it isn't. Even my old office is gone, the space now doing double duty as a supply and records room. After what I did to Lily in there, I'm glad the desk that was underneath her when my lust-vision cleared is long gone.

I shake off the thought of her and train my eyes on the screen in front of them, trying not to remember anything about that night. Or to imagine all the times I pulled a chair right up to Dad's elbow when he was in the seat I'm now in, a sponge for absolutely every move he made.

I cue up the security log, every step of doing so exactly as I remember it. Dad's two employees, his new nurse Nathan and Evelyn the office manager, each have their own distinct codes. I can see when each of them has entered a code into any door or changed a setting on the security alarm. The access log shows nothing for today since the clinic was closed.

I scroll through the video footage of the exterior cameras. Every possible point of entry, including windows, has a designated camera. The only blind spot on the building is the back side, where there are no windows or doors. To enter the clinic from behind, you *have* to go through my house. Like someone attempted to do tonight.

I play back the footage, starting with the time I arrived home from the youth day event. My car passes the clinic, slowing just beyond the front parking lot and disappearing behind the wall of pine. Outside of that, no cars even tap their brakes, and I don't see anything on any of the other cameras outside of a stray leaf blowing by on the occasional breeze.

For good measure, I check the interior cameras that watch over the waiting room. Nothing has tripped the motion sensors today.

I turn off Dad's computer and make my way back toward my house, setting the alarm before I step into the breezeway and listening for the click of the deadbolt on the steel door when I shut it behind me.

Satisfied that the clinic is secure and uncompromised, I move toward my old wooden door. My hand cups the knob a fraction of a second before the smell assaults me. I was too worked up to catch it earlier, my senses all adrift, but the scent lingering in the air isn't a remnant of this afternoon's encounter with Lily. She's been here.

I move through the house at a hurried clip, nose sucking air through my nostrils like a straw. I smell her everywhere, but faintly. It's as if she sprayed her perfume in the breezeway and the odor snaked its way from there into the rest of the house. Even my bedroom.

I run to the front of the house and pull back the dusty blind on the bay window. The night is dark, a wall of black rising on the other side of the lawn where the forest starts. Was it Lily in the woods earlier? Did she send someone to spy on me so she could sneak in?

The wind picks up, that dark wall of trees slowly swaying. The forecast is calling for a dusting of snow tomorrow night, the temperatures plummeting tonight and the day significantly cooler tomorrow. No one would stay out there in this.

Chest tight, I go back to my bedroom and retrieve my phone, searching the house a little better this time. My poor housekeeping skills are basically an alarm system, but with Lily on the loose and doing...whatever it is she's trying to accomplish, I think it's time to install a real security system.

I dial my dad, putting him on speaker when he answers. "Hey, old man. Were you sleeping?"

"Close to it," he replies, his voice conjuring a vision of him sitting in his recliner with his glasses perched on his nose and a book in his lap.

I open the door to my old bedroom. The walls look the same as they did before I left for college, and the dust on my shelving is thick. The rest of the room is mostly full of boxes and books, and there's a nice layer of dust atop those, too. I inspect the room for fingerprints. "I won't keep you long, Dad. I just wanted to check in on you and see how things are going at the clinic."

"Oh, things are just fine. Nathan is one heck of a nurse. Thanks for sending him my way."

I don't see any fingerprints, so I go back out into the main part of the house, walking through the kitchen and opening every drawer. "You're welcome, I'm glad he's working out. Evelyn still keeping the place running for you?"

He yawns. "Yeah, she keeps the schedule on track and me pointed in the right direction. How about the hospital? You have a north star over there?"

I continue my inspection in the kitchen, opening cabinets. "I don't think a guiding light is the kind of help I need."

He chuckles. "Sounds to me like you're prime for one, then."

I grab a hand towel and wipe up the water stain on the counter beside my old glass coffee pot. A metallic sound pings off the floor. I squat down and check the linoleum, picking up the small screw. It doesn't belong to the coffee pot so it must be part of what fell from the microwave this morning. "You might be right, Dad. I've had a crummy day and it would have been nice if someone was around when I got home."

There's rustling on his end of the line this time. "Want to talk about your day?"

I roll the screw between my fingers, contemplating how to bring up Lily. "My microwave caught fire and I had a flat tire. Busted actually." I think about the tool that was under my car and how it might have gotten there. *Who* might have put it there. "I saw Lily Beller at the youth day event this morning."

"Is that so?" I can hear the smile in his voice. His lips always did turn up whenever she was around. "Then your day wasn't too bad after all."

I lift off the floor and make my way to his old recliner, sitting down with a thud. He's not going to believe anything bad about her, *I* don't want to believe it, but I can't ignore what's practically written in neon paint on my wall.

I scratch my jaw, thinking of how to ease into this. "Lily left early. She didn't stay for cleanup, and my day was definitely terrible from start to finish."

He yawns again. "If you're still using those old appliances, it's no wonder your microwave caught fire. And I imagine Lily did have to leave early. She's one busy young lady. Her family is getting ready to go on some kind of world cruise. Her Uncle Avery bought a new yacht and invited the whole family to break it in."

My heart rate picks up a little. "Lily's leaving?"

"No, no," he corrects. "She's one of the few who aren't going, though. I think a couple of cousins are staying behind, but her parents, brother, sister-in-law, and the rest of the lot are all going. They've been having some get-togethers before they shove off, seeing who they need to see because it sounds like this is an open-ended cruise. People will come and go as they please, but the yacht will likely remain at sea for the better part of a year."

Dad is one of the few people kept in the loop of what the Beller family is up to, so I'm not surprised he knows their travel plans. They all probably asked for physicals before the trip. This cruise information doesn't exactly help me with Lily's thieving ambitions, though. And she was very clearly trying to get into the clinic today. She just didn't think I'd also leave the youth event early. "So you've seen most of the family lately, but not Lily?"

"Aw," Dad chuckles. "I see my girl quite often. That's how I know she's not going with her family and probably had to leave the hospital's event today to go spend time with them. They've kicked up quite a fuss about her not being with them. And her brother more than her dad, if you can believe that."

I can't. I know John Beller, so I have firsthand experience with him not living up to his overbearing reputation, but I also know that he *can*, and doesn't have a problem surpassing it when it comes to his family. His son Mikey was always laid-back, but that changed after the girl he ended up marrying was attacked while they were still teenagers. I saw both Mikey and Dani quite a few times after the attack and they seemed to be recovering from the trauma, but recovering doesn't mean the scars go away and you return to who you were. Trauma changes us, and recovering means finding a new path forward.

I wonder if the wounds suffered by others in her family have trickled down to Lily, turning her into a dark version of the person we all thought we knew. "Sounds like Lily should pack up and go yachting around the world with her family." The line goes silent. I check the phone. "Dad? You there?"

"Yes, I'm here. But it's getting late and I doubt you called to talk about Lily's travel plans. Tell the old man what's really bothering you and then maybe we'll both get some sleep."

I lean back in his familiar recliner and remember all the times as a small child when I'd sit on his lap and read whatever book he was reading, the two of us quietly rocking the night away while Mom lounged on the couch and knitted. We truly had a perfect life. Then Mom died after being mowed down in a crosswalk by a distracted driver. That trauma changed Dad and me. Me more than I realized.

If I tell Dad that Lily tried to break into his clinic, there's a chance the emotional toll of losing his trust in her will be more damaging than having a stranger successfully breach the clinic. But her attempt was a failure, so there's really no reason to involve Dad. I'll confront Lily on my own. "I just needed to hear your voice. I miss you, Dad."

"I miss you too, son. Why don't you come over for dinner tomorrow night?"

"I'll be there. And I'll bring a fresh deck of cards so you can't cheat me again."

~10~

I'm sitting in Dad's recliner, staring at the bare walls of this living room, trying to reason out why Lily would attempt to break into the clinic. The steel door has always been there, so she knows about it but still decided to attempt accessing the clinic from here. There must be something inside she really wants. Whatever it is, simply asking would have most likely procured it. I doubt Dad would deny her anything, and a part of me wouldn't either. A part I may need to cut out and burn at the stake.

My phone rings and I glance at the screen. It's Jill, who should be at work right now. I hit the speaker button, forcing concern into my voice when all I feel is drained. "Everything okay?"

"No," she groans. "I'm sorry to wake you up, but Mr. Vass has crossed a line. He's downright belligerent tonight."

"Is there no doctor on call?"

She inhales. "There is. We were able to order Mr. Vass some sedatives so he's calm now but...he shook my nerves. He grabbed my breast and when I spun around to get away from him, he took a big handful of my backside. He listens to you because he's scared of you, so I was wondering if you could talk to him?"

"Not while he's under the sedative."

She sniffs. "I know. But will you talk to him sometime tomorrow?"

The pain in her voice prods my humane side. "I'm sorry you had to experience this, Jill. I'll let him know to keep his hands off of you and everyone else. Make a note in his chart that he needs male nurses assigned, and then see if you can use your new supervisor role to make sure a man is always on night shift. Mr. Vass won't be our last vulgar patient."

"That's unfortunately true." Her voice cracks. "We don't have any men here tonight. Lily said she'd take him and I told her no, but she swears his behavior doesn't bother her."

My jaw tics. "Doesn't bother her?"

She sighs. "Lily has a way about her. A way that men *like*, if you know what I mean. She's too young to know how flirting with people the way she does will get her into trouble. That's why I was in the man's room to begin with, I'm the supervisor so when he got belligerent with Kassidy, I took her place. Lily reprimanded me for it, like *she's* the supervisor, and said I should have just let her handle it. But I already knew how she'd *handle* it and I wasn't comfortable sending her in there only to encourage the man."

I flex my fingers, keeping them from clenching into fists. "Let the sedative do its job and there shouldn't be any more problems tonight. I'll have a talk with Mr. Vass once he's alert enough for it."

Jill sniffs again. "Thanks. It's been a really tough night already and I...I just don't know what's happening. The wheels are coming off the bus and I'm...worried."

"What else is happening?"

She lowers her voice. "You remember Mrs. McGhee?"

I swallow. "Yeah, she was due to be discharged."

"Not anymore," Jill huffs. "She coded an hour after my shift started. She's in ICU now. And Keirstyn, our pregnant hospital nursing supervisor, doubled over right inside the fishbowl, puking her guts out. So now she's a patient, and thankfully not on this floor because our refrigerator stopped working and all of our milk spoiled. Keirstyn is *known* for how much milk she drinks."

"Did the refrigerator get moved? That plug is a little loose and it seems like I recall there being a similar problem a few years ago."

She takes a beat, inhaling deeply. "I'll ask Lily. She's the one who told me the thing was a furnace, almost like it was running but putting out hot air instead of cold."

"Lily, huh?" I contemplate whether or not she could have come into my house before, tampered with my microwave, and that's why the screw was out of the back of it. "You might want to keep Lily away from the appliances. All the rest sounds like par for the course, so don't worry about it. Just follow protocol and you'll be fine."

I hang up with her and go to my bedroom, pull clothes out of the closet, and head for the shower. I'm not going to get any sleep tonight so I might as well do something productive with my time. Lily can't run away from me while she's working, and I'm going to use that fact to my advantage. I don't know what I ever did to her but I'm tired of being manipulated. If she wants to break into my house, I'm going to break into her life and shine that little spotlight of hers right onto the calculating heart inside of her.

~

Trudging into the hospital cafeteria before heading upstairs, I stifle a yawn. If I'm going to confront Lily, I need enough caffeine in my veins to keep me alert enough to consider the odds that my microwave kicked the bucket the same morning that my car had what looks suspiciously like an intentional flat, followed up with a break-in. I'd say those odds are slim. More likely, Lily wanted me away from my house, by fire or flat. Once she explains why, she can explain what made her scheme against me five years ago.

I stifle another yawn and punch buttons on the coffee machine. Compared to what I make at home in my old glass pot, this brew is pretty decent. Dad keeps telling me to upgrade to one of the single-serve machines like he has in his clinic, but I rarely ever bothered with those flavored pods when I worked in the clinic so I'm good with this dark cup of sludge.

Fitting a lid onto my cup, I glance around the sparsely filled cafeteria. When I'm here during the day, this place is bustling. Tonight, there's maybe a dozen people...and Lily. She's in a booth at the end of the room, the lanky redhead from the brewery beside her. His arm is fitted around her shoulders and his lips are hidden in the crook of her neck. He moves the hair away from her ear and whispers. She laughs. His mouth dips forward, covering hers.

A strangled gurgle lodges in my throat, a tick in my arm slamming the fisted cup of coffee into my chest. The lid pops off. Steaming liquid explodes over the front of me. I drop the mangled cup and pull the tail of my button-up from my slacks, fanning it away from my body. The sound of footfalls rushes toward me and I cringe. It's *them. Her.*

"I've got it." I swat Lily's hand away when she tries to help keep my scalding shirt off my body. "The coffee here is barely warm."

"Not unless they've changed it recently." She calls out the lie and grabs a stack of napkins, dabbing at my shirt as I hold it out.

The redhead snatches a handful of napkins and lowers down to clean up the mess on the floor. I study his lightly muscled arms, one of them covered in a sleeve of tattoos. He looks up at me with a grin on what I guess Lily considers a handsome face. "The java here is terrible, so you're lucky this landed on the floor instead of in your stomach."

Lily laughs, a sardonic sound instead of the melodic one. "Dr. Mansfield despises even the possibility of spilled coffee, no matter if it's your fancy imported beans or this cheap hospital fare."

The boy straightens to his full height, about an inch taller than me but not remotely close to my weight class. My arms are thicker than his thighs, and I bet my thighs are larger than his scrawny waist.

I move away from the couple, angry that I even care to size the boy up. I unbutton my shirt and clean off my chest, unable to keep myself from side-eyeing the two of them. They throw their napkins away and Lily slips her hand into his, smiling up at him. He dives toward her lips and I spin in the opposite direction. I have a spare collared shirt upstairs and it's in my best interest to go change because I do *not* need to see them making out. I need to keep my cool tonight, approach Lily with a clear mind, and focus my thoughts solely on getting her to expound on why she's made it her life mission to destroy me.

I exit the cafeteria and move more composed than I feel to the elevator, getting inside and allowing my finger to smash against the buttons unnecessarily hard. "Hold the elevator!" Lily rushes through the closing gap, forcing the doors to open wide. I trail my eyes to where she just came from, her boyfriend heading out of the hospital through the main doors. That's a relief, because my pulse is already raging and the pounding in my head might manifest outside of my body if I have to see her kiss that boy one more time.

I stare straight ahead as the elevator begins its ascent. "What are you doing, Lily?"

She holds a thermos up, showing the extra cup in her hand. "Gideon is a coffee snob so he brings me a special blend about every shift, and he asked me to share with you. So here."

She shoves the empty cup toward me and I don't take it. Nor do I look at her. "Coffee isn't why you went out of your way to make sure you got into this elevator with me."

She twists the top off of her thermos and holds it up to my nose. "What do you smell? Gideon is always asking but to me, it just smells like plain coffee."

I break, setting my gaze on her and tightening my jaw as a reminder that I'm against her, not in love with her. "Get your excuse out of my face. I don't want to smell your coffee, the same way I don't want to smell *you*. Not at work, in my car, and sure as hell not in my house."

She tips the thermos to her lips, green eyes watching me overtop it. "Are you telling me that I stink?"

I move closer to her. A mistake. "I'm telling you that I don't buy for one single second that your boy Gideon just *happened* to be here making a special coffee delivery. Is he waiting for you outside? Or heading back over to my place?"

The elevator door opens on our floor and she inches toward the hall, eyes staying on mine. "Gideon uses the coffee as an excuse to come see his girlfriend, and the last time I checked, that's me. Not you. So no, he isn't heading to *your* place. Unless you're calling Jill's house yours now? Is that what this is about? Is your girlfriend making up stories about Gideon the way she's making them up about Mr. Vass?"

The muscles in my neck tense, the headache at the base of my skull intensifying. "Jill and I are not a thing, and I'm tired of you making snide comments about us."

She steps fully into the hallway, twisting the lid back onto her thermos. "Take your own advice, Doctor, and keep my name out of your mouth. And define for Jill what *not a thing* is, because she talks about you incessantly and Emelia Alice is almost as bad. Seems your indecent display in their living room left quite the impression on *both* twins."

I follow Lily into the hall, gripping her arm and swinging her into my chest, voice rumbling from deep in my throat. "What about *your* indecent display? I saw you at the brewery, but you already know that. Does your daddy also know? That you tempt grown men and wear dishtowels for dresses?"

Her eyes glitter like the hard surface of an emerald. "I buy most of my clothing from my mother's boutique, and since my father is by her side every single moment of every single day, he's well aware of what's in my closet. But you feel free to take any grievances you have about me up with him. I'm sure he'll be *thrilled* to hear from you. Especially after he hears about the harassment charge you're leaving me no choice but to file."

I release her arm and slam my palm against the wall, face lowering into hers, that infernal intoxicating scent of ambrosia tearing through my flared nostrils. "Right back at you. Because among many other things, you broke into my house. So don't pretend you're the only one with a harassment claim, *angel.*"

$$\sim 11 \sim$$

Voices echo down the corridor and I drop my hand from where it's planted on the wall in front of Lily's face, my still unbuttoned shirt hanging open while shock leaps from her eyes down to her open mouth. My resolve falters, the cursed part of me wanting to believe the innocence I see in her. I never meant to get so angry with her, just enough to keep from whispering this. "Lily, I need you."

Her lips quiver. "What?"

I drag a hand through my hair and clear my throat, stepping away from her as footsteps fall closer to us. "I need you to come with me. To the doctors' lounge so we can talk, because I can't take much more of this. I'm already a mess."

"You think I'm not?" she hisses. "You treat me like——"

"I know." I stop her with a nod to where footsteps are growing ever closer. She doesn't want to be caught out here any more than I do. "Please give me one ounce of mercy and come with me because I need this like veins need blood and lungs need air. "

Silent as a corpse, she follows me down the tiled hall to the doctors' lounge. I seize the door handle and yank it open, breathing in a lungful of relief at finding it empty. I thought it would be, but my luck is usually anything but good.

I usher Lily inside and shut the door behind us. She stops in the center of the room and spins to face me, anger simmering behind haunted emeralds. I turn toward my locker to keep from following through on the urge to drag her into my arms and fit my mouth over hers. She just kissed that redheaded string bean anyway. Her tongue probably tastes like him and his coffee.

I strip out of my stained shirt and toss it into the bottom of my locker.

"I didn't know you had a tattoo," she mutters.

I pull a fresh shirt over the kraken that covers my entire back, its tentacles reaching to the edges of where even just a t-shirt will cover it. The tattoo is personal for me. No one has ever seen it except for the tattoo artist who spent months using me as a canvas.

I face Lily again, working the buttons of my clean shirt into place. "What's happening between us ends tonight. I'm sorry for any and all emotional damage I caused you five years ago, and any that I've caused since you started working at Pemberton. But you're pushing me past every breaking point. I recover from one just to have you push me further. You have to stop, Lily. Especially where my job is concerned. I'm not letting you take my job away again."

"Again?" she balks. "I don't know what your problem with me is but I do know your issues are not *my* problem. I've never taken a single thing from you and I certainly haven't ever *pushed* you into anything. The choices you make are your own, the same as mine are my own."

I walk toward her. "Until the choice you make is to manipulate me. Then your choices become mine, and you've already taken *every* single thing from me. So fess up to what you've been doing and let's resolve the situation because this hospital isn't a battleground. We can't bring our personal issues here and turn them loose, letting my job become collateral damage."

Her eyes narrow. "What exactly are you accusing me of? Because all I'm doing in this hospital is *my* job, though I know that's hard for you to believe since you think the only thing I have to offer is my last name."

I stop short of being within touching distance. "I don't care about your last name, but you can't be oblivious to the fact that people like Angela do. From what Jill says, Angela is basically stalking the med-surg floor these days. That level of interest has everything to do with you."

Lily folds her arms. "Or it could have more to do with your girlfriend's incessant complaining. She's practically a part of Angela's ear now, always talking about what needs to change and how things should be better."

I groan. "Not my girlfriend. And isn't that what supervisors are supposed to do? Go to bat for their nurses and make things better?"

Lily laughs. Genuinely. "I didn't say she was championing the cause of nurses the world over. Jill champions Jill. She doesn't like having to use the nurses' lounge as an office, like every other floor supervisor in this hospital. Jill thinks she deserves a private office, like Keirstyn has. So Keirstyn came to have a chat with Jill and instead, puked all over her shoes, which gave Jill a whole new thing to complain about. In fact, you're about the only thing Jill doesn't complain about. When it comes to you, it's more of a brag. Congratulations on doing what no one else can. You make her very happy."

Lily's audacity makes my blood boil, the heat coiling through my insides and forcing my feet to not stay a safe distance away. I move into her space, palms itching to touch her. "Stop using your slander of Jill to deflect from the answers you *are* going to give me. Why were you in my house earlier? You know you can't break into the clinic from there, and as far as I can tell, you didn't steal anything. So what were you doing, Lily?" My heart thuds with a sudden thought. "Did you plant some sort of incriminating evidence in hopes of framing me?"

Her breath grows shallow. "You think I was in your house today?"

I study the emotion on her face, head tilting closer to her as if feeling her breath on my lips will clear up the muddy look in her eyes. "Hours after the youth event, I came home to find the place smelling just like your perfume." I inhale deeply, closing my eyes to savor every particle of her scent. "You left the breezeway door open, too. So don't deny what I already know to be true. Just tell me why." I meet her eyes, speaking softly. "Why, angel? Why are you doing so many terrible things to me?"

She glances at the clock on the wall, eyes rimmed in red when they swing back to meet mine. "I wasn't in your house, I don't wear perfume, and I'm late getting back from break."

She moves right and I slide in front of her. "You smell, Lily. So try a different lie because you've used the same perfume since you were sixteen."

She yanks a handful of her coppery locks forward and smashes them into my nose. "*This* smell? It's called shampoo, and I've been using it since I was *fourteen*, when my friend Madge gave me a bottle to try. I liked it, and because I'm a creature of habit, I've kept buying the same thing all these years. Like *thousands* of other women. Maybe one of them broke into your house, but *I* didn't!"

This scent is hers and hers alone, no one else has it. I know because I've never been tempted to lick anyone else, but Lily makes my tongue loll out of my mouth like a damn puppy.

I back away from her and run a hand down my face, swallowing my pooling saliva. "Lily, I've never smelled that smell on anyone else. And in a small space like that breezeway, the scent is overwhelming. Like walking into a room where an older lady who hoses herself down in perfume has been, or a teenager using body spray. So explain that to me because forasmuch as I *truly* don't want to believe the worst of you, the worst is all you're giving me to work with." I meet her fiery eyes. "Why are you trying to destroy my life? Did I do something to you when you were a kid? Not let you recite an encyclopedia to me or something?"

Her eyes swell with tears and she cups the thermos to her chest. I remove what little distance I put between us and trace my knuckles down the side of her face. "Don't cry. Just talk to me. Tell me what I've done, what you've done, what *we* can do."

Defiance lifts her shoulders, despite the shake in her voice. "What you can do is stop going out of your way to make me your enemy. Then you can act like a professional and get yourself under control because if I wanted to get inside the clinic, I'd use my key and walk through the front door."

She moves around my stunned frame and opens the door. "Ask your girlfriend about the smell. Her sister borrows my shampoo and maybe Jill is now helping herself to it, too."

I recover from the shock of her having a key to the clinic and chase after her. "Lily!" I run into the hall outside the lounge and dart toward the corner. Lily disappears around it and I skid as I scramble after her. Jill and Kassidy both jump, wide eyes watching me. I straighten, buttoning the last button on my shirt and tucking it into my slacks. Jill's eyes drag over my movements, head slowly turning toward where Lily was just seconds ago. Kassidy is fairly new on this floor and I don't know her very well. She's young and currently trying not to make eye contact with the doctor who looks like he just got caught in a compromising position with a nurse.

I straighten my clothing and walk toward Jill and Kassidy. "How's Mr. Vass? After your call earlier I thought I should come in and be here in case he wakes up."

Jill shifts her eyes to my face. "He's sleeping. We just checked on him since Lily was nowhere to be found."

I clear my throat. I don't want a rumor spreading about Lily because of me. "Sorry, that's my fault. I ran into her when she was coming back from break and held her up."

Jill's lips flatten. "Is everything okay? Or is there something going on that I should know about?"

"I was asking Lily about Mrs. McGhee and getting an update on Keirstyn. I'm going to run upstairs and check on both of them after I check on Mr. Vass," I lie, lifting a lock of her hair. "Have you ever borrowed Lily's shampoo?"

Her eyes narrow. "No. Why? Do I smell like Lily?"

Not even close. I let the hair drop. "You smell like a summer day in a forest full of California redwoods."

"Aw," Kassidy coos.

My stomach flips. Jill is smiling ear to ear. "So I'm a place you'd like to spend your time?"

Life would be a lot easier if she was, but hers isn't the skin I want to lose myself against. I already tried to, and I barely remember the encounter. Yet I remember how every strand of Lily's hair glows in every light in which I've ever seen her. I glance at Kassidy. She looks away. I raise a brow at Jill. "I'm going to go. I'll probably try to nap in the doctors' lounge later so if Mr. Vass wakes up, give me a call and I'll come nurse him for you."

She steps forward and presses a palm against my chest. "If you're asking about me borrowing Lily's shampoo, then she obviously told you about Emelia Alice using it. My sister did borrow it without asking, but in her defense, when Lily moved in, she told Em and me both that we were welcome to whatever she had. So it's hardly fair that she keeps droning on about it like Emelia Alice is a thief. My sister apologized and neither of us will ever touch anything that belongs to Lily again. So don't..." Her face falls, voice lowering for only me to hear. "Don't believe everything she says. Look at the facts and see what makes sense because I think Lily is a compulsive liar. And a good one."

~12~

I want to believe that Lily is a darling little ethereal creature with a button nose and eyes that shine because she is light itself. But if I believe Jill, Lily is anything but divine. If I believe Lily, Jill is the liar. Then there's the writing that's practically jumping off the wall and slapping me in the face. I worked with Jill for a long time before Lily came around and all was well. Now the ground is shaking again and Lily is standing in the epicenter.

Two years after my departure from Mansfield Clinic, Dad proudly announced that Lily had completed her RN training and was off to work in a rehabilitation center. I spent that whole dinner weighing the decision of whether or not to ask for my old job back. With her gone, I could go back to fulfilling the dream Dad and I had always talked about. But that dream only worked when I thought I was a good person. Or at least not a despicable one. So I didn't beg for forgiveness and ask to return. Just like I didn't consider whether or not he deleted her access code, I made the assumption that doing so would be standard practice. But Lily specifically used the word *key*. That I know of, the clinic is solely coded access, the only keys being an emergency set that Dad has.

"Uh-oh," Dad winces from the other side of his dining room table. "Looks like you had a rough day at the hospital, son."

I push a piece of chicken around in the alfredo-sauced pasta on my plate. Lily is possibly trying to make me lose my medical license if not burn down my house in the process, and yet I want nothing more than to hold her and tell her everything is okay. That I'm sorry. That I deserve everything she's done to me. And that I love her.

Love!

I drop my fork onto the side of my plate. "Dad, was there ever a time in your life when you felt like nothing was going to work out right? Like you wouldn't ever have love, a family, or even a career?"

He nods. "Oh, sure. I think those feelings are normal for any man. We worry we're not good enough, *handsome* enough, smart enough." His eyes crinkle. "But you're a lot more handsome than I ever was and with the way you're always studying the latest developments in the medical field, you're a whole lot smarter too."

I'm only proactive in scouring the literature because he taught me to be a doctor who never stops learning, citing the unfortunate truth that by the time research makes it into the education system, it's already outdated. "I care about people. I want to help them, but I don't feel...like I can do this job anymore."

His head tilts. "You think you're making mistakes in the care of your patients?"

I swallow. "No, nothing like that. *Yet.* But I'm not in a good place mentally or in my personal life, so am I really capable of administering the best care?"

I want to fight for my job the same way I want to fight my growing attachment to the green-eyed angel who cloaked me in shame to begin with. I don't want to love Lily. Her academic accomplishments and her clearly brilliant mind are where I want my admiration to end.

I stare at the man who has always been my best friend. I've told him everything, except for anything about Lily. It's bad enough to know how much I've hurt him, I couldn't handle it if he despised me.

He scratches the scruff at the base of his chin, wise old eyes thinking about my question. "Before I met your mother, I was lonely. People used to commend me for working long hours but I had nothing else to do, no family obligations or anyone I wanted to see. So my dedication was more to do with lack of engagements than anything else. Looking back, if I'd met your mother sooner, I may not have learned enough to feel comfortable opening my own practice." He sits forward. "I guess what I'm saying is your life will come together when it's time. While you wait, all you can do is involve yourself in the things that interest you. The right person for you will fit into the life you live, and you'll fit into theirs. Now if the mental issues you're having aren't in regard to being as lonely as I used to be, then we need to do a little more than wait on your perfect match to show up."

Tension feathers through me. Lily is my perfect match. But she might be trying to ruin me. And she has *Gideon.* Considering she thinks *he's* kissable, she probably thinks I'm gross. Some old, creepy doctor with a chip on his shoulder that she's plainly stated she's tired of. "The decline of my mental health has everything to do with my personal life, but having dinner with you helps lighten the mood." I point at my plate and hope my face doesn't look as strained as I feel. "We're not too shabby when it comes to following Mom's old recipes."

He mops up the sauce on his plate with a garlic breadstick. "There's no replacing the nostalgia that comes from sharing a meal like the ones we used to get from her."

Just like we lost her, I know one day I'll lose him. I'm hard-pressed to want a life beyond the day when I'll lay him to rest. I'll be completely alone then. I don't even have Jeremy's friendship anymore. We haven't spoken since he walked away from the parking lot and left me to change my tire by myself.

Along with the last bites of my food, I swallow down the lump of emotion in my throat. "You ready to chase this meal with a few hands of rummy?"

Dad leans back in his chair, hand resting on his stomach. "You bested me last time. Old age is making me lose my touch."

I clear our plates and place them in the dishwasher. "Me taking away your old deck of cards made you lose your touch. I think you had the very feel of those cards memorized."

His eyes crinkle with amusement. "Maybe so. By the time you have kids, you can have this new deck memorized."

I shuffle the cards. Me having kids has been a sore spot. Mom used to ask all the time if I'd met anyone because she wanted to live long enough to meet her grandchildren. Back then, I thought I had plenty of time to make that happen for her.

I feel horrible about losing the opportunity to give her the one thing she asked of me, and I know Dad has the same request, although he doesn't ever put it into exact words. But I only want children if I can be a dad like mine was, and it's evident that I'm incapable of even coming close.

Clearing my throat of the ball of emotion that's determined to live there, I deal the cards and think of how best to bring up Lily. If she has some kind of key for the clinic, that means she also has a code for the alarm. If she has those two things, she can easily go through the clinic and enter my house. That I know of, no one but Dad has ever done so. I didn't see Lily on the camera feed either, but maybe she somehow erased the footage. "I ran into Lily again last night. Or this morning rather." I shake my head, the effects of too little sleep and too much caffeine. "I had to go into the hospital a few hours early, so our paths crossed."

Dad leans back in his chair and takes a sip of his sweet tea. "I suppose that's going to happen from time to time. Pemberton is a big hospital but you two are working on the same floor."

I chew my lip. "Yeah, imagine the odds of that."

His brow cocks. "I thought you'd be pleased. I was. She gets to spy on you for me." I cock my brow right back at him. He chuckles. "You know I stay well and good out of your business. But I *was* pleased that the two of you would be reunited again. It's been what, going on five years since you worked together?"

I shift, muscles bristling under my skin. "I never worked with her. She was your intern, unofficially, and I tolerated her presence."

He sets his glass down. "If you insist on semantics, fine, that's how it was. But even as a mentee, that girl worked. And I know for a fact that she works even harder today."

I pick up my cards and sort them in my hand. "Do you now? She says she has a *key* to the clinic. Is that true? Or is she working hard at spinning tales?"

He sorts his own cards, picking his glasses back up and perching them on his nose. "Lily has a spare key. The other is locked up in my safe since we all have codes to the doors. There's no worry about either key getting misplaced, if that's what you're worried about."

My gut tightens. "Lily has one of the emergency keys? You gave it to her for safekeeping instead of giving it to me?"

He lays a spread of sevens on the table. "You have access to my safe so it didn't make sense to also give you the extra key."

"Maybe not. Buy why *Lily*? I know you're fond of her, but she isn't family. I am."

He takes a beat before answering. "Lily may not be my blood but I consider her family. And even when she doesn't have to, she still works for me. So giving her the spare key in case something ever happened and no one could reach me or you was an non-decision. I trust her with everything I have. Everything I am."

Shame and anger slither over my skin, feeding off each other. His implication is clear. I left the family practice, therefore I'm not dependable. "What do you mean *Lily works for you*? I thought she left for the rehab center a few years ago, and I know she's working at Pemberton now because I have to see her face every aggravating day."

He gives me a disappointed look. "Your tone is uncalled for. Yes, Lily worked at the rehab center and she left there to work at Pemberton. But she also works for me part-time. Always has. That's why she works night shift at Pemberton the same way she worked nights at the center, so she can be at the clinic during the day."

His words are a knife that draws blood two ways. "She's been working at Mansfield the whole time and you didn't tell me?"

His fingers drum the table. "I don't recall ever telling you she didn't."

"That's something one would naturally assume when told she was taking another job," I balk. "I've barely heard her name come off your lips and suddenly she not only works for you, but is the keeper of your emergency key? Is she your emergency contact on all of your accounts, too?"

He picks up his cards again. "Rarely do we discuss the ins and outs of the clinic itself, and I wasn't aware that you cared to know about them.

That's why when it comes to the clinic, Lily is second to only me. In all of my other matters, I still have my son named as my heir." His eyes land on mine. "Is that what this is about? Your inheritance?"

My spine goes ramrod stiff. "Of course not. I make more money than I need and I don't want your things, Dad. I want *you*. But it feels like you've written me off...replaced me with Lily freaking Beller."

His features draw down. "When it comes to the clinic, Lily did replace you. That girl is darn good on home visits, same as you used to be, even when they had you out both early and late. Most of my patients prefer her to me, and I can never decide if that's because she's a better doctor than me or because she's prettier." His lips turn up into a sympathetic half-smile. "I encouraged her to take on other positions when she was content to stay, and at eighteen, any day she had off from the rehab center she was in the clinic seeing how she could help. So neither she nor I planned for things to turn out how they have, it just evolved this way and now I depend on her the way I used to depend on you."

My jaw tics. "Except she's a nurse, not a doctor, so she *can't* replace me."

He folds his cards onto the table. "Son, when was the last time you were in the clinic?"

Sadness crawls through me. "I told you I'd help anytime you needed me."

He takes a sip of tea. "And I just told you that I had Lily, so I didn't need to call on you. Besides, when you left the practice, you did so because you didn't want to do the type of doctoring I do. And that's okay. You made your choices and I made mine. I won't sit here and second-guess yours any more than I'll tolerate you second-guessing mine. I tried to get Lily to go, thinking she'd want to spread her wings the same as you did, but she didn't. Not entirely."

I toss my cards onto the table. "Therein lies the problem. Have you ever questioned *why* Lily keeps herself weaseled into the clinic? She's not who you think she is. I don't trust her, and you shouldn't either."

He slowly lifts from his chair. "It's late, it's time for you to go."

My jaw falls slack. "You're kicking me out? Over *Lily*."

He scoots his chair in and grips the back of it, mouth turned down. "I love you, son. With every fiber of my being. But I love Lily, too. That girl has been good to me and the least I can do is refuse to hear ill of her in my own home. I'm going on to bed now, you can see yourself out."

~13~

Next to me, Lily is the closest thing Dad has to a progeny so I understand his attachment to her. I'd like to think that if someone darkened his doorstep with my name on their lips, he'd send them away too. But why should he? I haven't done a single redeeming thing since I fell for Lily. I keep messing up, and the evening I spent with him last week proved just how dire the situation is. We've barely spoken since then. And not only because of what happened that night. It's also because I replaced my back door, putting a keyless lock on it and setting the code to something completely different than the one I've always shared with him. When I asked him to not give the code out to *anyone*, the line fell silent. He knows I meant Lily, which widened the gulf between us.

I flop a pillow over my head to silence the pounding in my skull. Moisture hits my lips, wet and...furry. I jerk the pillow back and open my eyes. There's a blob of bloody gray fur protruding from just beneath my nose. I swat it away, shoving out of bed as the mouse splats against the wall, its innards trailing out of its body. I spit into my hands and claw at my lips, rushing into the bathroom to wash the tang of its bloody intestines from my mouth.

The pounding from earlier continues. But it isn't in my head. "Hold on!" I yell to whoever is at the door. Outside of the occasional delivery person, I don't get visitors. And it's too early for deliveries.

I take my washcloth with me to the door, still running it over my lips and nose when I pull the old oak slab open. I probably should have looked to see who was out there first, but unless someone brought a gun to a hand fight, I'm not too worried about anyone getting the drop on me. Especially Lily and her little boy Gideon. Or this woman standing in front of me. She looks to be in her late fifties, her scraggly brown hair tickling the top of her round-rimmed glasses. She's just staring at me, eyes somewhere around the waistband of my boxers.

I motion toward the frost-covered porch beneath her feet. "It's a little chilly this morning, so is there something I can help you with?"

She adjusts her oversized denim jacket. "I'm delivering papers and well, you're the doctor who runs this clinic here, right? I brought my boy here once when he got a bad case of the chicken pox."

I glance down the long driveway and see an old blue SUV with a yellow caution light on top of it. "Yeah, I'm one of the Dr. Mansfields. What can I help you with?"

Her eyes dart to my lower torso again, her tongue flicking over her chapped lips before she has the decency to stop ogling me. She points at the back of the clinic. "I deliver papers here, and well, there's a dead cat right on the welcome mat." She taps her foot on the solid black mat in front of my door, as if to show me what a welcome mat is. "I figured you'd want to get that cleaned up before any patients came. You know, diseases and all. Looks like it might have been hit by a car and rambled over to your clinic trying to get some help." She laughs at her joke. I don't.

"Thanks for letting me know. I'll get it cleaned up."

She tugs on her ill-fitting jeans and I say enough of a goodbye to be somewhat professional. It's barely dawn and I'm basically naked, so I doubt it really matters.

She backs out of the driveway and I wait until her headlights disappear before I close the door. "Maybe the cat and mouse had a fight, and they both sought medical attention." I make the joke out loud and look around the empty house. In all the years I've lived here, I can't recall having such bad luck. Of course, the parts that include Lily aren't luck but intelligent design. I can't fault her for the dead animals, though. I'm not entirely sure I can fault her for the microwave. But I can sure as heck blame her for stealing my own father right out from under my nose.

Going back into the bedroom, I inspect the mouse. Its stomach is ripped open so it's likely it *did* have a run-in with claws. How it got to my bed in this condition is a mystery, though. It's times like these that I wish I wasn't a deep sleeper, but when I can finally get my brain to shut off, it's usually because my body has no choice but to shut it down.

I tug a t-shirt from the dresser and pull on a pair of sweatpants, fitting the shirt over my head and grabbing a pullover from the closet. I ramble into the kitchen, washing my hands and starting a pot of coffee.

Armed with a roll of paper towels, I go back into the bedroom and wrap up the mutilated mouse. He's getting dumped in the woods. If a scavenger doesn't find the body, the smell of decomposition won't bother me. When you live in an area like this one, you get used to the occasional waft of decay on the wind. Things die in nature, it's part of life. Kind of like my soul. Not all men get to have dreams.

~

I'm not inclined to leave this little kitten out in the woods where a scavenger can pick it apart. It's well and dead, its head crushed on one side and its body splayed awkwardly over the clinic's mat. The impact of the car must have tossed its lifeless body to this exact spot.

I use the end of my shovel to move the tabby onto a waiting towel and then gingerly wrap the soft blue fabric around the body. I don't have to work today and I'm in no rush to be anywhere, so there's plenty of time to give this little guy a proper burial.

I dig a hole at the edge of the woods, cushion the dirt with a layer of leaves, and gently place the blue towel inside. The marbled orange cat entombed here can't be more than a year old. Too young to have had a fulfilling life. "I'm sorry, little fella," I whisper to him, wondering if there's a family somewhere missing him. He didn't have a collar but it could have been ripped from his neck when the car hit him. I'll have to check the parking lot and ditch line.

I take my time selecting rocks, circling them first around the mound of dirt and then placing them on top of the grave to deter critters from digging the cat up. I've never had a pet before but maybe I should get one. Something to keep me company so I'm not alone with my thoughts. I could talk to the cat about my fractured relationship with Dad and how it's Lily's fault. And about how I put tears in her eyes, something I'd rather be in this grave than ever do again.

My phone rings. I settle the last rock into place and slide the phone out of my pocket. It's Jill. I've done a pretty good job of avoiding her at work, thanks to our different shifts, and she isn't contacting me overly much, but she's called a few times and I always regret answering. Not because she's flirting, she's as normal as I think the two of us can be, given how I practically inhaled her. But I don't want the friendship she seems to be seeking. If Lily moved in with Jill because of me, any attention I give Jill, even friendly attention, could make Lily act out. For what purpose, I have no idea. When I cornered her in the doctors' lounge she didn't show any fondness for me. Not that I gave her a chance. Maybe she wants me to, though. Or maybe Lily inserting herself into my life again for the sole purpose of gaining my attention is only wishful thinking on my part.

I let Jill's call go to voicemail, listening to it when it pings. "Hi, Darren, it's Jill. I know we've had some tension lately and you aren't Lily's biggest fan. Neither am I. But Emelia Alice has gone totally overboard with this *roommate welcome party* and...and if you're not here, I'm going to be alone because you're the only person on my guest list. So will you please come? You're the only person I know who sees Lily for the conniving little girl she is. And trust me, after you hear about what I just found out, you're going to finally understand why she was so eager to rent my spare room."

~14~

Jill's driveway is full and two other cars are parked on the street, so I pull in behind the last one and tamp down my apprehension. When I returned her call, hoping to get the information about Lily without coming here, Jill only begged me to show up. She promised it was a low-key affair, and I promised her the size of her party wasn't what concerned me.

I take the bottle of wine from my backseat. This was given to me by a doctor I interned with in medical school and has been tucked in an unpacked box ever since. I'd forgotten about it until I went searching the boxes in my old bedroom to make sure Lily didn't plant something incriminating in my house.

Wind swirls fallen leaves across the yard, the chill nipping at my nose as I approach the door of the Tudor house. Soft music is playing but sounds like it's coming from outside instead of inside where it's warm.

The front door opens and Jill tightens a blue blanket around her shoulders, eyes bright and smile wide. "You made it!"

I hand her the bottle of wine. "I told you I was coming."

She scans the wine, taking my arm and pulling me across the threshold. "This will pair perfectly with our dinner. Thank you."

Her lips plant on my cheek and I cringe. "I see the cars outside, but where are the people?"

She nods toward the back of the house where lights glow through a glass-paned door. "Em wanted one last night under the stars, so she set up heaters on the deck."

I glance at Jill's blanket. It's cold out and I didn't wear a jacket, but she's in a dress that flares around her knees, her legs bare, so I follow where she's leading and exit the door with her. A mistake. One quick scan of the scene reveals what this event really is. A low table sits in the center of the deck, pillows and blankets surrounding it. Lounging on the pillows are five clear and distinct couples. Jill and I will make the sixth. Meaning this is a date I never agreed to.

My eyes want to face Jill so I can tell her I'm not okay with this, but they're glued to the vision at the end of the table. Lily is draped in a flowing green dress that pools around her, the color making her eyes practically glow. My pulse goes haywire, the beast inside me wanting to rip her from the chest she's reclined against. Gideon is behind her, legs open and arms around her. I expected him to be here, but was hoping I wouldn't feel the itch to rip his hands from his arms and shove them down his throat.

Jill tugs me forward, kneeling in the only open spot for us. I break Lily's stare, her eyes on me the way mine are stuck on her. It's bad enough that my brain wants to play the Lily show all day and I'm stooge enough to glue myself to the screen, I don't need the live show. Especially while she's in someone else's arms.

I drop down beside Jill, numb and unfocused on the chatter around me, my heart a caged animal. My muscles contract, coiling as if they're preparing to rip free of my flesh. "...Camilla?" Jill's voice sounds too close.

I close my eyes. "What?"

She laughs. "Camilla? Jeremey's wife? You've met, right?"

"We have," Camilla answers for me. "I go to the gym with Jeremy sometimes and ignore everything he and Darren tell me about weight lifting."

I open my eyes and take in the faces of the people around me, resting on Jeremy's. He's still not speaking to me, and if I wasn't drowning in a tumultuous sea, I'd care about that. I shift my gaze to Camilla. "Good to see you again."

"You too." She smiles, and Jill continues with introductions. Em's date is Freddie, a neighbor. The two other couples are unknown to me. Allen and Edith, and Bernice and Henry were introduced as *friends of ours*. I'm not sure if that means they're friends of the twins' or of Lily's too. Outside of her family, I've never met any of her friends. I was under the impression that she was like me and didn't really have any.

"Nice to meet all of you." I acknowledge the introductions and nod as the other couples repeat a version of my sentiments. My throat constricts as I look to the head of the table once again, Lily's eyes ready for my return. "Where is your family, Lily? I expected them to be at a party that's supposed to be for you."

She rests a hand on Gideon's jean-covered leg. Everyone else here is dressed nicely, the men in collared shirts and the ladies in dresses. But Lily's *boy* is in faded jeans and a t-shirt. "I know you're eager to speak to my father, but it's doubtful you'll get an in-person audience, you'll just have to call him."

"Good luck getting him to talk to you," Gideon mutters.

Lily shoots him a look and I can't help but smile. If Daddy Beller doesn't like Boyfriend Gideon, that relationship isn't going anywhere. And according to my own father, Lily's brother is worse than her dad. I just hope that applies to her current relationship.

Not that them breaking up does anything for me. This isn't an *if I can't have her no one can* situation. It's an *I want her* situation. I want her out of my dad's life, out of *my* life, and so help me, I want her living in my house and having my children.

I cast a glare at the sky and curse the gods, hand reaching for what I hope is a shot. I throw back the liquid, coughing against the burn. Emelia Alice grabs her own shot glass, raising it into the air. "You heard the doctor. Let's throw one back for Lily and her *very* sexy boyfriend."

She winks, I assume at Gideon, and I turn to Jill. She shrugs. "I told you my sister is a bit of a...hound."

Emelia Alice tsks, drawing the laughter of the table. "I can't help it. I like men."

"Hear, hear," Freddie sings from next to her, holding up his own shot and throwing it back. He takes a bottle from the table and refills his glass, doing the same for Emelia Alice before passing the bottle down the table. Jeremy and Camilla give themselves refills, all other couples doing the same until the bottle reaches Lily and Gideon. They pass it on without refilling and Jill does the same, handing the bottle to me. I begin to pass it on, but Emelia Alice's voice brings that action to a halt.

"Lily, tell everyone how you met your tattooed prince. It's the best story, y'all. They're high school sweethearts."

My hand shakes. High school means long-term relationship. Long-term means serious. And it also means that when she was sixteen, he was kissing her carefree while I was despising my own flesh for having done so.

I refill my glass, and Jill's, downing both shots and refilling them one more time before passing the bottle back to Freddie.

A melodic sound leaves Lily's throat, shaking its way inside me and pluming out, making me want to hear it again. To be the cause of her happiness. I look up to the end of the table, her body more entwined than ever with Gideon's. His arms are a barricade of branches around her, the twinkling tea lights strung across the backyard casting a golden glow over the two of them. *Lily's light.*

"We knew each other in high school, but we didn't date," Lily confirms while looking up into Gideon's face.

"No way," Camilla coos. "You two are basically newlyweds. And young ones at that, so you have history."

Jill leans into me, whispering, "When Lily rented the room, she didn't even mention having a boyfriend. Yet he's here enough that I should have charged double the rent."

I bite down, jaw clenching when Gideon silences the chatter with his own denial that he was Lily's teenage love. "It's true." He runs his fingers along her arm, peering over her shoulder to look into her face. "She barely knew I existed in high school."

She blushes. "I knew, I just didn't know you *liked* me."

His lip ticks up. "It was hard to get your attention, but I finally managed it."

She groans. "You managed to mortify me. And you paid for it."

"Do tell," Edith giggles. "This sounds like the juicy part of the story."

Lily's gaze drops and Gideon tightens his arms around her. "Though Lily is a brain, I managed to graduate ahead of her. Since I wouldn't get the chance to be around her after that, I pulled out all the stops." His chest rises in a chuckle when she rolls her eyes at him. "I graduated with her brother so I knew she'd be in the audience that day. I hacked the school's computer system and made all of the diplomas print with the names changed to '*Lily Beller will you go out with me?*'"

The table erupts in applause from the men and hands over hearts from the women. Gideon grips Lily's chin and turns her face up to his. "See? That's how you were supposed to react. I was being sweet."

"Hardly." She swats his hand away. "This one is so cocky he didn't even have to sign his little stunt. Everyone knew who the computer genius was, including every single member of my family. The ones who also had to take home graduation day programs with the exact same question printed right there on the front of them."

Gideon laughs. "I was just covering my bases, making sure you saw it."

A smile splits her face. "You made sure the computers had a bug that ensured the school couldn't reprint anything until after graduation. And only one of us was graduating so I had to endure the rest of my high school career seeing 'Lily Beller will you go out with me?' written on every surface you can imagine. Even right across the front of my locker in big block letters."

He shrugs. "You should have said yes to me and then I would have swatted anyone who thought about messing with you."

"Swatted?" Jeremy asks. "Is that what the kids are calling punching these days?"

Gideon's lips pull into a wide smile. Lily's face goes slack. Emelia Alice wags a painted nail between the two of them. "It's worse than punching. Swatting is that thing hackers do when they break into everything you own. Your bank accounts, computers, credit cards, even security systems and placing emergency service calls that get people in all kinds of trouble." She sucks a breath between her teeth. "You're dangerous, Gideon."

"Criminal," I correct, my blood moving from a low simmer into a rapid boil. If he's as good as he's portraying, he could have cleared all traces of Lily on the clinic's security feed. "That's why her dad doesn't like you. You're a criminal."

His posture straightens. "Who said he doesn't like me?"

"No one." Lily moves onto her knees and stands. "The setting is beautiful and the heaters are nice, Em, but it's still too cold out here. Everyone grab a dish and let's go inside."

Without waiting for a response, she picks up a basket of naan and a bowl of rice, handing both to Gideon. He follows her into the house, Jeremy and his wife close behind and followed by every other couple save for Jill and me.

Jill inhales a deep breath and looks up at the sky. "That was awkward."

I take the remaining shots from the table, hers and mine. "There's no help for it up there in the stars. So make this night worse by telling me what you found out about Lily and the *real* reason she's in your house and getting this special little party thrown for her."

"Angela promised her my job."

My hand stills with the second shot halfway to my mouth. "When?"

Jill adjusts her blanket. "When she hired her. Angela knew that Priscilla, the former supervisor, would be leaving. She used that inside information to lure Lily in. But because Priscilla didn't leave before Lily started working at Pemberton, Lily came in as a floor nurse. I have more seniority, as do many others, so Keirstyn forced Lily's name out of the running for the job."

"That's why Angela is watching you. Trying to force the situation back into Lily's favor."

Jill swallows. "Lily's *in* my house. We signed a one-year lease and her family has lawyers I can't even think about without applying for a loan. I have to live with a spy for a whole year. One who keeps dragging my sister back in like a black widow. Em will notice something is off and we'll talk about it, and then the very next day she acts like Lily is the most darling kid." Jill's watery eyes lift to mine. "Gideon is a *criminal*, and everyone is acting like it's fine. Like it isn't dangerous to have someone like him around. What am I supposed to do? I'm scared to even go to sleep half of the time."

~15~

I wish I got the same surge of electricity from being near Jill as I get from just *thinking* about Lily. It would make my head stop wanting to rend itself from my neck. If I have to watch Gideon whisper in Lily's ear one more time, I might relieve *his* neck of the burden of a head.

"You need a refill?" I ask Jill, the two of us sitting on the couch we fell onto the last time I was drinking.

She holds her wine glass up to me, the downturn of her lips now present in the curve of her eyes. She's really worried about Gideon. I lean into her. "Don't worry, we're going to figure everything out. In the meantime, I'll get us both a double."

I take her glass, throwing a sidelong glance at Gideon. I'm still not impressed with the computer guru, and I'm still pissed as hell that he's touching Lily.

I grab a stuffed olive from a tray on the kitchen counter. I stayed outside with Jill long enough that neither of us ate anything when we finally rejoined the group. They'd all finished eating by then, and Jill's appetite was as ruined as mine.

I set the wine glasses beside the tray and pick up the bottle of wine I brought. Empty.

"There's more back here." Lily directs me around the side of the refrigerator, disappearing into the shadows. I don't hesitate to follow

95

her. I round the corner, setting course for the flash of her dress as it slips behind a slender door.

The pantry is cramped, only room enough for the two of us to stand shoulder to shoulder in front of the wine rack. "See anything you like?" she asks.

"You," my tongue spits. "Instead of an angel, you look like a goddess of the earth tonight."

Her face whips to mine. "Pretending to be nice isn't going to make me forget how you've proclaimed to practically everyone how worthless I am, and it certainly won't wipe the slate clean regarding the *gall* you have to think you have any right whatsoever to say a single word either *to* or *about* Gideon."

My teeth grind. "Trust me, I'm not being nice. I didn't tell you how good you look because I'm happy about it. And I never told anyone that you're worthless because I'm not a liar. As for Gideon, someone needs to inform the *boy* that it isn't polite to whisper."

"Maybe he's just following your lead. You can't seem to keep your mouth off Jill's ear."

I move to face her as much as possible in these tight quarters. "Are you jealous, Lily Beller?"

She folds her arms. "Are you drunk, Darren Mansfield? Because not a single word that's come out of your mouth tonight makes any sense."

"Because *you* drive me to the brink of insanity. Did you have that punk in there erase the clinic's security footage?"

She throws up her hands, whisper-shouting in my face. "Gideon is *not* a criminal. He works for the United States government. Why would I waste his time and have him erase footage of me *not* breaking into your house?"

My shoulder bumps the shelving as I try to muscle my way closer to her. "If you planted something in my house, I'm going to find it. And there's nothing your *boy* can do to erase that."

She jams her finger into my solid chest. "If I wanted to hurt you, in *any* way, I'd do so. And there wouldn't be anything *you* could do to erase *that*."

"I. Know." I force between clenched teeth. "You already left your mark on me and I doubt burning in hell will remove it, but it sure might feel better."

She steps away from me, finger falling from my chest. I suck air through my nose and run my hands through my hair, elbows knocking cereal and rice from the shelving on either side of me. "I didn't mean that. I'm just..." *hurting*. "I'm drunk, Lily. And I wasn't in a good headspace before I got drunk."

She lifts her shoulders, hands clasped tightly in front of her in a way that belies the confidence she's trying to portray. "Move, please."

"Lily——"

"There you two are." Emelia Alice claps her hands behind me. "Come on, we're taking a tour of the jewelry studio."

Lily isn't looking at me, she's looking past me to the presence of the audience we now have. I back out of the small pantry, wincing when Lily bends down to pick up the items my too-big frame knocked into the floor. "I'll get those, Lily."

She ignores me, placing the items back where they came from and sliding a bottle of wine from the rack. With her eyes still nowhere near mine, she exits the pantry and hands the bottle to Jill. "I'm no sommelier, but this should be close to the bottle you two have already shared."

Lily floats down the hall in a cloud of green and I stay where I am. My track record on saying and doing the right thing is complete trash whenever she's around, and because of the alcohol, I'm bound to make it even worse.

Jill presses into my side. "So? Did you confront her about harassing me?"

I rub my neck, headache now a full-body migraine. "No, I need to be sober before I speak to Lily again. And she isn't *harassing* you, she's only making you uncomfortable."

"In my home," Jill huffs. "But you're right, we should only approach her with clear heads. We've blown that for the night so do you want to go on the tour? Or take this bottle to my room?"

She raises onto her toes and I press my hand to her arm, stopping the path she's trying to blaze toward my mouth. "We've both had entirely too much to drink, and we know what happened the last time I drank without putting anything solid in my stomach, so I'm going to call for a ride home and wait outside for them. Is it okay if my car stays parked out on the street for the night?"

She lowers back onto her heels, tracing my jaw with one finger. "It's fine. But are you sure you don't want to stay and sleep off the buzz with me?"

I take her touch from my face and cup her hand in mine. "Positive. Go on upstairs with your sister, she seems pretty animated about showing off her jewelry."

Jill walks in the direction Lily went and I slog back to the living room. Gideon is sitting on the loveseat. Alone. Face buried in his phone. I sit in the chair across from him and lean my forearms onto my knees. "You didn't want to see the jewelry collection?"

He glances at me. "I've seen it."

"Too bad none of Lily's family could make it tonight or they could have seen it too. As close as all of them are, it's curious that none of them are here."

He clicks his phone off and slides it onto the seat next to him. "Lily didn't add them to her guest list, I was the only one who made her cut. And just as soon as she comes back, the two of us are cutting out of here."

I shift forward. "What's the rush? Lily seems to be enjoying herself, and this is where she lives, so where do you expect her to *cut out* to?"

He leans back and stretches his arm across the top of the loveseat. "Trust me, Lily wanted to skip this noise altogether. Which is why I've told her she should move in with me. I won't ever make her sit through a party she doesn't want. But since she's been a real trooper for these roommates of hers, I'm going to reward her with a party she does want. A private one that starts as soon as she *cuts* into her room with *me*."

The muscles in my back coil into tight knots. "What does her dad think about your offer to have her move in with you? Because if you're asking her that, you must be thinking about marriage, and *that* sounds like something a lot of people are going to have opinions about."

His mouth tilts into a crooked grin. "Who would those people be? You?"

"You can count on my opinion being one that you'll feel deep down in your bones."

He smirks. "Here comes my sweet girl. Ask her what she thinks about other people having opinions on our relationship. And then disappear. We don't need an audience, and my soon-to-be fiancée doesn't need another babysitter."

~16~

My mouth is dry, like it's full of cotton. Dirty, sticky cotton. I roll my head to the side, trying to get air from the fan I keep beside my bed. It isn't on. I reach out and instead of hard plastic, my fingers bump against soft flesh. My eyes snap open. There's blonde hair splayed over a pillow that isn't mine. The silver sheet covering what looks to be bare shoulders isn't mine either.

I roll onto my back, the silken sheets shifting over my also bare chest. I slide a hand down to my legs. My pants are still in place. I let out a shaky exhale and glance toward the soft warm flesh beside me. I can't see Jill's full body to know what state her clothing is in, but I'm going to assume I didn't put my pants back on after...

My teeth clench and my stomach rolls. I peel the sheet off me and sit up, bile rising into the back of my throat, my depravity battling the hangover to see which will make me puke first.

I have no memory of what happened here with Jill. The last thing I remember is Lily sitting on Gideon's lap, the folds of her dress covering his legs and his arms sliding into place around her waist. I tried to look away but as he whispered in her ear, she made a point of staring at me, some unreadable expression in her eyes that felt like a chasm opening between us. I couldn't sit there watching her with him, feeling as if I lost her before ever getting a chance to truly be with her. I got out of my chair with every intention of leaving the party. I apparently didn't, though.

I claw my hands down my face, digging my fingers into my eyes. *What in the hell is wrong with me?* I took advantage of Jill, *again*, and don't have so much as a fuzzy recollection of it.

I push to my feet, slowly turning toward the bed. Jill looks more the part of an angel, if one was to be cast for a movie, but my stupid heart insists that Lily *is* one, no matter all the evidence to the contrary. Whether she is or isn't, I have to stop fighting my feelings because doing so is leading me into darker waters than the ones I was drowning in before I pulled Jill into the deep with me.

I scan the room. My shirt is on the floor three feet away. I slowly bend down to pick it up, vision spinning as my stomach turns upside down. I tuck the shirt into my fist and search for my shoes. One is by the door and the other on its side at the end of the bed, as if I came into the room already stripping my clothes off and chucking them.

I gather up the shoes, sliding them onto my feet as quickly and quietly as I'm able to. The last thing I need to do is wake Jill up. I need to get out of here, collect my thoughts, and do my best to remember exactly what happened last night. Then I'll call her and express how sorry I am, though I already know it won't do any good. Because there are no words that can make up for the appalling way I've treated her.

I move to the door and don't bother looking back. Shirt clutched in my hand and Jill's woody perfume lingering on me, I slip out of the bedroom and softly shut the door behind me. I lift my eyes as I step away. The front door of the house is directly in front of me, and off to the left is the kitchen. The place from where a robe-clad Lily Beller is watching me.

I wish I could tell her that this isn't what it looks like, that I'm not bare-chested and sneaking out of her roommate's bedroom. But that's exactly what I'm doing and it's all because of *her*. She turns my brain to mush. When I'm anywhere near her, I'm incapable of rational thought. Facts that don't absolve me of blame. My actions are my own and I'll take responsibility for them, with Jill and Lily.

I walk toward her, her robe too thin to keep my eyes from imagining exactly what's underneath the satin folds. Despite how deplorable my actions have been since I first walked into this house, my fingers ache to tangle into Lily's copper tresses. Her eyes narrow on me and she turns away, popping a little pod into a coffee machine like I'm not advancing on her with lust in my eyes. It's there, I can feel it. And it's okay if she despises me for it. All I can do is lay myself at her feet and accept her choice, even if she stomps me until nothing but dust is left of my bones.

"Lily," I whisper her name.

She smoothes her hands down the sides of her robe, keeping her back to me. "We're all adults here, Doctor. Who sleeps in Jill's room isn't any of my business."

I stop at the corner of the kitchen island; if I get closer to her, I'm going to touch her. And I shouldn't do that. Same as I shouldn't choose this moment to tell her that I love her, but my tongue is begging me to and I feel so utterly broken right now that I don't have the strength to stop the words. I might as well finish burning down my life in one fell swoop. "Lily Beller, I—"

"Someone's been hitting the gym too hard." Gideon pointedly looks at my overmuscled torso as he strides by me, his own chest bare and loose black shorts riding low on his hips. "Nice ink, though."

My skin crawls. Since I got my tattoo, I haven't been caught shirtless, but now both he and Lily have seen my ink, and probably Jill. The newspaper lady saw the parts of it that wrap around me from the back. Similarly to how Gideon's long arms are wrapping around Lily's floor-length robe, the delicate flowers of the fabric crushing as he pulls her back against his chest. "Babe, you're not drinking that garbage. Give me five minutes and I'll hook you up with the good stuff. I put some cold brew in the fridge so I can make you one of those iced coffees you like."

Emelia Alice darts around the corner, her short robe open and the lacy pajamas she's in catching the light as she falls against Gideon's tattooed arm. "Me too! Please? I've been waiting all morning for you to get out of bed."

My mouth goes dryer than it already was, the cotton spinning down my throat and mixing with the bile. Emelia Alice has been standing in that hallway to the pantry and she would have overheard every word I said to Lily.

Gideon smirks in my direction. "I've got you covered, Em. But Doc over there is getting something hot, with melted butter in it because he needs some body fat. What are you, like point five percent? That's not healthy, dude."

"I'm not a *dude*, and I don't want your coffee."

His eyes spark, falling away from me as he presses his lips to Lily's cheek. "Looks like you're not the only one who is a grump in the morning, babe."

She pulls her cup from under the coffee machine and takes a big sip, spinning in his arms and looking up at him as she does it. "Girlfriends are less grouchy when boyfriends don't take jobs in Tokyo."

He cups her cheek. "You and mornings weren't getting along before I told you about this job. And you know I *have* to go. So just come with me and I'll make sure you get to sleep in every day."

I ball my shirt more tightly in my fist, chest heaving, eyes on the glint of Lily's as she looks up at the lanky redhead who's going to lose limbs if she says yes to him. Emelia Alice leans on the counter beside them. "Before you take Lily off and use your sexy self to persuade her, I need you to hit me with the good stuff." She holds a mug up to him like it's a chalice. "Freddie too. He's upstairs sleeping."

Gideon dips his head, pressing his lips to Lily's before letting go of her. "Three iced coffees coming right up, but only one of them is being served with plane tickets and diamonds."

I step forward. Lily's eyes dart to mine. Emelia Alice nudges her. "Even if you leave the country, you still owe rent."

Lily moves away from the counter. "I've already paid for the full year, and I don't plan on needing a refund. I also don't want your iced coffee, Gideon. Because I only liked your coffee *before* you decided to run away to Tokyo."

She walks by me, stomping back toward her bedroom. I turn around and watch her go, a smile spreading over my face when she slams the door and Gideon lets a string of curses fly. The smile fades just as quickly when an arm slides around me and fingernails trail across my abs, picking their way along my muscle with tantalizing precision. "Em," I growl.

"Em?" Jill's lips press against my neck. "It's me, love. Let's go back to bed."

~

I wish Lily was the woman asking me for a commitment because despite what Jill is insisting upon, fear of commitment is not my issue. I sit forward on the edge of her bed, from where I'm attempting to explain that every single interaction we've had outside of Pemberton was unintended.

"I know my apology isn't enough, so I won't ask you to forgive me. I won't be forgiving myself either, if knowing that is any comfort. But the truth is exactly what I've told you. I asked you out but had no intention whatsoever of having a second date or letting anything intimate happen between us at any point. It was only supposed to be dinner, and then back to being just coworkers."

She fiddles with the fingers she has clasped together on her lap. "I don't understand how you could do this to me."

I blow out a long breath, staring at the far wall and trying to conjure any memory of last night, but I'm empty inside. Hollow. "I'm broken, Jill. I've been this way for a long time now. Maybe even my whole life, I don't really know."

Her hand rests on my back, gently rubbing. "We're all a little broken in some way. So don't let me slip away all because you're human. I like you, and I *know* you wouldn't be with me the way you have been if you didn't like me too. We're good together, Darren. *Very* good."

I stand up and walk away from the bed. I don't want the comfort of her touch and I most certainly don't deserve it. I face her. "I have absolutely no idea how I ended up in your bedroom. The last thing I remember is that I was leaving."

Her face scrunches. "You don't remember sitting on the front porch sharing a bottle of wine with me while we waited for your ride to show up?"

"No."

She huffs. "Then I guess you don't remember sending the car away either? Or smarting off to the driver when the man showed annoyance that he'd driven all the way out here for no reason?"

I lift my shoulders. "He still got paid, right?"

She sighs. "That's exactly what you said last night, that you paid him for a job he only had to complete half of, so he should be *thanking* you, not griping about it."

The words sound familiar. I have a flash of saying them, the taste of bitterness on my lips. And something else. My eyes fall to Jill's mouth, I'd already been kissing her by then.

I look past her to the crumpled sheets on the bed. "How far did we go? I woke up with my pants still on but...what exactly happened after we got in here?"

She crosses her arms around herself. "You're making it sound like I took advantage of you."

I walk toward her and place my hand on her cheek. "You responding to whatever it was that I was doing is not wrong. *I* took advantage of *you*."

She glances up at me. "I didn't mind."

I step away as she tries to tuck her hand into the bottom of my shirt. I pulled it back on the instant we got inside this room. "That's the problem, Jill. You *should* care that I keep doing this to you. You should care that I have no idea how *far* I went with you."

She blushes. "You went far enough that I slept naked last night." Her head dips. "You passed out before we got *your* clothes all the way off, though."

My throat constricts. She looks back up at me, cheeks still pink. "I wanted it, so you didn't take advantage of me. And I also want to help you with whatever it is that's causing you so much pain. Is it the alcohol? Do you have a drinking problem?"

I cross back to the bed and sit beside her, letting my hands fall between my knees as I prop myself up with my elbows. "I wish drinking was my problem, but I'm not an alcoholic. And you're much too good to ever chase a man or to put yourself in the position to have to deal with their garbage. You deserve better, Jill." I look at her. "You deserve someone who will wake up next to you without an ounce of regret. I'm not him, and believe me when I say I feel the loss of not being him because I wish like hell it was me."

$\sim 17 \sim$

Shame is something you can't run from. Once you break the seal, it permeates every part of you, hiding in the dark crevices where it waits until you have hope, and then it strikes you down again.

After my behavior last weekend, the entity that is my shame is well fed. If Dad knew, he'd be so proud to learn that between insulting women and making them cry, I barely have time to be a mediocre doctor.

I snatch my keys from the bowl on the entryway floor, noting the dark scuff on the wall where my keychain has bounced up and hit it too many times. My lack of motivation to even repaint the house keeps me from updating anything else, but maybe if I care about the shabby state of my living quarters I'll figure out how to properly care for the people in my life.

Jill has been gracious, polite, and professional to a fault when our paths cross at Pemberton. And I've stayed away from Lily while licking my wounds and letting the turmoil of my badly broken moral compass subside. With our different shifts, there have been few times when my duties as a doctor have required me to speak to either of them. During the times when I've been forced to speak to Lily, I've managed not to be controlled by the idiocy that befalls me in her presence. I can only hope the trend continues because today I'm going to intentionally speak to her. I need to tell her that I'm leaving Pemberton.

I start my engine and step out to clear the snow from the windshield. The smell of burning flesh wafts up from the hood. I turn the car off and pop the hood open, shining a flashlight inside. "What in the heck?" I use the end of my ice scraper to poke the mass of fur. Another kitten. "Is your whole family dying?" I pull the cat off the engine, freezing in place when I see what's underneath it. At least a dozen little mice skewered on a metal spike. All of their heads are missing.

~

I scratch the day-old scruff of my jaw. The cat under my hood died of blunt force trauma to the head, the injuries similar to what I saw on the one I already buried, leading me to believe the first young cat hadn't been hit by a car at all. The skewer of mice certainly weren't. Someone decapitated them and left the dead animals on my engine. And that someone likely killed the first cat. But the first mouse was on my face. I might be a heavy sleeper, but I would have known if someone was in my house. The way I knew when Lily came in. Right?

More ludicrous than thinking I could sleep through someone putting a mutilated mouse under my nose is the very idea that anyone would try to mess with me. I'm not prone to intimidation. If anything, my general personality is intimidating to people even though it's unintentional on my part. I'm simply matter-of-fact, and that comes off as abrasive. And it's disturbing to question for even a fraction of a second that Lily might be capable of killing those animals. I considered Emelia Alice, since she apparently borrows Lily's shampoo. But if any woman was going to attempt to terrorize me, Jill would be the one with the most cause. She wouldn't slice up mice to do it, though.

Lily's feet stall as she approaches her vehicle and finds me leaning on the hood. I hold up my hands. "I'm not drunk and I'm not here to harass you. I'm actually hoping we can call a truce."

She stays a few paces away. "You're the only one who is at war, so call your truce and get off my car."

Her words sting. I move away from the hood and nod to the thermos of coffee I placed above her door. "It isn't what your boyfriend makes, but it's the pod flavor I saw you use the other morning. I figured you could use it considering you're probably going to work at the clinic now instead of going home to sleep."

Her head tilts, her green eyes catching the light, but she remains silent. I brush a hand across the back of my neck. "Is Gideon gone yet? To Tokyo?"

She doesn't answer, the set of her jaw sharp enough to cut out my heart. I take a beat, letting the silence become a thing I can hold in my hand. I've made my decision. I don't care if she broke into my house. I don't care if she tried to set me up as one of her brother's next predator marks. I'm not a sick pervert who lusts after little girls. I don't even lust after grown ones. All I want is her. If Gideon is gone, then I have time to figure out how best to tell her that I'm utterly in love with her. Doing so trumps dealing with mutilated animals. I'd like the killing to stop, for the sake of the animals, but I'm not afraid of the coward refusing to directly engage me. "Are you planning to go to Tokyo with Gideon? Because that means giving up your job."

She adjusts her shoulder bag. "So that's what this is, then. You're here to remind me that I only got this job because I come from a wealthy family, and that because of that wealth, I'm taking up the job of someone who needs the money it provides. I guess I should quit then."

My mouth opens and she slams a hand up between us. "Don't. I've already heard enough of your opinions from Jill and I'm fully aware that I'm professionally expendable. That doesn't give the two of you the right to campaign against me. Surely you and your girlfriend have better ways to spend your time."

She storms toward her door and I move to her side. "I don't know what Jill said to you but I'm not campaigning against you."

"What then?" Her eyes blaze. "Did I leave an open container somewhere? Is that why you're insisting on harassing me once *again* instead of just letting me get on with my life? Or is this punishment because I *dared* to recite a few stupid books to you when I was kid? I didn't realize that was such a problem for you, but you could have said no."

"Part of me thinks I should have," I whisper, fingers lifting to brush against her cheek. She moves away, startled by my touch. My heart grinds to a mournful halt. No matter how hard I try not to, I just keep poking holes in my life raft. "Will you have dinner with me?"

Her brows pinch together. "Why would I do that?"

I shove my hands into my pockets to keep them from touching her. "Because you affect me in a way that no one else has ever come close to. Sometimes I think knowing you is the worst experience of my life and others...I feel like the wrecking ball of a teenage girl who crashed through my world is the only challenging thing I've ever had to face. I want more. I want you."

Seconds draw out as she stares at me. I swallow emotions I'm never going to be done with, taking my hands from my pockets and running them through my hair. "I know I'm a lot older than you. And I know that you're in a relationship. But there's a moment in time that's forever seared into my soul, one that causes me every problem in the world but yet I can't move past it." I take a chance on moving closer to her. "I'm beyond caring about anything, Lily. Except for you. So please talk to me. I need to know if you're repulsed, indifferent, intrigued... Whatever you feel, tell me."

She folds her arms against her stomach. "You're in a relationship too. With my supervisor, who also happens to be my landlord."

My heart musters the courage to spark back to life. "That didn't sound like repulsion. Maybe not indifference either."

Her eyes widen. "You accost me every other day. And accuse me of the most absurd things. And we *both* have significant others."

I tentatively cup her face, moving slowly so I don't spook her. "I'm not in a relationship with anyone, but I'd like to be in one with you. How long will Gideon be in Tokyo?"

She rests her hands on my wrists but applies no pressure to remove my touch. "What does that have to do with anything?"

My pulse accelerates. "While he's gone, date *me*. See if I'm better suited for you than he is because I already know you're perfect for me."

She backs into her car door. "You want me to cheat on Gideon? With *you*? As if everything you've done to me doesn't matter?"

I let my shoulders lift, keeping my hands on her warm skin. "Everything I've done to you matters, and I want you to tell me about it from your perspective, so I truly know the extent of the damage. And I want you to dump Gideon. Then you're not cheating while you decide that you like me better."

She opens the door behind her and shuffles back until she's inside the car. I reluctantly let go of her. She slams the door closed. I tap on the window. She rolls it down with a huff. "You're unbelievable, Darren Mansfield."

"Would you prefer I lie? You're the one who tore back into my life and *you're* the one who didn't go to Tokyo with Gideon when we both know that if he meant that much to you, there'd be nothing stopping you from going."

She backs out of the parking space and I fold my arms over my chest. "So you'll think about it then, angel?"

~

I replay my conversation with Lily. Because of the dead animals, I forgot to lead with the news that I was turning in my resignation. Angela gets to be the first to hear the announcement since she's outside of Keirstyn's office. "After I check in on Keirstyn I was coming to see you, but I might as well give you this now." I hand Angela my resignation letter.

She snatches the envelope with an aggravated sigh. "Keirstyn has a doctor and it isn't you, so what exactly are you here to check on?"

I let her question hang in the air as she looks over the resignation, the dawning of what it is making her usually grim-lined mouth turn up at the corners. "You plan to stay on until your replacement arrives?"

I nod. "Providing said replacement doesn't take too long to get here."

She steps away from Keirstyn's door. "They won't. Go ahead and begin saying your goodbyes. I'll see to it that replacing you is top priority."

This conversation is going about as well as I expected it to. "While I'm grateful that you're finding it in your heart to be intolerable right up to the bitter end, I'm not here to say goodbye to Keirstyn and I don't plan on announcing to any of the other staff that I'm leaving. I'd appreciate it if you kept this information on a need-to-know basis."

Angela checks her watch. "Fine by me, Dr. Mansfield. Now how about you get to the med-surg floor and begin doing your job, while you still have it."

~18~

Mr. Vass's thin lips press into a smile. "I get to go home today?"

I shake my head at him. "In the morning. And I'm surprised you look so happy about being discharged, you seemed to be enjoying the company of our nurses."

"I did." He works his wrinkled hands over the folds of his blanket. "When they were female. And pretty. Like that little blonde number who pranced around here. I haven't seen her in a while. Think you can send her in before I get out of here?"

"The blonde one? Not the copper-haired one? I thought the latter was *friendlier* than the other nurses."

The old man laughs. "I had one like her when I was younger and woo! They chew you up and spit you out. Not like the nice ones. The trick is to get one of those good girls, 'cause they do what you say."

I haven't been treating any of the women in my life kindly lately, but I'm not intentionally abusing them. And I'm taking steps to remedy forcing my failures on anyone else. If Lily doesn't want me, I'm not sure what I'll do with my life, but it will start with isolation and end with lots and lots of therapy. "A woman doing what you say doesn't make her good, it makes her unfortunate." I adjust his pillow for him. "I'll send in one of the male nurses to finish going over your discharge with you. Keep your hands off of them, too."

I stroll out of his room and check the time. My day is over and I don't intend to spend an extra minute here. I head straight for the stairwell and jog down the flights.

"Doc!" Jeremy catches up with me. "You hittin' up the gym?"

I glance at him as we exit into the lobby. "You're talking to me again?"

He runs his shoulder into me. "Don't make this awkward. I miss you, big guy. I need someone to spot me on my bench press."

"Not today," I mutter.

He moves ahead of me as the sliding doors open and we step out into the waning evening sun. "Because you're holding a grudge you're not entitled to? Or because you have plans with a set of long legs that you won't notice because you'll be too busy staring into Jill's ocean-blue eyes?"

"Do me a favor and have Camilla put a muzzle on you."

He chuckles. "Jill would prefer a muzzle for you. She was telling us how badly you snore. Like a bear wielding a chainsaw."

My jaw tics. Considering how my overnight with her ended, I didn't expect Jill to spread any information around. "Good thing she only had to endure it once."

He plants his feet. "Good thing she doesn't have to depend on you to drive her around. What did you do, back into a building?"

I inspect my crumpled bumper and the white paint etched into the dent along my side panel. "Check my windshield for a note," I direct him, kicking the pieces of a broken taillight over the asphalt. Whoever hit me took some damage to their vehicle too.

"No note." Jeremy comes back to my side. "Want to see if the hospital caught anything on camera?"

I look up at the sky, tracing the rim of a low-hanging cloud. "Do you believe in higher powers?"

He shifts. "Yeah, but I doubt God hit your car. If he did, he'd probably leave a note."

I shrug. "Or maybe he puts marks on certain people and sits up there laughing every time their day gets ruined."

Jeremy cups a hand over my shoulder. "You okay? You've been morose since the party. Is it because things are moving fast with Jill? She's been practically glowing this week."

I press the heels of my hands into my eyes. "Her glow isn't because of me and I don't feel like looking at security footage today. I'll see if I can look at it tomorrow."

His grip becomes a pat. "Alright. I'll leave you to it then, but if you need to talk later just give me a shout. Camilla put me through my paces before she walked down that aisle, so I know what these early days of relationship building are like."

I shrug him off of me. "I'm not in a relationship with Jill, so just stop. I'm tired of hearing her name."

He squints at me but I ignore the scrutiny and take out my phone, getting pictures of the damage and location of my vehicle before getting into my battered car and backing out of the spot. Jeremy walks off in the direction of his own vehicle and I turn out of the parking lot, setting a course for home.

My phone rings. It's Jill. I drag in a breath and let the call connect through the car speakers. I shouldn't, but after what I've done to her I feel obligated to speak to her whenever she wants. At least until I'm out of Pemberton and away from the situation altogether. One she's making worse. I understand that I embarrassed her and that making it seem like we actually have a relationship saves face for her, but it's getting old. Even if everyone at that party saw me go into her room, it wasn't that many people.

"Hey, Jill. What's up?"

"Hi," her breathing is heavy. "Are you still at the hospital?"

"No, I just left. Why?"

She pauses, talking to someone else in muffled noises before answering me. "My neighbor collapsed. We've called an ambulance and Lily is with him, but if you were still at the hospital, I was going to have you meet the ambulance so Freddie would have a familiar face there."

"Freddie?"

"You met him at Lily's party. Tall guy with curly hair and a squeaky little voice?"

"Right. Emelia Alice's date." I remember his voice not matching his exterior. "I can go back and meet the ambulance. Has it arrived at your house yet?"

"No," she whispers. "And I don't think Freddie's going to make it. He's already unresponsive."

I U-turn and hit the gas. "I'm on my way."

~19~

I figured it would be unlikely that I'd beat the paramedics to Jill's house, but there was no point in taking the chance when a man's life is at stake. I might be a shoddy person but I'm a doctor, and I used to be a good one.

I whip into the driveway behind Lily's car, eyeing the scene in the neighboring yard where two paramedics are lifting a stretcher, Freddie lying limp on top of it. Emelia Alice is holding his hand, tears streaming down her face. She goes with him, loading into the waiting ambulance with the paramedics.

Lily and Jill are at the base of Freddie's porch. Lily's face is drawn into hard lines while Jill's brows are furrowed. I walk toward them. "What happened?"

Lily doesn't take her eyes off the ambulance, watching as the lights and sirens race down the street. Jill wraps her arms around my neck. "You didn't have to come, but thank you. Seeing Freddie like that... It's always hard when it's someone you know."

I let my hands give her a little pat, relieved when I pull away and she lets go. "Lily? You okay?"

Her head shakes, eyes slowly making their way around to Jill. "Is Freddie a diabetic?"

Jill sighs. "Honestly, I don't know. Em probably does, they've been getting close lately."

I watch the wheels turning behind Lily's lids. "You think his collapse has something to do with diabetes?"

She finally meets my eyes. "Insulin overdose."

"Overdose?" Jill gasps. "Emelia Alice was with him all afternoon and she would have mentioned if he was having problems, mental or medical."

Lily rubs the back of her neck, a smear of blood on her wrist. "I know, and I appreciate you having the presence of mind to ask her if she recalled anything, but insulin can be fairly fast-acting, especially in a large dose. If he gave himself a shot right after he returned from Emelia's loft, the timeline from that point to when he stumbled out his front door could make sense."

"How long was it?" I ask.

Lily frowns. "Em said he left no more than forty minutes before she saw him fall." She nods to the stairs behind her. "He was helping her craft jewelry today, and after he left, she took some of the pieces to a local store that carries her line. The owner wasn't in so she came back home and that's when she spotted Freddie staggering out of his house. She said he looked confused and when she called his name, he collapsed and thumped down the stairs."

Jill nods. "I heard Em scream but Lily was in the backyard, so she got here before me. Freddie convulsed a couple of times and then went unresponsive."

I internalize their account of what they saw and heard. Without knowing the man's medical history, it's impossible to say what happened to him today, although Lily's theory is certainly plausible. I move toward her. "Hopefully Emelia Alice will call with an update soon. Until then, we need to get you cleaned up." I point to her wrist. "I assume the blood is Freddie's?"

She checks the smear on her arm. "Yeah, he cracked his head pretty good when he fell."

"Which could be why he went unresponsive," Jill points out.

Lily nods, wheels still turning behind emeralds that have only looked at me once. "I'm going to go take a shower. If Emelia Alice calls, let me know."

My fingers flex in Lily's direction but I keep my hand at my side. I'm not above taking a hint and I wish Jill wasn't either. Instead, she's taking my hand and lacing her fingers through mine like I didn't just treat her abominably. "I really appreciate you coming over here. It means a lot that you dropped everything to rush to my aid."

I shrug overdramatically, hoping the motion will make her let go of my hand. It doesn't, and I don't want to have to yank out of her grip. "I'm a doctor, helping people is what I'm supposed to do. Plus, I got here too late so I didn't aid anyone."

I take a step away from her, making a second attempt to break the hand contact as I look around at the other homes. With how the Tudor house sits on its deep lot, Freddie's house is the only one close by. "I'm going to take off. You can't really see any of your other neighbors, but if they should also happen to drop, I'll trust the paramedics to get here in time."

She walks beside me, fingers tight where mine are limp. I should have tamped down my instincts and never come here. I don't want to keep ripping open Jill's wounds and pouring salt in them but I'm not quite sure what else I can do. I've been completely truthful with her but she's still choosing to live in a reality she wants to be true rather than the one that's actually true.

I open my door with my free hand and give the one she's holding a firm shake before sliding into my seat. "See you at work." I close the door, an action that forces her to back up. Yep, jerk move, but I've done worse.

I reverse out of the driveway, angling down the street and away from the house. I glance back to where Jill is standing, watching me go, and wish it was Lily. Even if she was only out there to flip me off. My eyes trail to her BMW. There's damage to the front right bumper. I slam on my brakes and shift into park, leaving my car in the middle of the street.

Jill runs toward me. "What's wrong?"

"Lily Beller," I growl, getting a good look at the damage on her front end. It's a perfect match to mine.

Jill places a hand on my tense shoulder. "Lily said someone hit her while she was parked at the hospital last night."

I straighten, staring at the house Lily disappeared into. She can be angry that I asked her to date me, but a solid *no* would have sufficed. If she hadn't pushed her way back into my life, I would never have uttered those words to begin with. "I saw Lily's car this morning when she left Pemberton. When she pulled out of her parking space, her vehicle wasn't damaged."

Jill's eyes flit to my car, her fingers trembling. "You think she doubled back and hit you? Why? Because of me?"

I grip her hand, sorrow for all the damage I've caused filling my chest. "No. Because of *me*. I honestly don't think Lily being here has anything to do with you. I think it's all because of me, but I'm working on taking care of it, okay? Just give me a little time and I'll fix this for you."

She points to Lily's car. "Whatever her motives for coming here, this is dangerous, Darren. She's *living* in my house. How am I supposed to sleep knowing she's capable of this? How am I supposed to not worry about my sister? Lily seemed so sweet before, but now I'm afraid I brought destruction into my own home."

I grip both of her hands tightly, staring down the unease I see on her features. "Listen to me, Jill. Lily isn't going to be here much longer. And that doesn't mean you're going to have to refund her rent. I know you depend on that money, so keep it, and if anything is said about it, I'll cover what's owed to Lily. But she hasn't actually *done* anything to you, right? You're just getting creepy vibes?"

Her throat bobs. "The creepy vibes are her *doing* something, but she's never crashed my car."

"And she won't," I assure Jill. "Lily has plenty of places to go, so ask her to leave. And don't mention to her that I saw her car. I'm going to get some pictures of it and when I'm ready, I'll tell her myself."

Jill tilts her head forward and rests it on my chest. "I'm scared. What if I ask her to leave and she attacks me?"

Visions of dead cats billow up, their preferred prey dead right alongside them. I can't imagine Lily ever hurting any living thing, but uncertainty crawls through my gut. I lift Jill's chin. "I don't think Lily is violent at all, but I'll go inside with you while you have her pack her bags. I'll even follow her to wherever it is she's going to go."

~20~

It's hard not to resent Lily. She has every good thing this world has to offer and yet she's taken away all of mine, including every chance of being happy with anyone but her. I sit in the parking lot of Mansfield Clinic and scroll through the photos of her car and mine. If Jill hadn't called me over Freddie, I would have never known Lily hit me. She has a family-owned car dealership at her disposal. She could have had the damage fixed or traded for something newer before I had any idea it was her.

This is yet another move on a board *she* designed, and further proof there's something dark underneath her angelic façade. For myself, I'm not worried. But Dad and Jill are different stories. Although visibly shaken, Jill didn't want me to help her confront Lily yesterday, citing Freddie and Emelia Alice as points of greater concern. When I left, Jill was heading to the hospital to be with her sister.

For Dad, neither of us will be able to reconcile our feelings for Lily with the disturbing truth, but I need to separate him from her. I intentionally left the hospital early so I could get home before the clinic closed. Lily's car isn't here, and I wonder if she worked at the clinic today. Or yesterday.

I walk into Dad's office. "Hey, old man."

His wrinkled fingers tip down glasses he only started wearing last year. "Well, isn't this a treat. Unless something is wrong?"

I sit in the chair in front of his desk. "Everything is fine, except that you need to fire Lily Beller. I don't trust her. Especially not around you."

A soft chuckle lifts from his throat, holding little humor. "Then I guess it's a good thing that you're no longer a part of my team here because I trust Lily implicitly. That girl has a doctor's soul and is whip-smart."

I sit forward. "And your son *is* a doctor and he's also smart. I had accomplishments when I was young, same as Lily. So her age doesn't give her spectacular credentials, certainly not ones that elevate her over me."

His eyes widen. "So you want me to fire her and hire you?"

His question takes me back. It should really be an easy answer, but until I reconcile the rot inside me, whether going down with my ship or puzzling out exactly what dark things are troubling Lily and helping her exorcise those demons, I can't work anywhere at all. "What I want is for you to take what I'm telling you seriously. Lily is dangerous. She rammed my car yesterday, drove straight into it and then just left. No note or even the slightest courtesy given, because she didn't hit me by accident. It was on purpose, Dad. Stable people don't do that."

His hands fold together. "She told me about the neighbor of hers that died. An insulin overdose. Did she run into you after that? Could be that she was more shaken up than she realized."

Anger burns my throat. This morning, Jill called to say that Freddie had died. She also told me that Lily had called his brother and made claims about an insulin overdose, prompting the grieving man to push the hospital to confirm the truth because he was originally told his brother had a heart attack. Understandably, the man wants an explanation as to whether or not his brother was misdiagnosed. But even if he was, from what I've heard, there is no case for the wrong care being administered because there was nothing that could be done for Freddie by the time he reached the hospital. Yet blowback landed on Jill, Angela claiming Lily's actions were Jill's fault because a supervisor should have better control of her nurses.

"Dad, I understand that you care for Lily. Trust me when I say I know exactly how hard listening to reason is when it comes to her, but you have to. Lily rammed my car *before* her neighbor collapsed. She *is* dangerous, in ways I don't even understand yet."

I show him the pictures of both vehicles. He gives them a cursory glance. "I'll discuss the matter with Lily. I'm sure there's a reasonable explanation."

My anxiety levels rise. "What aren't you telling me? Does Lily have some sort of leverage on you?"

His eyes crinkle. "Son, I know you've been struggling lately. You're short-fused and bristly, and I've been letting you have your space, waiting for you to come talk to me about what's really going on with you. Whatever it is, you can leave Lily out of it. If you have a problem with the decisions I'm making, those problems are with me, not Lily."

I push out of the chair and pace the room. "Lily *is* the problem, Dad. *She's* the one with serious issues. And it will be much less stressful to figure out her end game if I know you're safe from her. That your clinic is safe. For all I know, she's trying to sabotage you and open up her own concierge service."

He leans back, the leather of his chair creaking under his weight. "Lily has no reason to sabotage the clinic. In fact, quite the opposite."

I stare at him. "What does that mean?"

He takes his glasses off and rubs his eyes. "The end of my time here in the clinic is nigh. I don't want to see the practice close, you don't have the calling to keep it open, so I've asked Lily to take over for me."

My legs give out. I grab the edge of my chair and sink back into it. "You what? You gave away the clinic? To Lily? She's not even a doctor!"

He moves his seat forward and places his forearms on his desk. "While Lily *does* have the skill to do the job, I'm aware that she doesn't have the credentials. That's why I'll keep the clinic open until she makes the decision on whether or not to go to medical school. If she decides not to, I'll close up shop. If she decides to become a full-fledged doctor, I'll continue on as best I can until I can pass the baton to her."

Tears threaten my eyes. "When did you plan on telling me this?"

His face falls and he suddenly seems older than he was moments ago. "I'm tired, son. Your mom is long gone and I'm ready to go be with her. If I have to close the doors, so be it. If Lily goes to medical school and

I can't make it until she's done, well then, I can at least let our patients know that one day Lily will be back to serve them."

A tear rolls down my cheek. "Why didn't you tell me any of this before? I can help you. I'll come back and do whatever you need me to do."

He smiles softly. "This clinic doesn't mean to you what it means to me, and that's okay. You followed in my footsteps as long as you could, then you blazed your own trail, and I'm so proud of you, son."

I lift from the chair and go to his side, gripping his hands together in one of mine, tears burning as they fall. "I didn't leave *our* clinic because I wanted to blaze a new trail. All I ever wanted was to live and work alongside you because you're the best doctor I know, and an even better father."

His brows furrow. "Then why did you leave?"

I rub my face on my shoulder, scraping away tears, and give him the only part of the truth that I can. "I don't measure up, and you deserve a son who does."

~

I'm shaken, the cold reality of what my decisions have led to cutting deep. I'm not good enough to walk in Dad's footsteps, but neither is Lily. We're two damned souls, marked and shackled.

I can pinpoint with excruciating accuracy the exact moment when the shift began inside of me and I accept my fault in carrying a painful spark for Lily, but I won't let the cursed love that pounds through my veins keep me from stopping her before she tears down what Dad built. I knock on her front door. It's late, but she should be getting ready to leave for work soon and I don't mind sacrificing my own sleep in order to end her reign.

I knock again, louder this time. There's scuffling inside the house and a curtain in the front window pushes aside. I lift a hand to Jill, her face pressing into the glass to get a look at who is standing on the porch. She smiles and my gut sinks. She thinks I'm here to see her.

The door in front of me opens. Jill slips on her shoes and moves outside, shutting the door behind her. "You really are the sweetest man, Darren, but I'm okay. I'm not as upset as I was after being chewed out by Angela this morning. Em loaned me some of her sleeping pills so I could rest and that really helped."

I clear my throat. "That's good. Did you talk to her about asking Lily to move out?"

Jill chews her lip. "Yeah. The two of them haven't been getting along either but Emelia Alice is worried that..."

I raise a brow. "Worried that...?"

Her eyes dart to Freddie's house. "Remember how I said that when Em screamed, I heard her, but when I got outside Lily was already with Freddie?"

I nod. "Lily was in the backyard and you were somewhere in the house."

Jill swallows. "Em said Lily was *beside* the house. *Freddie's* house. As in sneaking from his house and into our backyard."

A shiver runs along my spine. "What are you implying?"

She pulls her jacket tight and zips it up. "I'm not implying anything, I'm only telling you what my sister said."

My jaw tics. "Where's Lily? I need to see her before she heads off to Pemberton."

Jill looks past me to the driveway where I'm parked behind Lily's car. "She's in bed. She ended up calling in last night and I just found a note a little while ago that said she was taking another personal day. It's like she's avoiding everyone. Emelia Alice didn't see her all day today. Right after Freddie died, Lily went into hiding, like maybe she didn't mean to kill him."

My teeth clench. "So you're skipping the implications and jumping straight to accusations?"

Jill's eyes flutter up to mine, frown deep and lines across her forehead bunched together. "I'm not saying she did it on purpose, but maybe she was helping him with the insulin dose and gave him too much? How else would she know *exactly* what happened to him minutes after it happened? She even outlined how a fast-acting insulin would work."

Lily did more than that. She called the man's brother, making sure the hospital got the cause of death right. *Guilty conscience?* "Do you mind if I go inside and wait for her to get up?"

Jill wipes a tear from the corner of her eye. "Despite how flirty my sister is, she'd be uncomfortable with you inside. After what happened between us, she's not your biggest fan and she doesn't really trust that you're going to help us get rid of Lily. She thinks you're going to cover for Lily. And it sure sounds like that's the case."

Emelia Alice isn't only poised, she's smart. I do intend to cover for Lily. On everything she's done to me, but not on murder, even if it was accidental. There needs to be actual proof of her guilt before she's accused of such a thing though. "I'll come back by later and see if I can catch Lily after the sun comes up."

~21~

I feel sorry for Jill, and even more determined to put a stop to the chaos. I walk her to her car. "I know you're uneasy over how everything seems to be going but I *promise* you that I'm going to set things right."

"Thanks," she smiles halfheartedly, lifting onto her toes and pressing her lips against the corner of my mouth.

I shift, opening her door and ushering her into the vehicle. "Try to put everything out of your mind and just focus on your job. Have a good night, Jill."

I close her door and head for my own vehicle before there's reason to interact with her further. I want to help her, and I have a hefty debt to pay where she's concerned, but my motivation to extract Lily from Jill's life is purely selfish. I want to separate them before things escalate and Lily does something that I *can't* forgive. Like murder a neighbor.

I start my engine and shift into gear, backing out the driveway and turning in the opposite direction of the one Jill will go. I drive slowly, fingers drumming over the steering wheel as I contemplate what time I should come back. I don't want to miss Lily. I need her to agree to have a long and honest conversation with me. My headlights reflect off a shadow, something darker than the night moving against the tree-lined street. A person clad in black. One who can't hide her shape, even under the bulky hood of the thick jacket. I pull alongside the curb and get out, slamming my door. "Lily Beller, stop right there."

She tosses the hood from her head, copper locks falling free over her shoulders. My heart forgets to beat. Even in near total darkness, she shines as bright as sun reflecting off snow.

Her mouth moves, drawing my attention before my ears bother to hear. "Darren? What's happened? Is it Jill?"

I shake loose the slow movement of time and remember why I'm here. "Is there a reason you think Jill *wouldn't* be fine?"

Lily stops short of me. "It's the middle of the night and you practically jumped from a moving car just now."

I close the distance. "That's right, it's the middle of a *cold* night, and you're missing work to wander around in it dressed like a burglar. Why?"

Her shoulders move under the fabric of her jacket, making her hair tumble in a way that catches the glow of the moon itself. "My clothes are warm enough and I like to walk at night, the cold air helps me think. What's your excuse for being out here?"

"*You're* my excuse. For everything." Anger ticks through me for having to admit this to her. "You're my *reason*, Lily. And it's pretty freaking annoying, so why don't you tell me what you've been out here thinking about. Your next move? Your partner in crime is in Tokyo, so I'm going to assume you weren't out nosing around my house tonight because you wouldn't have anyone to erase the security footage for you."

She slips her gloved hands into her pockets. "The clinic's system is hooked to the internet so Gideon could hack it from anywhere. But I don't know all the particulars of how his skills work so I'll give you his number and then you can accuse him directly." Her lips turn up into a smirk. "Then I suggest you hold onto your figurative hat because he'll prove our innocence by swatting you down from the perch you've placed yourself on."

I narrow my gaze on her. "You're the one who walks through this life doing whatever you want, angel. And you don't care who you stomp all over in the process."

Her jaw clenches. "Name one person I've *stomped* on, Darren. One."

"Jill, for *one*," I nip. "What you're doing to her makes me wonder about how many lives you're willing to destroy in order to hurt me."

Her chest heaves under her jacket. "I applaud you for going out of your way to defend your girlfriend, it's a definitive change from the day when you said *I* was the one you wanted to be with. And somewhat of an about-face from me being your *reason*."

I move forward, chest rubbing against the lapel of her jacket. "Despite how appalled I am that I feel anything at all for you, I've meant every word I said to you. So you can keep calling Jill my girlfriend even when you know she isn't, but that won't change the fact that I only have to defend Jill because you're not just stomping on her, Lily, you're taking away everything that's good in her life the same way you ruined *my* life."

Her chin quivers. "Everything that goes wrong in this world is not my fault. I don't have some nefarious plot to ruin *anyone's* life. All I'm doing is trying to live *my* life, and I don't know why you and Jill and everyone else seem to think I'm not entitled to that."

I press a hand to her cheek. She backs away. One step, and then two more. My heart thuds. It's hard to want to be her everything while also trying to drain her venom from your veins. "You *are* entitled to live a life you choose, Lily. And I want that for you, I always have. As long as you don't think that you're entitled to hurt people." I motion to the cold night around us. "You're renting a room in a house that's in a neighborhood that even I think is sketchy, and I'm a big man so I'm not prone to being creeped out." I take one steady step forward and speak calmly. "You're not living in this place because you can't afford better. So what's the real reason you're here? And why are you traipsing around at night dressed so as not to be seen?"

She swallows. "You saw me."

I move forward again and this time she steps backward. The emotional pain of her determined distance rubs my throat raw. "Is it too much to ask for all of us to be happy, Lily? For everyone to get to live a good life?" I take half a step, flooding with relief when she doesn't move. "Please tell me where you've been tonight. If you've really just been out wandering around in the freezing cold by yourself, explain to me why you would do such a thing. Your family doesn't exactly have the best track record when it comes to people trying to kill them. So why this neighborhood? Why the risk?"

Her voice trails low, tears glistening in her eyes. "I know better than you what my family has gone through. I also know the strength it takes to face each day without fearing every person you meet has designs on ending your life. I won't live in fear, though being constantly accused of making the wind blow or the seasons change is starting to scare me." She takes a breath. "I rented a room that was offered to me. So I could have a new experience and see what it was like to live with people I'm not related to before..."

Her head dips and I reach forward, sliding my hand under her chin and gently bringing her eyes up to meet mine. "Before you move in with Gideon."

She nods, the motion slicing through my chest and ripping my heart in two. "Emelia Alice overheard me talking to my brother about Gideon's offer. The conversation didn't end well. She said she had a room and suggested I try living with her and Jill, and it seemed like a good idea at the time. This way I can figure things out and keep everyone else appeased." She slips her hands from her pockets and wipes her eyes, reclaiming the personal space I invaded as she does. "I didn't know it was going to be like this or I wouldn't have signed the lease."

"You didn't know it was going to be like what? Because Jill said you were the one who suggested renting the room. At least, Emelia Alice represented it that way."

Lily chews her lip, brows drawing low over her eyes. "Em isn't as nice as I thought she was, but she isn't a liar. Jill must have misunderstood. She has a tendency to do that, or a tendency to claim that's all it was."

I shake my head. "I don't know who to believe. Jill hasn't done anything to make me question her but you have, Lily."

Her eyes fill with tears. "So you do know who to believe and it isn't me. Well, that's why I'm out here, Darren. Because no matter what I do, I'm in everyone's way. Everyone is always angry with me and apparently that's because me simply existing ruins their lives." She motions around us. "So I'm out walking alone in the middle of the night where no one has to be bothered by my presence while I attempt to decide if anything in my life is worth fighting for because the stupid room in your girlfriend's house isn't! But I don't know where to go when I leave here. Gideon's penthouse is empty but if I move in there..."

Her eyes close and I move forward, bumping against her, the contact shooting stardust through my veins. I grip her arms, tightening my fingers in the fabric of her jacket. "Don't, Lily. Don't go to his place. Please."

She opens her eyes, breath fluttering over my lips. "Why not? All you care about is getting me away from here. Away from you."

I loosen my grip and run my hands up her arms, fingers tangling in hair they haven't threaded themselves through in five years. "I want you away from here, but not away from me. I don't ever want to be away from you again."

She stares at me, electricity building between her breath and mine. "Lily," I whisper. "Can I kiss you?"

~22~

My mouth crashes against Lily's in a frenzy. She opens her lips for me, arms circling my neck. I drag my hands down her sides and pull her against my throbbing body. Her fingers dig into my shoulders, holding tight as I lift her onto my hips. I hold her close, pulling her deeper into me as my mouth breaks free, diving to her neck while my feet move toward my car. She's intoxicating.

Just like that night in my office at the clinic, if I don't take my mouth off of her I'm going to start working very hard to get her clothes off. I slide her down between the car and me, chest heaving in time with hers. Thankfully she has a jacket on because that night in the clinic she didn't and my hands... I close my eyes and take a deep breath, letting her scent fill my lungs while she steadies her feet back on the ground, remaining pressed between my body and the car. I open my eyes and sweep her jaw into my palm, lifting her face to mine. "Everything about you is worth fighting for. I know because I've been at war over you for five years." I kiss her again, slowly, savoring the burn of desire as the meaning of her lips on mine seeps inside, mending my bones and sewing me back together. I don't need her clothes off to feel this. All I need is her.

I press my forehead to hers, staying close enough to keep feeling her breath on my lips. I don't ever want to breathe air again unless it's straight from her lips. "I'll fight to the death for you, Lily. I'll take your pain, suffer for you, do anything you want me to do. All I need in return is for you to *stop* hurting other people. No more gaslighting. Just be honest with me because good or bad, I'm going to be here for you."

She pushes me away, stumbling sideways as if her knees aren't cooperating. I reach for her and she swats my hands away, wide, watery eyes questioning. "Gaslighting?"

I take a step forward and she stumbles again, clearing the back of the car. I reach out a hand, hoping she'll anchor to me the way my soul is anchored to her. "You rammed my car, Lily. The white paint and the damage done to the back are perfect matches to the color and damage to the front of your vehicle. Yet you didn't leave a note or bother to tell me about it because just like I *know* you were in my house, I know that you're poised to deny intentionally hitting my car. But you can't do things and then just deny them. You're caught, so be honest with me and let me help you figure out where you should go when you leave Jill's house."

Her eyes stay steady on me despite the shake in her legs. "You did this on purpose. You hit my car so you could then accuse me of hitting you. This whole time, you've been gaslighting me and trying to make it look like I'm the one..."

She presses a hand to her lips and I shake my head, begging her. "Don't do this, Lily. Have a heart. Borrow mine if you need to. Just don't lie to me anymore because I swear to every god under the sun that shines on you that I will blow up every part of your world if you don't stop messing with me. And Jill, my dad, and everyone else. Just leave them alone, Lily. Whatever your problem is, it's with me. So handle it with me."

She backs away, putting more distance between us with each long stride. "You're delusional."

I move forward. "Yeah, I am. Compliments of falling in love with you. What's your excuse?"

She rushes down the sidewalk. I keep a steady pace behind her, calming my nerves and reminding myself she just once again proved how easily she can break me. How easy I want to make it for her to crash my body against the rocks, breaking my bones while her siren song pours down my throat and spreads through my soul on wings of pure ecstasy. She felt good on my lips. Tasted better. And left me in pieces, still sporting a smashed car, a violated home, a stolen clinic, and not a single explanation for any of it.

She turns up the cobblestone path leading to her front door and I grab her arm, spinning her to me, brain on the fritz and words rioting in my mouth. "We're not finished talking, angel. You have a lot of explaining to do."

She shoves a hand into her pocket and draws a canister of pepper spray, finger on the trigger. "Let go of me. Or you'll end up in the same place as everyone *else* who threatens my family. And I care about your dad too much to watch him have to bury you."

I pull her closer, snuffing out the distance and folding my palm over the top of her hand. I hold her stare, dragging my fingers downward and plucking the canister out of her grip because even my pinky is stronger than the whole of her hand. "Did you just threaten to *kill* me? Is that your end game, Lily? Drive me slowly mad and make sure my life comes to an abrupt end?"

"My end game is to get away from you," she screams, tears battering her cheeks.

I ease my grip on her waist and open her pocket, dropping the canister back inside. "My end game was to get away from you, too. It didn't work. So here we are." I run a thumb beneath her eyes. "Don't cry. Just tell me why you're running around ramming parked cars and stealing clinics out from under their rightful heirs. I'll let you keep doing it, Lily. *If* you let me be the only person who ever feels your wrath. Leave everyone else alone because they didn't ask to be tortured by you any more than I did, but they also don't love you like I do. So let this torment be reserved for me."

"Torment?" She sniffs.

I press my forehead to hers. "You're a sickness in my brain, a mark on my soul, and I'm willing to let you do your worst because you've already taken everything from me anyway. All I have left is what's standing in front of you, so take it. Let me be enough."

A sob heaves from her chest and my teeth grind. "Don't, Lily. Don't make me watch you cry like this when I'm already cursed to love you." I fist my hand in her hair. "Just tell me that I'm enough. That you're going to move out of Jill's house and——"

She rips free of my hands, leaving copper hair draped over my fingers. "Lily!" I run after her, chasing her onto the porch. "Stop! I need to check your head. Why did you pull away like that?"

Tears drip from her chin and run down the front of her jacket. "Don't touch me. I swear I'll scream. I don't care how big you are, I'll kick and fight."

I look at the fist of hair I hold. "Fight?"

Her teeth grind. "I don't know what I've done to make you hate me this much, but I'm not going to take this abuse from you."

"Hate you? Have you heard anything I've said?"

She nods, sobs breaking from her throat. "You hate everything about me. You despise every part of yourself that cares about me. I make you miserable and you're punishing me for it."

I drop her coppery strands and stretch out my hands, tears flooding my own eyes. "I'm punishing *me*. Because not a single time in my life have I wanted to harm you, yet I have. And the worst of it was five years ago when you were so young... Lily, please. Let me check your head and then afterward maybe I can say things without them coming out all wrong."

The door behind her opens, a sleepy-eyed Emelia Alice staring between us as Lily rushes over the threshold.

I move forward. Emelia Alice blocks my path. I glare at her. "Move!"

She plants a hand firmly into the center of my chest. "Stop. Shouting."

I lift my eyes to the end of the living room where Lily is about to disappear from sight. "Lily, wait. Please, just wait. I'll find the words to explain myself better, just let me come inside with you. *Please*."

She steadies herself with a hand on the wall, glancing over her shoulder, the weight of her tears crushing my heart. "I'll turn down your dad's proposal, Darren. He can leave the clinic to you." Her eyes dip to Emelia Alice. "Jill can replace me there, too. Which should make all of you happy."

I press forward but Emelia Alice shifts, moving her entire body into my path. I can remove her, but I don't want an assault charge and she looks close to filing one already. I point over her head at the space Lily has disappeared from. "I can't leave her in that condition, so don't make me have to move you, Emelia Alice. Get out of my way so I can go to Lily."

"You left my sister in that condition," Emelia Alice bites. "So go wipe *your* tears and remember which one of them made you cry." She slams the door in my face, clicking the lock before I can grip the handle.

I rap my fists against the slab. "Em! Open the door!" She doesn't. I yank on the handle, half tempted to break this door in half. Instead, a string of curses flies from my mouth. I jump off the porch and jog around the side of the house to where I know Lily's bedroom window must be. There's a dim glow behind a set of ruddy-brown curtains. I press my palm to the glass, tapping my rough fingers hard enough that she has to hear me. "Lily."

The light turns out. I press my other palm to the glass and use all of my fingers to tap, forming fists and using my knuckles when she still doesn't answer. "We need to talk, angel."

Silence answers from inside the house. I take out my phone and dial. She's had this same phone number since she was a young teen and it's one of the few I know by heart because when it comes to Lily, I can't eradicate a single thing about her from my mind. She's stuck in the deep recesses like inoperable cancer. And I explained the weight of that to her all wrong.

"Please answer me, Lily," I beg, hanging up and calling her again. I want so badly to dry her tears. "Please, angel, please talk to me. On the phone, in your room, in my car...I'll stay out here in the cold all night if I need to because I don't want to leave you crying." I press my head to the siding. "I don't hate you. I hate me. And I'm not mad at you for anything. I just need answers." I close my eyes. "I need *you*, Lily. For better or worse, I need you."

The call ends and I stand completely still, waiting for the faintest noise, proof she's inside and listening to my message. Emelia Alice is one click away from reporting me for a domestic disturbance and she's probably already called Jill, so if Lily answers me, I'll do my best to get her out of here. We need privacy. Time. Things we'll never have if she moves out of this house and into Gideon's.

I pry my eyes open, silence heavy around me. Something glints in the shine of the grass below me. I squat, running my fingers along the patch of earth, smoothing my way across the blades until my fingertips trace over something familiar. A shiver crawls along my spine. The barrel of the syringe is intact, and I can see that a cap covers the needle even though the tip is partly buried as if someone stepped on it and embedded it into the soft earth. *Lily was on the side of the house.* Jill's words float like ghosts on the edges of my mind.

I glance to the left, where the corner of Freddie's lot meets with the gate of the backyard Lily was supposedly in the day he stumbled from his front door. If someone was exiting his house from the back door while he went out the front, Emelia Alice's scream could have deterred them from entering the gate. Could prompt them to smash the syringe into the earth in a place it wouldn't be found while they swooped in like a saving angel.

If Lily accidentally administered a fatal dose of insulin, would she take the needle from Freddie's house and bury it in her yard?

Muscles stiff, blood curdling in my veins, I tug off my shirt and use it to pluck the needle from its grassy grave, wrapping the entire syringe in the folds of the fabric. I straighten, coming face-to-face once again with Lily's dark window. Will she know I found this? And if she does, what will she do?

Skin prickling, I walk briskly back to my car, glancing around me before getting inside. Lily could be watching me, and if she killed Freddie, she could use this needle to frame me. For all I know, she broke into my house to plant some other form of evidence. Like the insulin bottle.

In a preemptive strike, Lily could have filled her syringe and then left the rest of the insulin in my house, waiting until she took Freddie's life and the time was right for her to escalate her deeds. But is the woman I kissed right here in this exact spot truly devoid of humanity? She definitely felt alive to me. And genuine.

~23~

Pebbles tip over one another in my mind, rattling around until my gut churns. The story Lily and Jill recounted to me on the day that Freddie died didn't have any smoking guns as to what caused his collapse. It could have been any number of things. Yet Lily said insulin overdose, even though she claimed to not know if he was diabetic.

She was also first on the scene to *help* him, outside of Emelia Alice, I suppose. But Emelia Alice hasn't inserted herself into Freddie's death the way Lily has, to the point of going over the heads of everyone at the hospital in order to contact Freddie's brother herself, telling him before any results were finalized that Freddie had died of insulin overdose. Why would a nurse do that? For the glory of being the first one to announce the cause of death? If so, the only way to reap that reward would be to know the official cause before it was ever determined.

I rest my head on Dad's desk, ulcers throbbing every time I think about the needle I buried in a cat grave this morning. I don't want it in my house, and since it's still wrapped in my shirt, my DNA is all over it. Knowing my luck, I'd report Lily and end up being the one to get arrested. But I don't think I'm going to report her, and that worries me more than the dead cats and decapitated mice. I suck in air. "I'm in love with an angel of death."

Dad chuckles from the doorway behind me. "Rough day at the hospital?"

I straighten, stroking my lips and dropping my hand when I realize that I'm once again unconsciously basking in the way Lily's murdering lips felt against mine. It's been a full day and a half and I can't shake wanting her any more than I can't force myself to go to the police. "Rough *life*."

Dad comes to a stop beside the table, brows pinching as his eyes move over my face. "I'm sorry, son. I tried——"

"Not because of you." I wave him off and scrub both hands down my face. "The best parts of my life are the ones I spent with you, most of them happening right here in this clinic." I scan the undecorated walls of his office. "I was thinking we could take another vacation together this summer? The way we used to?"

He sits down in his chair, the worn leather too broken in to make much of a noise. "You know I haven't been much on traveling since your mom passed."

I swallow. Before she died, all of our vacations were spent together. Since then, Dad hasn't left the state and after two solo trips, I haven't either. "Me neither. I think I might just spend the summer fixing up the old house."

He nods. "Don't forget to replace that old bedroom furniture. Especially since you were just muttering something about love. I'm going to guess the rough part of your life has to do with that, and any woman will appreciate a nice house and furniture that doesn't hold the ghosts of your parents."

I spin my pen in a circle on the desktop. "I have a new mattress so it isn't as creepy as you're making it sound. But there's also no woman to introduce my mattress to so..."

He folds his hands on the table. "I thought things were getting serious between you and the young lady from Pemberton?" My eyes snap up and his brow furrows. "Jill, right?"

I swallow. "No. I mean yes, the lady I had *a* date with is Jill. But it isn't serious and she's not young. She's my age."

He chuckles again. "Son, when you're *my* age, everyone is young. You and Jill have barely gotten started on your lives."

I pinch the bridge of my nose. "There isn't a Jill and me, and Lily is the young one who hasn't gotten started on her life. Yet she's out doing all sorts of things and is in a serious relationship with a boy who has most definitely been introduced to her mattress."

"I thought this meeting was about business." Lily's voice slices through the air behind me. "I didn't realize we were discussing my personal life."

I spin in my chair, shock dragging my tongue down my throat. Lily didn't work at Pemberton again today so I assumed she wouldn't be here either. It never occurred to me to ask Dad if she would be. He called to see if I could meet him here and I assumed it was so we could mend the divide that's been steadily growing between us.

I clamp my hands on the arm of my chair so as not to lift from my seat and drag Lily into my arms. When I spoke to Jill this morning, she hadn't seen or heard from Lily, though Emelia Alice did relay the scene Lily and I created while Jill had been at work the night before. I was hoping Lily's lack of interaction with her roommates meant she was packing, though Jill is worried that if Lily leaves, she'll only retaliate, using the full weight of her family name to sue, resulting in the home the twins have spent all of their money on being taken away from them. An understandable fear, but one that pales in comparison to what Lily could be capable of if she really did murder Freddie.

For now, I'm not telling anyone about the syringe. I'm keeping all the worst parts of what I think Lily may have done to myself, the reasons why growing ever more complicated as I look at her swollen red eyes. She's cried recently, and I'm most likely to blame for that.

I watch her every move as she rounds the desk and leans over, pressing a kiss to Dad's cheek. He accepts it with a bright smile on his aging face, giving her cheek a pat of his own and slipping one of his hands into hers. "I remember a time when your father was about Darren's age. Your grandmother called me, madder than a bulldog, wanting to know what I knew about this strange woman your dad had moved into his house." He lets out a whistle. "She was dead set on having the woman removed. Your dad was dead set on the woman never leaving his bed, let alone his sight."

Lily smiles, though it's forced. "I've heard this story about seventy-eight thousand times. Mom *still* insists she tried to leave, but the rest of us suspect she didn't really want to."

Dad chuckles. "As someone caught in the middle of your parents' whirlwind, I can assure you that if your mother wanted to leave your dad's sight, she would have. But those two are possessively co-dependent." He winks at her. "And more in love every time I see them. So you get no lectures from me on your personal choices because at the end of life, all that will matter to you are the people you've cared for. If you've found someone to share your life with, I'm as happy for you as your grandfather will be when I get to heaven and tell him all about it."

She kisses his cheek again. "You're going to have to wait a long while before you go, because telling him something like that now will only be a rumor." She casts an annoyed glare my way and then pulls a chair to the side of the desk where she'll be positioned between Dad and me. "I know how the people in this room *hate* to spread rumors."

I shift uncomfortably in my seat. "If you're implying that I spread rumors about you, go ahead and say them aloud. We'll let Dad be the judge of who is right and who's the psychopath."

A gasp of air sucks through Dad's lips. "Darren!"

I shrug, intentionally avoiding looking at Lily because doing so breaks my heart and it's already crushed. "If Lily is who you think she is and who I wish she was, then let her give an account for herself. Let her look you in the face and tell you that she didn't intentionally ram my vehicle because when I tried to ask her about it the other night, she blamed it on me."

She rises from her chair. "You accusing me of hitting your car isn't even close to *all* that you've been saying. But if it will stop your incessant whining, I'll buy you a brand new car. Any that you choose. I'll even buy your girlfriend a brand new car. And because *I'm* not the psychopath in the room, I'll have a cleaning service come take care of the odor in your breezeway. I know how much you hate it and everything it represents."

My eyes snap to hers, tongue heavy in my mouth. Her eyes are redder now than they were before. She's holding her resolve, but barely. I stand, keeping my feet planted so as not to allow myself to get any closer. "You know that isn't true. I *love* that scent."

Dad slams his palms onto his desk. "I thought I was going to bring the two of you in here and talk about you working together to take over the clinic for me. Not see you fighting about cars and smells. What is going on between the two of you?"

She removes her eyes from mine, shoulders squaring to Dad. "Yesterday, when I said I'd stay on until you found a replacement, I made a mistake. I won't be able to come back." Her features soften and tears loose from her lashes. "I'm really sorry."

I move but Dad pushes out of his seat and rounds the desk himself, holding Lily's hands in his. "I know you've been on edge since your neighbor died, and Gideon being out of the country isn't helping. But instead of making an emotional decision, why don't you take a couple of weeks and go visit Gideon in Tokyo? Or track down your globetrotting family and spend some time on the boat with them? When you get back, we'll try this meeting again because if my son is going to take this place over, he's going to need you."

The bottom drops out of my stomach. Lily shakes her head, more tears softly falling. "He needs *a* nurse, not me. Darren can hire Jill. The two of them working together will go a long way in solidifying their relationship."

Anger flashes in my chest. "I don't *have* a relationship with her and no matter how many times you try to say that I do, it will never be true."

Lily shifts, green eyes narrowing on me though her words are still directed at Dad. "Just this morning, Jill was telling me how sweet your son is to her. In addition to the *housing* advice he's giving her, he gave her an expensive box of macaroons. Between the sugar high and the rise of her pulse when she filled me in on all the things they enjoy doing together, I wasn't so sure she didn't require medication. Seems two people have never been so happy together, not even my parents."

Needles prick along my spine. "Medication? Are you threatening Jill now?"

"Darren," Dad snaps loudly.

I ignore him, the ulcer in my stomach throbbing. "Lily, if you hurt Jill——"

She turns toward the door and marches out. I move in that direction but the swell of Dad's voice and his grip on my arm stops me. I face him, meeting eyes as hard as stone. Never in my life have I seen him this angry. "Darren, I don't know what all this nonsense is about, but I will *not* sit here and let you abuse that girl any more. *I* gave Lily this job and whether you decide to come back or not, this is still my clinic. And right now, you're the only one I don't want in it!"

My jaw clenches. "I know you don't, which is why I haven't asked to come back even though Lily is the only reason I left in the first place."

"Lily? You said——"

I yank my arm free of him. "I know what I said. But Lily was sixteen so I didn't have much of a choice back then, but I do have one now. And my choice isn't to abuse her, Dad. I'm trying to do the opposite. But she's already broken me down. I am what I am because of her and that guts me because *you* are the only person I ever wanted to be the product of. But it's too late for me. I'm done. You aren't, and I refuse to let her hurt you." Emotion crawls into my throat. I sit back into my chair, shaky legs no longer wanting to hold me. "Lily might have something wrong with her. But I can't figure it out because I lose my flipping mind when I'm around her." I throw a hand at the door. "You can't spring her on me like this. I have to have time to think before I see her because if I don't, this is what happens."

I bend forward and press my face into my palms. "Don't tell her to go to Tokyo. Gideon isn't meant for her."

Dad kneels beside me. "Now I understand the problem. But yelling at a woman is not the way to convey your love to her."

I don't say anything. I'm too defeated to even speak. He takes a long breath. "I didn't see it until just now, but your grievances with her started around the time she took the position at Pemberton. I'm guessing you saw her again and it stirred something in you, but she has a boyfriend. A pretty serious one from what I've seen of them when he comes into the clinic to see her."

I run a hand to my forehead, gripping my temples between my thumb and ring finger, massaging the ache banging inside my skull. "Of course he comes in here. You probably have dinner with him all the time."

"Not all the time."

I look at Dad. The gray hair at his temples raises, a smile tugging his features upward. "A couple of times. And I wouldn't have liked him so much if I knew my own son had designs on Lily. Did you tell her and she rejected you? Is that why you're mistreating her, because you're hurt and dealing with it in the wrong way?"

I wipe my sweaty palms on my slacks. "No. Not exactly. I've tried to talk to her but my feelings for her are intense, so we usually end up arguing. And it stems from..." I close my eyes. "I crossed a line with her when she was sixteen. I...did more than only kiss her, but not...*everything*. From what I'll allow myself to remember, I did enough, though." A tear slides from underneath my lashes. "I'm so sorry, Dad. I've never felt anything for anyone underage except Lily." I look at him. "I swear, I've never touched another kid. Only Lily. And I left your clinic so I'd never do it again. So I knew she'd be safe from me."

He swallows thickly, raising from his crouched position and moving around the desk. He sits back in his chair, eyes fixed on a spot over my head. I wipe my face. "I'm a disappointment to myself so I know how much this hurts you. I hoped to never have to tell you. I wanted it all to go away. For me to accept that I couldn't carry on your legacy and that I couldn't have Lily. But she's back in my life again and I'm unraveling. Hurting her makes me want to physically harm myself, but there's this storm raging and it's starting to scare me because I don't know if I'm going insane or if Lily already is. And after five years of heartbreak, this is killing me. That's why I put in my resignation at Pemberton. I can't work there, or here. I can't be a doctor anymore. I'll finish my contract with Pemberton and then I'm done. Especially if Lily runs off to Tokyo. I don't think I can survive that."

His throat bobs. "Both of you are emotional, that's evident. So after you fulfill your obligations at Pemberton, why don't you take time off too. Maybe Lily will go on that vacation with you."

I gape at him. "I just told you that I took advantage of her when she was sixteen years old and this is what you have to say about it?"

He rubs the back of his hand across his mouth. "If you'd told me back then, I would have said something different. But some things make better sense to me now and," he throws up his hands, "this is about Lily, not you. You've done enough. She'll decide where she lives and works and whether or not any of that is with you is something you'll accept without question. Do you understand me? If I hear one more bad thing about that girl come out of your mouth, I'm going to slap you upside the head the way I apparently should have done years ago!"

My eyes burn with the sting of my tears. "Understood. And I hope you understand that I would give anything to go back and take away that one night."

I reach the door and his voice stops me. "Son, it's going to be tough, but if those tears I saw in Lily's eyes mean what I think they do, you'll keep trying to earn the privilege of apologizing to her. And if she lets you, you'll apologize to that girl every day for the rest of your life. You understand me?"

I nod. "I doubt I'll ever earn the privilege of even speaking to her again, but I do plan on trying, though I realize she's still too young for me. And that she has a boyfriend I'll never admit *might* be better for her than I am."

Dad steeples his fingers. "A boyfriend isn't a husband. And when Lily is thirty, you'll be forty-two. When she's forty, you'll be fifty-two. When she's seventy, you'll be eighty-two."

I raise a brow. "So are you telling me to break up her relationship? Or giving me a math lesson?"

He sighs. "I'm saying you should stop pulling Lily's pigtails because this isn't a question of math anymore. It's a matter of her deciding if you'll be celebrating birthdays together or apart. So have a nice long conversation about everything you've been keeping bottled up."

I rub my face. "I'm trying to, but what you saw today is the aftermath of my efforts, so it might be better if I put a cap on the bottle and ship my feelings to the middle of Siberia."

"Then you better let me meet this Jill that you're buying expensive macaroons for because when Lily all but resigned yesterday, she said you wanted to come back to Mansfield Clinic. And I got a little excited thinking maybe one day you'd have a child who would find his or her way back to this old place, too, following in *their* dad's footsteps."

I grip the door, throat so tight I can barely speak. "The only way I get to live that dream is if Lily lives it with me because she's the only woman in this world I'd buy anything expensive for."

~24~

Dad may not believe there's so much as a sarcastic bone in Lily's body, let alone a dangerous one, but whether he's right or suffering from the same ailment of the heart as I am, at least we have some closure on the past. He knows I didn't leave the clinic because I outgrew him. He also knows I haven't lived much of a life since I walked out the doors of Mansfield Clinic. I only wish I'd confessed everything to him five years ago. He would have made sure I stayed away from Lily and possibly called the law on me, but if he knew, if her parents knew, then maybe her life would have taken a different path. A happier one.

Dad knowing how I feel about Lily also eases the stress of my emotions, though it doesn't lighten my burden. I'm still the man who put his mouth and hands all over an underage girl. I've punished myself, but not enough. I hurt Lily. I continue to hurt her, and she continues to intentionally destroy me. I've searched every heat vent and under every rug in my house, pulling back loose corners of carpet in the bedrooms and searching the attic. If Lily hid something in my house, she was slick about it.

I wish I was as smart as she is. Instead, I'm hiding a possible murder weapon and keeping my mouth shut about dead and mutilated animals. I can't even bring myself to ask her about them because even if she refuses to let the words of affirmation pass her lips, I'm afraid I'll still see the truth in her eyes. I'd rather not be burdened with that knowledge.

All I want to see in her eyes is love. For me. Even if it's twisted and all of her plans concerning me are vile, I want to look into her gorgeous face and know I'm the reason for every single thing Lily does. I want to hear her say that she only took the job at Pemberton to be close to me again. I want her to tell me that the only reason she stayed at Mansfield all of these years was for the hope that I'd come back to her.

I walk into Pemberton and take the stairs to my floor. Lily either bought a new car or didn't show up for work again today. I checked the entire parking lot twice and didn't see her BMW. Part of me was relieved, a bigger part wholly disappointed.

There's a small crowd of people gathered outside of Mrs. Meadows's room, Jill among them, her hands folded over Kassidy's shoulders as they talk in hushed tones to the right of the group. I move toward them, wishing I had a tissue to offer Kassidy. Her eyes are leaking as if a faucet is on behind them. "What happened?"

Jill glances at me, taking a breath and moving Kassidy and herself farther away from Mrs. Meadows' door and the other bystanders. I follow along, cringing when Jill finally stops and faces me. "Mrs. Meadows had a reaction to penicillin."

"Penicillin? She's allergic. I made a note that she should only receive Cipro."

"We know," Jill groans, teeth clenching as Kassidy's tears fall harder. She turns back to the young nurse, doing her best to wipe them away. "Everything is going to be okay, Kassidy. Go on home and get some rest. I'll cover the end of your shift and if anyone needs to speak to you again, I'll call you."

Kassidy nods, eyes lifting to mine. "I'm really sorry. I did check the order, I swear."

I fold my arms over my chest and wait for the nurse to leave. Jill does the same, leaning against the wall once Kassidy is gone. "If I had known being a supervisor would end like this, I would never have taken the position."

"Are you the one who administered the penicillin?"

She huffs, keeping her eyes on the wall across from us. "No. *Lily* did. But I can't talk to you about this because there's clearly something going on between the two of you and you'll be just like Angela, covering for Lily while blaming everyone else for her mistakes."

A stone drops into the pit of my stomach. "I don't understand how Lily *or* Kassidy could have made this mistake. The notes in the patient's file are clear, and I ordered *Cipro* for Mrs. Meadows."

Jill presses her shoulders against the wall, lifting her chin to glare directly up at me. "Before you spoke to Mrs. Meadows's husband about the allergy, you had already placed a pharmacy order for penicillin. You changed it, but too late I guess, because the pharmacy sent it. Kassidy caught the mistake and noted that the wrong order had been filled, but she left the penicillin lying on the cow she was using. Along came Lily, *helping* Kassidy because it was a rough night and everyone was behind. Lily then administered the penicillin because unlike Kassidy, Lily doesn't bother following protocol. She didn't bother checking if the medication was right because nothing matters to her. So what if she loses her job? And do you think this hospital's administration would dare fire her? *No.* They'll ensure that this mistake falls on any shoulder but Lily's."

The white tiles of the hall roll like waves beneath my feet. I peel my arms from my chest and place a steadying hand against the wall. The blame for this is on my shoulders. "How severe was Mrs. Meadows's reaction?"

Jill pushes off the wall. "Severe enough that it was obvious *something* triggered the shortness of breath. Like being given a medication she was allergic to."

I run a hand through my hair, my fingers as shaky as my legs. Instead of burying needles in cat graves, I should have reported my suspicions about Lily. Or, at the very least, stopped being too much of a coward to outright confront her. "How is Mrs. Meadows now?"

Jill flicks a wrist toward the woman's room. "As good as one can be when their flippant nurse says *oops, I almost killed you but hey, we all make mistakes.*"

I look toward where the hall curves, leading to the fishbowl. "Where is Lily now?"

Jill tugs on my shirt, a tear in her eyes when I look back at her. "Not suspended like she should be, but I did send her home early. So she's at *my* house doing who knows what." She drops her hands. "Darren, I'm scared. Even more so now that I know you...and her...that you're..."

I press my palms against Jill's cheeks, keeping her looking into my eyes and hoping she'll find comfort in what I have to say. "I promised you before that I won't let anything happen to you, and I'm going to keep that promise. You did the right thing in sending Lily home. Pending an internal review, I'll personally see to it that the hospital follows protocol and officially suspends her. I'll *personally* see to it that she moves out of your house, too. If that ends with a lawsuit, I'll be in your corner for it." I swallow, knowing that if it comes to a lawsuit, even if it's only Mrs. Meadows suing the hospital, I'll have to confess everything I know and even what I only suspect. And in turn, Lily might confess to what happened between us that night when she was sixteen.

I wipe my thumbs under Jill's eyes. "After Lily administered the drug, did she stay in Mrs. Meadows's room? Did she try to *save* her?"

Jill's head shakes. "No one even knew the drug had been administered until afterward, when Kassidy checked her cart and noticed it was missing. Lily admitted she was the one who gave it to Mrs. Meadows, but at first denied that it was wrong. She said she followed protocol and everything was correct. But since it obviously wasn't, she threw up her hands and said it was only a mistake. Then she had the gall to call Angela at *home*."

My brows draw together. "Lily reported herself to Angela?"

Jill's mouth turns into a snarl. "How else would she spin her sob story? Keirstyn is too smart to fall for it and refuses to let Lily's money affect her judgment. She's also not being seduced by Lily the way you are so that keeps her judgment sound also."

I remove my hands. "Being angry with me isn't helping this situation. Tell me *exactly* what Lily said happened."

Jill folds her arms. "She told Angela she was unusually tired, and Angela said I should have known that since Lily both lives and works with me. I couldn't deny knowing the girl never sleeps. How can she? Lily works ten-hour shifts here and then moonlights at your dad's clinic.

And she's apparently helping her cousin set up some kind of store in his ice cream shop. *Ice cream.* Like that's more important than resting up for a job that's literally life and death."

I take a breath. It's no secret that nurses are overworked, but Lily is inflicting this particular overexertion on herself. "Did you mention Lily's extracurriculars to Angela?"

Jill unfolds her arms, worrying at the ends of hair falling over her now slumped shoulders. "I had no choice, but Angela already knew about the clinic so she decided to *cut Lily some slack*. Then she took that slack and wrapped it around my neck, faulting me for everything that happened because it's *my responsibility to know the physical condition of my nurses*. Which means *I'm* being held responsible for Lily's carelessness. So if Mrs. Meadows decides to sue the hospital, Angela is making it pretty clear that I will lose my job. And she's liable to have me fired even without a lawsuit."

If Mrs. Meadows knows the wealth of Lily's family, that would only be more of a reason to sue the hospital. Both the hospital and the Bellers would want to settle out of court to avoid the scandal, and they would do so lucratively. "You don't deserve to be held accountable for what Lily did, and I'll make sure to voice that opinion. But until this blows over for you, show the hospital that you're taking steps to ensure nothing like this happens again. Hold a meeting with your nurses and have them all sign off on having read the proper protocols. And keep Lily off the schedule. I'll catch up with her after my shift ends and let her know, so if she's at your house when you get there, don't say anything to her. The less you engage, the better."

"What about you?" Jill steps closer to me, lowering her voice as people pass by us. "I'm confused about why you and Lily were both in tears the other night, like you were having a lover's spat when you had seemed to abhor her before that."

I work my hand over the back of my neck, all too aware that the part of me that loves Lily has too much control over the rest of me. "I'm as confused as you are, Jill."

Her face falls. "Then you do have feelings for her. Strong ones if you're still confused about them after all of this." She glances toward

Mrs. Meadows' room. "I would think you'd at least be worried about your dad. Lily is working for him so he's at risk. And more so than me or this hospital."

I nod. "I'm aware of all the risks, Jill. I'll handle them for my dad the same way I'm going to handle them for you."

~

Angela doesn't try to hide her contempt when I enter her office. I didn't used to take her disdain personally, but now I'm sure I've deserved all of her disrespect. She's been in the hospital business a long time and she's probably dealt with despicable men like me before, so she had me pegged right from the start. "Is there going to be an internal investigation regarding Lily Beller?"

Angela leans back in her chair. "The medication orders you placed for Mrs. Meadows are being reviewed. That's your part in what happened and all you need to know."

I cup my hands over the back of the chair across the desk from her. "That means you aren't going to let anything blow back on Lily. You'd rather frame her supervisor, or even me. But did it ever occur to you that Lily could have planned this whole thing so she can snatch the supervisor position you apparently promised her?"

Angela laughs, a loud cackle. "No, Dr. Mansfield, it never occurred to me that Nurse Beller would intentionally harm a patient in order to receive a title. What *has* been clear is that the standard of care on the med-surg floor has gone down since Jill took over as supervisor."

"Which happens to coincide with you hiring Lily Beller."

"I'd appreciate it if you would shut my door on your way out, Dr. Mansfield, lest anyone else thinks they should bring their girlfriend's unwarranted plight to my attention."

I feel anything but qualified to have a moral argument, but I promised Jill I would stand up for her and she deserves this from me. "I'm not in a romantic relationship with Jill, and you can't fire her simply because Lily wants her job."

Angela's beady eyes grow smaller, head tilting to the side like a viper watching its prey. "I'm under the impression that Jill leaving Pemberton is *your* doing. She's to start working alongside you at Mansfield Clinic."

My muscles seize. "My dad's clinic?"

Angela fixes her glare. "*Your* clinic. Isn't that why you're leaving here too? Nurse Beller said you'll be taking over for your father and poaching Jill to go with you."

My throat tightens. "No. On both charges. All that's happening at my dad's clinic is *Lily* is leaving, and it would be in your best interest to make sure she leaves Pemberton, too."

I turn toward the door, gripping the side of it to drag it closed as I exit. Angela's voice snakes over my shoulders. "Thank you for your service at Pemberton Medical. You'll be paid for the remainder of your contract, but we won't need you back after today."

~25~

I don't need the distraction of running through the forest anymore, and my gym equipment is worthless. Now that I've opened the Pandora's box that is my love for Lily, there's no hiding. I am what I am. She is what she is. And I can feel the darkness coming for us both.

I roll my neck, the tension in my shoulders unyielding as I once again stand in front of the door behind which both Lily and Jill live. I rap my knuckles firmly. The turmoil of loving Lily while also knowing I should despise so many things about her makes my stomach feel like a canoe being tossed around in stormy seas. I don't trust that I can keep my thoughts straight long enough to *make* Lily move out of this house, and before I confront her over everything else, I have to get her away from Jill.

Jill opens the door, face long. I resist the urge to reach out and offer her comfort. The mistakes I made in regard to her keep getting thrown in my face, and they're the reason Lily's words concerning Jill are always laced with veiled threats. Ones she seems to be making good on. "Lily's car is here, so I assume she is?"

Jill opens the door wider and I walk inside, cringing at the narrowed eye glare from Emelia Alice. "*Both* women are here, so which one are you going to choose?"

"Em," Jill's tired voice lowly chastises.

Emelia Alice shakes her head, her hair whipping wildy. "*He's* the reason all of this is happening. He's pitting you and Lily against each other and then waltzing off into the sunset while the rest of us have to live inside this toxic environment."

I break my no contact rule and rest a hand on Jill's arm when her lips purse to respond to her sister. "Emelia Alice is right, I'm to blame for all of this." I meet the stare of the other twin. "I didn't pit them against one another, though. Believe that's true or not, but I am here to help. That starts with me seeing Lily. Privately. Is she in her room?"

Jill leads me to Lily's door and knocks softly, head tilted down. "Darren is here to see you."

Lily doesn't answer. Jill looks up at me. "She does this sometimes, won't answer us when we knock. I don't know what to tell you."

I press my palm to the door. "I've got it. Go on back to your sister."

I wait for her to leave and then try the knob—it's unlocked. I open the door a few inches. There's a light on beside the bed, illuminating a stack of dog-eared books. One thing that's always been true about Lily Beller is that when her nose is in a book, someone could steal the seat out from under her and be three states away before she ever noticed.

I move inside the room. The bed is made, two suitcases piled atop it. One is half full and the other empty. I glance around, eyes falling on her heavily blinded window. The night I found the syringe, Jill had thought Lily was in her room. Maybe Lily snuck out through the window that night and did so again today.

I move to the open closet door. "Lily?

"What do you want?" Her voice crosses the room to me.

I turn toward the only other door in here, halting my steps when I reach the bathroom threshold. Lily is sitting in the floor, back pressed against the wall by the toilet. Her eyes are red and puffed with tears. I ache inside, ulcers and heartbreak flaring against the willpower I'm pretending to have. "What's wrong? Are you sick?"

She places her forearms onto her bent knees. "You're in the wrong room. Jill's is off the main living room and should be easy enough for you to remember your way to."

I push a hand behind me, motioning toward her bed. "Are you packing? Or did you never unpack all the way to begin with because you knew you wouldn't have to stay here very long?"

She picks at a nail. "You don't need to try to scare me off, if that's what this is. I'm leaving of my own free will. This place and its remaining occupants are all yours."

I walk toward her. "I have a house of my own, so let's cut the crap because none of what's happening has anything to do with our lack of housing options."

"No?" she challenges. "Because since the day I moved in, all I've heard about is how *insulted* you are by my presence."

I squat in front of her. "I *questioned* Jill about why you'd rent this room the same way I questioned you about it. And in all fairness, Lily, you never gave me a straight answer. *That's* what's insulting."

Her tear-soaked face turns into a mask of resolve. "I don't owe *anyone* an explanation of the choices I make. Especially *you*. So when your head is resting on Jill's pillow at night, spend your time doing something more creative than talking about me."

I swallow the weight of her emotions, the accusations her words hold. The shame over what happened between Jill and me is mine to carry and even without Lily pointing out my past actions, I feel as if I've robbed myself of only having ever tasted Lily's lips. She's the only memory I want. "I didn't buy macaroons for Jill. A patient's mother brought them in for me and I left them at the nurses' station for *all* of the nurses. I in no way implied they were only for Jill, and even if I did, how can you hold *anything* against me after what you've done?"

"What I've done?" She sniffs. "What about the things that you *are* doing? What exactly is it that you want from me?"

A lump forms in my throat as her tears fall. "The truth, Lily. I'm willing to help you. Too much. But you have to give me reasons and explanations, something I can hold on to so when I'm promising to take all of your secrets to my grave, I know why you have those secrets to begin with." I reach forward and grip her fingers between mine. "What happened with Mrs. Meadows?"

Lily's gentle sobs cut through the silence, a pang of guilt throbbing deep in my chest. I don't want to see her cry like this. I move forward and wrap one arm around her shoulders, pulling her away from the wall and against me as I press my other palm to her tear-soaked skin, my fingertips skimming her hair. I can feel her heartbreak. It isn't fake. She's genuinely upset and that makes my heart swell in relief. "It was only a mistake." I say the words for her. For me.

She shakes her head, voice cracking over the syllables. "I could have killed her. Her family could be burying her right now because of me."

I press my lips against the crown of her head. "Accidentally. It could have happened accidentally. Right?"

She draws her face up to mine. "What? Of course it was an accident. You think..." Her breath catches, eyes wide. "No. No, no, no, no, no! I would never...how could you..."

I dip my forehead down to hers. "I don't. But I'm a mess, Lily. There's so much weird stuff going on and you're right at the center of it all." She tries to pull away but I hold her tightly. "Please don't, angel. Just sit here with me like this and let's talk, because there's not going to be a time in my life when I don't love you. I think the day you were born, I was marked for you. So if you're not okay, I'm not okay." I brush my lips against the corner of her mouth. "Please let me help you."

"Am I interrupting?" Emelia Alice's voice cuts over me.

"You seem to have a knack for interrupting," I mutter as Lily scrambles out of my arms, pushing against my chest until I lean back onto my heels. "Better?"

She stands, keeping her back pressed to the wall, eyes locked on Emelia Alice. I glance over my shoulder at Jill's twin, unease winding between my ribs as she stares at Lily. "Can we help you, Em?"

A switch flips and Emelia Alice smiles, prim and pretty. She produces a flat white box. "I made this for you, Lily. When I was restocking Zach's merchandising section, he said you'd been in and admired a piece like this." She takes the lid off the box dand tilts the cocooned white chain bracelet toward Lily. The links are tiny ice cream cones. "I've been short with you, because of my sister." Em's eyes dart to mine and then back to Lily. "But most of what's happening isn't entirely your fault, and I can see you're just as upset as Jill, so I made you both a new piece. Twin pieces."

Lily swallows. "Then you should have it, Em. To match your sister's."

Emelia Alice slips the delicate bracelet from the box. "You both attract the same men, so you're more alike than Jill and I ever have been."

I grind my teeth. I'm tired of hearing Jill's name attached to mine. "Lily didn't steal me from Jill, I'm just not compatible with your sister."

Lily holds her wrist out to Emelia Alice. "She *knows* I didn't steal you because there is *nothing* going on between us. At least not anything that's keeping you from Jill."

My tongue stills, lying heavy in my mouth as I land on the memory of kissing Lily. It's enough to keep me from everyone, and it should be solid enough proof for her that we have *everything* going on.

I straighten and lean against the sink while Emelia Alice affixes the bracelet to Lily's wrist, showing her how to adjust it before excitedly revealing the matching earrings underneath the tissue paper.

Eyes barely attempting to dry, Lily takes the earrings from the box, removing the tiny diamond studs she was wearing and replacing them with the ice cream cone studs. They look odd on her, but I get the novelty of them. Her cousin Zach was just a boy when he opened Scoopz. Everyone thought he'd hire people and not be a kid prodigy, but I always knew Zach would be the one doing all the work. His last name might be Kingwood instead of Beller, but they're both one and the same. Like her, Lily's family works hard. So why am I so surprised that she's working two jobs and still finding time for Zach?

Emelia Alice sweeps Lily's copper hair aside. "They're beautiful on you. Don't you agree, Darren?"

I watch the hands of Jill's twin almost petting Lily's hair. It's creepy. "*Lily* is beautiful. Especially her hair. Is that why you borrowed her shampoo? Without asking?"

Emelia Alice rounds on me. Lily turns with her, hand flattening against her stomach. "How much do I owe you, Em? I'd like to leave here with a clean slate."

Emelia Alice drops her eyes back to Lily, admiring the bracelet now clinging to Lily's wrist. "The jewelry is a gift. And I really wish you'd reconsider leaving, I'm sure you and Jill can reach an understanding."

I place a hand on Lily's shoulder, ready to convince her otherwise, but she leans away from me and toward the toilet, dropping to her knees and barely managing to get overtop it before dark liquid heaves from her mouth.

Emelia Alice jumps backward. I drop down beside Lily, tugging her hair up into my fist to keep it from her vomit. I press my free palm to her back, rubbing softly as I turn to ask Emelia Alice for a cool washcloth. She's gone.

I take my hand from Lily's back and brush her cheek. Her skin is clammy, muscles straining in her neck as her stomach rebels. It's hard to say if she was feeling fine earlier, considering the tears, but right now she seems so frail, like a little mouse who needs to be protected from the cat. And from whatever killed the cat.

Lily's muscles relax and I rearrange myself to a seated position, tucking her between my bent legs. She steadies her hands on my knees. I let her hair drop down her back. "Were you sick earlier? Is that why I found you sitting in here?"

She nods. "I haven't been feeling good for a few days. Tired mainly, but vomiting today."

I curl an arm around her waist so she can rest her weight on me. The force with which she just emptied her stomach left her shaking. "You're working two jobs and apparently helping Zach, so I imagine you are tired."

Jill rushes into the bathroom, kneeling beside us and paying no mind to my arms around Lily as she offers pills and a cup of water. Lily doesn't take either. Jill frowns. "It's Zofran. Em said you were throwing up so I thought you could use this."

"I'm fine." Lily rocks forward, pushing up onto unsteady legs. I raise with her but she snatches her arm away from my grip, steadying herself instead with a hand pressed to the wall.

I take the medication from Jill. "Thanks. I'll have Lily take this later if she needs it. Right now, I think she just needs to lie down and rest. I'll stay with her."

Lily pushes away from the wall, taking a towel from beside the shower and using the whole thing to wipe her face. "I said I'm fine, and this room is technically still mine and neither of you have been invited inside. Please leave."

Jill gives me an *I told you she was weird* look. "We're just trying to help, Lily. Darren is right that you need to lie down. You've been vomiting every morning for a week."

"A week?" I question. "You told me only today."

Lily's fingers stroke over her abdomen, the dark rings under her eyes more pronounced now. Jill makes a gurgled noise, halfway between a yelp and a gasp. My insides scream. Lily's fingers are absently doing what expectant mothers' often do. "You're pregnant."

$$\sim 26 \sim$$

I'm not sure who uttered the words, Jill or me, but they turned my skin into brittle glass, and the only way not to shatter over Lily carrying another man's child was to push anger into my veins, let it soak up all the hurt until I could get out of that Tudor house and retreat to my own.

Every time Lily lets me get close to her, it's only to crush me. And I keep falling right into her trap. I tell her things I never intend to say and resolve myself to keep my mouth shut about things I don't even know the depths of because the part of me that burns for her is unwilling to be doused by buckets of ice water or accusations of murder.

I need a way to break the command she has of my heart. A way to scrub the want of her from my soul. Especially if she's going to have a child. I won't be able to stick around for fear of seeing that unfold, and I won't be able to utter a single word to anyone about any suspicions I have about her because I can't be responsible for sending a pregnant Lily to jail. I'll leave this place and live with the shame of taking my suspicions to the grave. The weight of it will be good company for the rest of my shame.

I'm no longer worried that Lily is framing me. At this point, who cares? I'm not even worried that her family will swoop in and save her from any real punishment should her evil deeds ever be revealed. I'm worried that they won't.

Hair still wet from my post-run shower, I make my way through the house wondering who could possibly be at my door this time. The postman come to tell me that a whole box of dead cats have been shipped to me?

It's well past dark and my porch light is apparently blown. I swing the door open anyway, no regard for my personal safety because I don't care what happens to me. I'm pretty sure I've lost the right to the air I'm being allowed to breathe.

My eyes scramble over the pale-faced apparition, freezing my muscles in place and stilling my lungs. On my doorstep, clasping a thick white shawl around her shoulders, is Lily.

I don't speak because I can't. Thinking about her is painful enough, seeing her is worse.

She takes a step away from the door. "I don't need to come inside, I just want to tell you a few things and then I'll go. Do you want to get dressed and sit in my car? So we don't let all of the heat out of your house with the door hanging open like this?"

My jaw tics, an all too familiar cyclone beating against every surface inside me as her eyes rake over my exposed torso. All I'm wearing is sweat pants, and they're not thick enough to create the barrier I need between myself and Lily. I need a brick wall reinforced with concrete and covered in steel-plated armor.

She pulls her shawl tighter, red-rimmed eyes lifting to meet mine. "We'll do this here then. Firstly, I'm not pregnant."

My grip on the door handle tightens. If she isn't pregnant, then while I'm rotting away as the lovestruck complicit accomplice to her crimes, at least I won't have to envision her having Gideon's baby. She'll only be getting away with murder because I'm too weak to do anything to stop her. "You took a pregnancy test?"

She brushes the lightly falling snow from her face. "Three. All negative."

I stare at her, the way the snow sprinkles over her hair in the lightest dusting of starlight. I should have married young, promised myself to someone else as soon as I could have, and kept myself out of the trouble I'm in now. I could have had a wife and given Dad grandchildren before he got too on in his years to keep up with them the way I know he'd want to. I should have had children before Mom died. Before Lily was written in blood on my soul, her name carved into my bones.

I step aside and motion for her to come in. She hesitates. I walk away from the door. "You hungry? I have some day-old takeout I was getting ready to heat up. Fajitas from Conchas."

I disappear around the corner and into the kitchen, the faint click of the front door reaching me. I open the refrigerator and remove the four plastic-domed takeout containers. I always order in family-sized portions and eat what I have for breakfast, lunch, and dinner until it's gone. Then I select a different restaurant and repeat the process.

I take a plate out of the cabinet and a spark of delight hits me dead center when I reach for the second. It burns a little stronger when I let it sink in that Lily is the one this second plate is for. It's depressing. I'll be long rested inside a box in the ground before the flame I carry for her will snuff out of existence.

I set the plates beside the food containers and go back to the doorway, looking around it to find Lily standing in the entryway, shawl pulled tight around her shoulders. "I thought you wanted to talk?"

She shifts uncomfortably, as if it's a struggle not to crawl out of her skin. "What I have to say doesn't require me to be inside your house. I can talk to you from here."

I crook a finger and beckon her forward. "It isn't like you haven't been in here before. And don't deny it because you're the only person I know that smells like heaven, and I doubt any other fallen angels found their way to my breezeway. So come here, and eat with me."

Her head shakes. "I'm not hungry."

I stomp across the floor and pluck the shawl from her grip, gently removing it from her shoulders. "You made the trip all the way here, so what you have to say must be important. At least come and sit down, and talk to me while I eat. You look half ready to fall over anyway. Are you still feeling nauseous?"

Her throat works. "No, not really."

"That's a yes, then."

I lead her to the kitchen and pull out a chair, draping her shawl over the back of it as she sits down. "I have chicken and beef fajitas with rice, beans, and a vegetable medley. Any of that sound appealing to you?"

She glances at the waiting plates. "I remember you used to eat at Conchas at least three times a week, but there isn't much about you that I recognize anymore so I wasn't sure if you still did."

I move away from her and decide to reheat everything, that way she can just eat off of whichever plate she wants. Family style. Or lover's style, the way a couple might enjoy eating together.

I swallow down the waves of an emotion that feels so much stronger than love. "I've definitely changed, but my stomach's preferences are the same. How about you? I know you're different as a person, but you used to like Conchas too. I remember us grabbing dinner there a couple of times after you'd gone out on a house call with me."

Her laugh is dry. "I actually had a craving for it earlier, but that's passed now."

I place the warmed plate of meat and vegetables onto the table, the spicy aroma making my stomach growl. "Craving?"

She massages her temples. "I'm *not* pregnant. I've had the tests, plus I'm on birth control."

I go back to the counter and heat up the beans and rice in my new microwave, plopping the tortillas in for a few seconds before going back to the table and spreading the rest of the meal in front of her. "You might not be far enough along for a drugstore test to be accurate, and we know birth control isn't one hundred percent effective. Keirstyn has four kids already and was just telling me how shocked she is to be pregnant with number five because she's been on birth control since her last child was born."

Lily pulls a warm tortilla from the stack, picking at the end of it. "I saw my obstetrician. Twice. That's what I was doing when I missed those days of work. Fretting and getting my drugstore negative testing confirmed. Based on the last time I was with Gideon, the obstetrician said I'd be far enough along that her tests would definitely pick up a pregnancy. But they're negative. Which isn't surprising, because Gideon always uses protection and it's highly unlikely that both of our precautions would fail in unison. I also don't want to talk about my sex life with you, so could you for once just believe what I'm telling you?"

I take the seat next to hers and scrub a hand down my face. "Believe me, I don't want to hear about you sharing a cup of coffee with Gideon, let alone anything more. You say you're tired and stressed, so maybe that's why you're feeling ill?" I prop my elbows on the table. "You should leave the hospital. You need time to sleep during the night when your body is naturally *supposed* to sleep."

She swallows. "I resigned a few hours ago. When Angela called to confront me about being pregnant with your baby."

My pulse jumps but I keep my voice even. "Did you tell her we're waiting until the honeymoon phase is over?"

Lily leans against the back of her chair. "This isn't funny. I was already being painted as a Jezebel, and now Jill is seeing to it that I become a *pregnant* Jezebel."

"You're saying Jill told Angela you were pregnant? Today?"

Lily nods. "After what happened with Mrs. Meadows, Jill was understandably upset. She kept talking over me and wouldn't let me explain anything, and Angela..."

"Is being extremely tolerant of you?"

Lily looks down at the tortilla. "Angela asked me to keep her informed about what was happening on the med-surg floor, bringing things directly to her even if the protocol would be to report it to the floor supervisor."

I set my fork aside. "Why?"

Lily's shoulders lift. "I'd already moved into Jill's house when Angela made the request, so it felt like she was asking me to spy. Which made me leery of both of them, so I never reported anything to Angela. Until after the medication mix-up. And that was only because Jill wouldn't let me speak. She just kept yelling at me and saying all I do is screw up my job and make her look bad."

"Hey," I place a finger under Lily's chin and lift her eyes, "My actions have been all over the map lately, but I hope you know you *can* trust me. With anything. And it sounds like Angela and Jill were both out of line in how they treated you."

Tears drip from Lily's lashes and she brushes my touch away. "This is all because of you, Darren. *You* did this to me. At least where Jill is concerned. She continually brings up my name to anyone who will listen, as if Pemberton is so big the rumors won't get back to me. They do. People are always asking me the most bizarre things or making snide comments. Because of you and Jill. So I confronted Jill tonight, told her how I feel about her spreading around business that would be none of hers even if it were true. Her excuse for calling Angela was that pregnancy brain was a good reason for me to have messed up with Mrs. Meadows, and Jill denied implying the baby was yours, but I don't see why Angela would lie about that."

I pick up my fork and move some of the rice around. "I don't see why Jill would."

Lily huffs. "I'm aware that you think she walks on water, but if *any* of the rumblings the two of you are spreading get back to my family, especially a false pregnancy rumor that implies I'm sleeping with so many men I don't even know who the father of my child is, my family *will* come for you. There will be nothing I can do to stop them. I tried to tell Jill all of this but she refuses to see the seriousness of the situation. I'm hoping you will. You know my family and that they do *not* tolerate being burned by anyone. They'll go completely scorched earth on you."

I wave a hand around the room. "My world is already burned to the ground so let them come, Lily. I'm not spreading rumors and I haven't heard any from anyone, so I doubt Jill is either. She has no business telling Angela anything about your personal life, but I'm sure she did so because of how hard *Angela* has already come for her. Jill is worried she's going to lose her job over what happened with Mrs. Meadows, and I think we can both agree that what you did has no bearing on Jill's job performance. *You* administered the wrong medication, and you did so either by your own error or on purpose."

Lily surges to her feet. "On purpose? Is that the next rumor I can expect to hear? Because if so, you really do have a death wish, Darren Mansfield."

I stand and face her. "Having a death wish is better than wishing death on others, *angel*. And if you want to talk about who is spreading rumors, how about *you* telling Angela that Jill is leaving Pemberton to come work for me at Mansfield Clinic?"

She raises her chin, indignance rolling off of her in waves. "Angela asked if I was going to continue moonlighting there because *someone* told her you were leaving Pemberton to resume your old job. I informed her that I would not, and she wondered aloud if Jill would go to work for you. I told her I didn't know, but that it would be a perfect solution for the two of you. Now that I've been better acquainted with the way you and Jill take up for one another, I can't help but see I was right. You two *are* perfect for one another. Maybe the next rumor I hear will be that *she's* having your baby."

Lily takes a step, the anger suddenly fading from her face, eyes going distant. I reach for her, barely catching her collapsing body. Her legs are as gone as her eyes. "Lily?" I hug her to me. She's burning up.

~27~

The magnitude of how many ways a life can fall apart is staggering. I find myself longing for the days when the only problem I had was a burning lust for a girl who was too young. As sick as that is, that time in my life was easy compared to now. All the anguish that came before pales in comparison to being forced to confront Lily.

I finish hanging the IV. "Does everything feel and look okay? I'm rusty at this compared to you."

She keeps her head resting on the back of the recliner, eyes fixed on the ceiling. "It's fine. Thanks."

I check the line. "We're lucky to be this close to a fully stocked clinic."

Lily makes no comment, her body still as stone. I shift closer, resting my fingers on the wrist of the arm without the IV. Her pulse is still elevated and a quick touch to her forehead tells me her temperature is still spiked, though the medication I retrieved when I got the rest of the supplies is already doing its job.

I stand over her, checking her eyes. The pupils are slightly dilated. "Any dizziness still?"

"A little."

"Blurred vision?"

"No."

"When did you eat last? And the sliver of tortilla you just ate doesn't count."

Her throat bobs and her pulse picks up again. "I'm eating normally. I'm just tired."

Unlike earlier, I don't feel like there's any truth to her words. I rest a gentle hand on her shoulder. "I can't help you unless you're honest with me."

Her lips part, silently at first. "My appetite comes and goes. When I'm hungry, I eat. When I'm nauseous or not hungry, I don't."

I move my hand from her shoulder to the curve of her jaw. "How long has this been going on?"

More hesitation. "A couple of weeks."

"My dad is your doctor, have you talked to him about it?"

Her head shakes and I reposition myself onto the arm of the recliner. "How much sleep are you getting?"

Sadness flicks through her eyes in a way that claws at my chest. "Considering recent events, not much. I'm stressed. Badly enough that Gideon's noticed from half a world away."

She misses him. I can hear it in her voice, and that sorrowful note makes my stomach hurt. "Just in case this is more than stress and lack of sleep, do you care if I draw some blood and run some tests?"

She sits up. "Thanks for the pretend concern but I'm sure I just need to eat something and get some sleep."

I stretch an arm across her and press her back into the recliner. "Lie still and let's finish getting these fluids in you." I take her hands in mine when she complies, gripping them firmly to quell the tremble of her fingers. "I know it's hard to be a patient, but you should really consider letting me do the bloodwork. You should also never dismiss my concern for your well-being as anything but completely genuine. I'm sure you think it isn't because of how badly I've been treating you, but I promise you that I care. Deeply."

"I could tell by the warm welcome you gave me when I started working at Pemberton."

I nod. "I was horrible. But it was all just an attempt to push you away, so I wouldn't have to see your beautiful face while I continued to fight every feeling I harbor for you."

I run my fingers through her hair. She turns her head aside. "Don't, Darren. You're only making things harder for both of us. If you're not with Jill, fine. But I *am* with Gideon."

I take a second longer to feel along her scalp where I'm relieved to find no scabs from where she yanked her own hair out using my fist. "I know Gideon is in your life and that there are absolutely no excuses for how I've treated you. I was wrong, Lily. To you and to Jill. I unintentionally led her on, but I did apologize to her and set the record absolutely straight because she's never been the person I want to be with. Which means I'm not defending her. I'm saying that if she's spreading rumors about you, I'm entirely unaware and entirely at fault."

Lily presses her hands to her stomach. "Apparently you're speaking to Jill in code because she believes that you two are madly in love but that I'm *forcing* you to stay away from her. She openly accused me of blackmailing you."

I study Lily's unreadable face. "Are you being serious? Jill said those exact words to you?"

"No, Darren, I'm sitting in your house making up lies so you'll be mad at her," Lily retorts. "Jill believes I'm blackmailing you because *you've* practically written it in the sky. *You* told her that I rammed your car. *You* told her that I've been chasing you, throwing myself at your feet and threatening to hurt you if you didn't choose me over her. *You* told her that I only moved into her house so I could disrupt your relationship with her and make her lose her mind as well as her job!"

"I did no such thing." I wince as the words ring false. "I mean, I might have said a few things that she misinterpreted..."

Lily pushes forward, ripping at the IV line. I take control of her hands. "Stop for a minute and listen to me, Lily, because saying that my head is messed up is an understatement. I haven't been able to see the damage I've caused you because I spend too much time trying to punish myself for falling in love with you to begin with. Even at sixteen, you ticked all of my boxes and kept me dreaming of a different life, one where instead of being taboo, you could be my wife. I know that's sick. That I'm twisted and should be in prison. But to the detriment of my own soul and everyone else's, I love you in a way that will never end." I slide one hand free of hers, pressing it against her cheek. "In every worst-case scenario that I run through in my head, I come out the other side still caring about you far more than I've cared for anyone or anything."

Tears fill her eyes. "Yet you have Jill and Emelia Alice spewing vile words straight into my face. That isn't love. It's hate. Maybe you don't know the difference but I do, so remove your hands and let me up because I'm not going to let you seduce me for your own sick gain. Again!"

Anxiety blooms in my chest. I take my hands from her but keep my body fixed in place so she can't get up. "I've done a lot of things that I'm not proud of, but I've gained nothing from my sickness, Lily. In the last five years, I've lost everything. Including my dad. He's rightly angry with me over how I've treated you and disappointed in me for leaving the clinic. I'm disappointed in myself, too. And angry. Confused. Lovesick. Jealous. I'm so mixed up that I can't be a doctor anymore. So you can blame me for a lot of things, but don't ever accuse me of not loving you because I'd open my veins for you. And if you were mine, I'd *never* be half a world away from you."

"Gideon didn't have a choice." She sniffs. "His job demanded he go."

"There are other jobs," I defend. "And you didn't go with him even though you could have. What does that tell you?"

Lines crease her forehead. "It tells me that I made another *mistake*. But at the time, I didn't know your future wife and her sister were going to begin bullying me. I didn't realize I'd come home at the end of a long day only to find things in my room had been *borrowed*, without permission or remorse when they suddenly couldn't return the missing items."

I swallow. "I'm sorry if they've been bullying you. I don't know about the borrowing things, but any hard words they've said to you are my fault. I'll have a conversation with Jill, and Emelia Alice if need be, because what's between you and me, even vehicle damage, is between you and me. They shouldn't be saying a word to you about it."

"If *you* stop accusing me of everything that goes wrong in your life, I'm sure they wouldn't."

I let my gaze bore into hers. "If *you* would provide some clarity on things like our vehicles having matching damage, then I wouldn't have to accuse you. I'd know. And I'd be able to support you instead of being pissed off about it."

She leans forward, face inches from mine. "The day the damage occurred, I didn't know about it until I got out of the shower after basically having a man die in my arms, and your *girlfriend* stormed into my bathroom while I was completely naked, shouting at me for hitting your precious car. I told her then what I'm telling you now. *I. Didn't. Hit. Your. Car.*"

I run my fingers along the side of Lily's face and into her hair, her breath fluttering over my lips. "Okay. I believe you. So if you didn't hit my car, let's figure out how we got matching damage. Where did you go when you left the hospital that day?"

"I was at the clinic for four hours, then I went to my room at Jill's house and slept for two before getting up to eat. I had fruity cereal that I bought myself, with milk that I also bought myself." She smirks. "For clarity's sake, since your girlfriend likes to help herself to my things but falls into despair if I use an ice cube that I didn't make myself."

I sigh. "Jill is nothing to me but a now *former* coworker and you continually saying otherwise isn't helping. But you two really are living in a toxic environment, aren't you?"

"Three," Lily bites. "There are two of them and one of me, and it makes the inside of that house *very* small. Which is why I chose to sit outside after I ate my cereal. I was having a cup of decaf and distracting myself with an article on stem cells when I heard Emelia Alice scream. I ran to help but was ineffective at saving Freddie's life, and then I showered and met with your ex's wrath. So I don't know when or how my car was damaged. Want to check the reading history on my phone? I can show you the stem cell article."

I lower my forehead to hers. "Don't be mad at me for wanting to know what's going on because despite my best efforts and anything that you may have done, I love you. You are my beginning and my end, and I want us to stop hurting each other. *I* want to stop hurting *you*." I move my fingers through her hair, gently letting the strands slide and pool. "I need to know where I'm right and where I'm wrong, so I know how to help you, angel."

Tears wet her lashes. "I don't need your help and I don't want your empty words. I came here tonight so I could have a clear conscience and know that I've done everything I can to settle this on my own because if the harassment doesn't stop, the consequences will be out of my hands." She pulls away, her jaw set. "I did break into your house. Twice."

I've told myself so many things over the years. Firstly, that I'm redeemable. That's a joke. And most recently, that Lily is in crisis mode and all of her behavior is a plea for help. Help I can give her if she lets her defenses down and opens up. So why her confession about breaking into my house is driving me away from her is yet another mystery. I don't want to botch this opportunity to get answers, but I need space. To not be touching her. Because doing so puts my brain on the fritz.

I check the IV bag. "Looks like this is done. Are you feeling any better?"

She removes the catheter, the picture of calm despite the storm thrashing around me. She presses a cotton pad to the spot on her arm. "Physically, yes."

"Good. Now you can explain this breaking and entering situation because I want to trust you, Lily, but you're making it hard. Why did you lie when I asked about you being in my house?"

She sits up straighter. "You didn't ask, you accused. And I wasn't in your house on the day you *accused* me of being here."

I lean against the squat rack, crossing my ankles in front of me and willing my nerves to pick a course and stay on it. I can't be both smitten and devastated. Not all at once. "So you lied because of semantics?"

She looks directly at me, as if to own every word of what she's saying. "I didn't lie. You never asked if I'd *ever* been in your house. You were rude and wildly insulting, and going on about the day of the youth event as if I'd really break into your house."

My eyes bulge. "You did! You just admitted to it not five minutes ago."

She blows out a breath that makes her bangs flutter. "Not recently. When I was a *kid*, Darren. The one you keep reminding me that I was. I came through the breezeway once when I was sixteen, and for the second and *last* time when I was eighteen. But I didn't touch anything, let alone steal from you. I just..."

My pulse picks up. "You just what?"

Her hands clench into fists in her lap, releasing and contracting again. "The first time, when I was sixteen, I came to leave you a note. I wrote it and had it with me but..." She drags in a ragged breath. "I wasn't sure, but I thought maybe I was the reason you left the clinic. Because of how you acted the night we...kissed. When you took your hand out of my bra, you looked...stricken. And then you just left. I didn't know if you were coming back. I thought maybe I did something wrong, or that you maybe went to get protection." She stares at the floor. "I laid on your desk for I don't know how long. Alone. Cold. Eventually I understood that you weren't coming back so I got dressed and went home. Then when I saw you again, you wouldn't look at me. Then your dad told me you weren't working at the clinic anymore so I wrote you a letter, asking if I was the reason why and promising I'd never even stand close to you again if you'd just come back to work."

Her words recall all of the pain I felt that night. In all these years I never thought about what she did in the wake of my departure. I ran out of my office as fast as I could and ended up crying on my bathroom floor all night. "I'm so sorry, Lily."

She shakes her head, wiping away a lone tear. "It was a long time ago, and wouldn't have happened if I didn't have a crush on you. So mostly my letter was just apologizing for ruining our friendship. Or rather, the friendship I thought we had."

I reflect on the chaos of that time. In my attempts to avoid her, I was hardly ever here. But I would have found a note. If not then, by now. "Why didn't you leave the letter?"

Her head lowers. "Once I got in here, I realized how stupid I was being. You didn't want a note from a kid, you just wanted me to leave you alone. So I did."

I swallow around the lump in my throat. "You leaving me a letter like that would have only added to my torture because I would have wanted you even more if I knew with certainty that *you* wanted *me*. Even if all you wanted was my friendship. So no, you weren't being stupid when you came to leave the note, you proved how smart you are when you didn't leave it. I can barely live with myself now, and if I'd..." I close my eyes. "What about the second time? When you were eighteen?"

Her voice trails softly across the room. "I came on my birthday. I knocked on your door but your car wasn't here and neither were you. So I went through the clinic again and let myself in to wait for you. You didn't have any furniture then, either."

I look around the space. I have everything you'd find in a serious modern gym——the squat rack, bench press, free weights, stair climber, rower. A maze of box jumps and battle ropes. "I've spent so many years running from you, Lily, that I never allowed myself to turn this place into a home." I meet her watery eyes. "You might say the irritating gods in the sky know what they're doing when they curse a man."

She sniffs. "That didn't take long. Glad to hear that I've already returned to being the bane of your existence."

I shrug. "We're finally being honest so I can't sugarcoat the situation. These last five years have been hell."

"I know. I've lived them, too." She runs her hand over the worn arm of the recliner. "This was here that last time I came. Only it was over in that corner." She nods to the space on my right where the recliner did used to be. "I sat in it for an hour before I realized that me turning eighteen didn't matter to you. In nearly two years, you hadn't said a single word to me. The stupid teenage crush I had on you was a one-sided infatuation I needed to get over. So I left, did my best to move on, and until tonight, I haven't been back here."

I push off the rack and kneel in front of her, the pads of my thumbs wiping away the liquid beginning to slowly trickle down her face. "I'm assuming that night in my office was your first sexual experience, and I was terrified at how close I came to not being able to stop myself from doing what I was doing to you. I was out of control, and you deserved so much better. You deserved a life that didn't include a grown man putting his hands on you like that." I rest my palm along her jaw. "I broke the law, your trust, and both of our hearts. Lily, your dad would have killed me back then and he still might, but if I'd known you held feelings for me those first two years, *I* would have been on *your* doorstep at the dawn of your eighteenth birthday."

"Stop." She pushes me away. "You think I'm a curse, Darren. The absolute worst thing that has ever happened to you."

Her voice cracks and I move forward again, cupping my hands along her face. "The underage girl was my curse. Not knowing if you thought I was just a creepy old man was a curse. But if you came here two full years after..." I close my eyes and drag in the scent of her. "I would have waited for you to turn eighteen. I *did* wait for you." I open my eyes. "I'm *still* waiting for you."

She slides her hands along my arms, fingers trailing over my biceps. "Part of me is still waiting for you, too. But I think I hate you."

My eyes water. "Love is crazy like that, angel."

Our lips brush, the salty wetness of her tears filling my mouth as her lips part. I kiss her deeply, fingers tightening in her hair. This isn't like last time, the pent-up desire prodding me to grope her in the middle of a dark street. *This* kiss is what futures are built on. It's what dreams are made of and fantasies are born of. And I want to live each of those fantastical dreams with Lily.

~

My brain shut off somewhere between the taste of Lily in my mouth and her hands trailing south of my border. We made it to my bed in a frenzy of tongues, hands, and what sounded like clothing ripping. That was hours ago, and my heart is still pounding against the prison of my ribs.

I rest on my side so I can get a better look at her, trailing the rough pads of my fingers over her elegantly bare back. She smiles, eyes remaining closed as I trace along her spine. "That feels nice."

I run my hand up and into her hair, curling my fingers in the silky tresses, trying to keep the darkest of my fears at bay while I paint the picture of what could be. So many things make her my perfect match. "We should have had a conversation a long time ago. I'm sorry I wasn't here on your eighteenth birthday, and that I fought my feelings for you as hard as I did."

Her eyes flutter open. "The first day I saw you at Pemberton, I thought I might see if you'd have a drink with me, catch up on life since I hadn't seen you in so long. Then I said hello and had to immediately go check to see if my head was still attached. You very clearly weren't interested in talking to me."

I slide her hair over her shoulder. "I was shocked to see you. I couldn't string a single thought together and I panicked." I still my hand. "You were so young before, and still are, and I've been beating myself up about that for so long I never wrapped my head around what I truly feel for you. That made it difficult to navigate seeing you again."

She smiles. "Then I wish you were here when I was eighteen, too. Because you're not that much older than me and even at sixteen I was a heck of a lot more *grown-up* than most of you thirty-somethings are now. Your good friend Jill and her sister being perfect examples of immaturity."

I trace my fingers along the outline of Lily's angelic face. "Maybe that's why I fell for you back then, because you're so much wiser than your years. The total package of brains and beauty." I shift closer to her. "Why did you move into the Tudor house? The real reason."

Her smile fades. "I already told you, I just wanted to see what it would be like to live with people I'm not related to. I now know that it sucks."

I rest my arm across her hips, palm wrapping around her waist. "Then I'm glad you didn't test it out with Gideon. I know he asked."

She lifts her head from where she's been resting it on her folded arms. "What did you say to Jill that makes her think you're in love with her?"

"I have no idea," I whisper, feeling a tug inside my chest. "In your version of events, she's repeating things to you out of context and with a lot of embellishment. In hers, you're basically trying to overthrow her life."

Lily shifts off her stomach, sitting up on her knees. I sit up with her and drag her back against my chest. "That's not an accusation, it's a question. Angela seems to want Jill gone for some reason, and Jill believes that reason is you. Because you were promised the supervisor position before onboarding at Pemberton. Is that true?"

She lifts her hands and massages her temples. "Angela offered the position but I declined, pending my decision on your dad's offer to buy the clinic from him."

"Buy it?"

She turns, first her shoulders and then the rest of her follows until she's looking into my eyes. "You thought I was stealing your inheritance. *That's* why you were angry. I told your dad I'd buy him out, at fair value, not some lowball one he made up because he's always so kind to me. How could you think I'd steal from you?"

I rest my hand along her jaw. "It wouldn't have been stealing. But I need you to listen to me, to hear my words and let them sink in because I've made my choice, and it's *you*. If being with you costs me my medical license or sends me to jail, so be it. Good or bad, no matter what, I *will* stand by your side. For *our* sake, and for the sakes of our families."

Worry lines splinter across her forehead. "Why would being with me cost you anything?"

"Lily," I whisper, tears burning in the back of my eyes. I finally made love to this beautiful creature and if I want us to have a life together, I have to get all the secrets out in the open. Now. Before any other darkness can claim us. "I found the syringe."

Her brows knit. "What syringe? And why do you look like you just lost your best friend?"

I slide my hands down her arms. "You're what I'm afraid to lose. So tell me again what happened with Freddie because I need to know if the woman I love is as good as my heart believes she is, or if she's in a crisis that we need to deal with immediately. I found the syringe outside your window, angel. Now tell me the truth. Did you inject Freddie with insulin?"

~29~

I wish I'd taken more time, basked in the glory of being allowed to worship at Lily's altar just a little longer. But now that I've been allowed to, I want to be a better man for her. Not the kind who is willing to keep putting people's lives in danger, but the kind willing to go to any lengths necessary in order to get her the help she needs.

I reach a hand out to her, beckoning her back to my side, heart breaking with every beat it takes as she frantically fumbles through the tangle of sheets and tosses pillows from the bed. "Lily, what are you doing?"

She springs off the bed, voice steady despite the panic on her face. "Where is my shirt?"

I lower my outstretched hand. "I don't think the location of your clothing is important right now."

Her teeth grind. "Where is my shirt?"

I scan the room. "I don't know. Somewhere between here and the recliner."

She stomps out of the room. I get off the bed and trudge into my closet, yanking a pair of joggers off a shelf since Lily wants to be dressed for this conversation.

I meet her in the kitchen where she's managed to pull her shirt back on, albeit sitting a little askew on her body. I grip the back of a chair as she snatches her jeans from the hallway and tugs them over her legs, face turning red when she finds the button is missing. "Sorry about that, angel. I'll buy you a new pair."

She zips them, stretching her shirt to try to make it hang low enough to cover the missing button. "No, thanks. I've had everything I need from you."

I fold my arms. "What's that supposed to mean?"

She throws her shawl around her shoulders. "It means we waited a long time to get that roll in the sack out of our systems and now the deed is done. We have no further reason to ever speak again."

I grip her shoulders and she shoves me off, both hands against my chest and fire in her eyes. "Do *not* touch me."

I hold my hands in front of me. "Fine, but don't run from me. I'm terrified for you, Lily. For *us*. Our parents. Your actions don't only affect you, they have consequences for everyone around you. Not to mention Freddie's family. Were you helping him with injections? Did something go wrong?"

A sob rips from her throat. "You're sick. *Disgusting.*"

I sling a hand out to the left, in the direction of the two graves outside. "What's *disgusting* is that I have a syringe buried with the rotting carcass of a cat right outside these walls. Do you know how messed up that is, Lily? How it makes me feel that I'm willing to hide that for you?"

"Whatever you're doing is *not* for me," she grinds through clenched teeth. "I didn't kill anyone, and I would have told you that before you took me to bed!"

I follow her to the front door. "So just like the matching damage to our vehicles, you don't know anything about Freddie's death? Is that the story you're going with? Despite you *accurately* deeming his death an insulin overdose right there on the spot?"

She spins toward me, eyes thick with tears and shining like an emerald sea. "I came here tonight as a courtesy, to clear the air and warn you about Jill, because that teenage girl inside of me never got over you. But she will now. Because not only did I *not* kill anyone, I also wouldn't cover up a murder for *anyone*. So what does that say about *you*?"

I cup her face. "It says that I am a desperate man who is *desperately* in love with you. I don't want to see you get hurt, Lily."

Her chest heaves, sobs crashing out of her. "Don't do that. You don't get to think I'm capable of murder and in the very same breath say that you love me."

I run my thumbs softly under her eyes, wiping the tears. "I've denied my feelings for you for too long and I won't do it anymore. You evoke such deep emotions inside of me that I don't care if you're a serial killer or just simply trying to frame me for murder. Whatever happened with Freddie and Mrs. Meadows, the cats... Just tell me, and I'll make sure you get the help you need."

She bats my hands away, backing into the door. "You think I murdered Freddie and attempted to murder Mrs. Meadows? Her medication was *right*, Darren. The pharmacy supplied *both* orders and I pulled the *right* one. Kassidy is the one who pulled the wrong medication. I don't know what she did with it but what I injected into Mrs. Meadows' IV was Cipro. I checked it *three* times. Jill is well versed in your kind of tactics though and she was gaslighting me into believing I mixed everything up. But I didn't! I *didn't*."

I hold up my hands. "Okay. I believe you."

She shakes her head, tears cascading over her red cheeks. "No, you don't. You came into my bedroom, telling me how I *shouldn't* feel so terrible about what happened when the whole time you thought I had tried to kill a patient. That I *did* kill Freddie."

I step closer but don't touch her. "Ever since you showed up at Pemberton, nothing has been right in my life. I've had so many strange occurrences and all of them somehow linked to you. But not a single time could I reconcile the girl I knew to one who would do harm to anyone. So believe me, I'm as messed up over this as you are. But I don't know what to do here, Lily. There's evidence that clearly points to you so I thought maybe you're in some kind of bad mental state that has you acting out of character because it isn't unheard of for nurses to——"

"No!" she screams. "Nurses don't kill people, Darren. *Murderers* do. So keep me out of your pathetic theories because your investigative work is weaker than your excuses. Stay away from me."

She tugs the door open and pushes out into the cold. I follow her to her car, bare feet leaving tracks in the snow. I want to force her to stay but I can't. All I can do is beg. "Lily, please don't go. Come inside and let's talk things through because if you're not messing with me, someone else is, and they're making it look like it's you."

She yanks her car door open. "Get away from me. I'm not falling for any more of your manipulation."

I drop down beside her seat, hands clinging to her legs. "Please, Lily. If you didn't hit me and I didn't hit you, then we need to figure out who had access to one or both of our vehicles. And the dead animals——"

She leans her head back on her seat, covering her face with her hands. "Now you're accusing me of killing animals?"

I rest my head on her thigh, muffling my curses against her. "Obviously, you didn't do any of this. I'm just a moron. A scared one, Lily." I look up, tugging her hands from her face and cupping them in mine. "All I think about is you. All I *see* is you. In every situation, every sunrise, every sunset, and all the moments in between, it's you and only you. Maybe I smelled you in my house because I *wanted* you to be inside it. Maybe I connected you to everything that's been going on because in my own twisted way, it meant that you were connected to me and I liked that feeling because I'm tired of being so far outside of your life. I don't know, angel. All I know is that dead cats are showing up on doorsteps and under the hood of my car, right along with decapitated mice. I also had a microwave fire, a flat tire, and other things that when I link them all together, I'm scared. Not for myself but for you. Something is happening, Lily. Something bad. I can feel it, and it terrifies me because it's going to take you away from me."

The hard edges fall from her features. Her lips part but her phone rings. She takes her hands from mine and picks the phone out of her console, pressing it tightly to her ear. "Hey, babe." … "No, I'm not at work. Mikey and Dani left for the yacht so I'm checking on their place." … "Yeah, I left my phone in the car. Sorry about that." … "No, I'm okay. Just tired." Her spine shoots straight. "You're where?" … "I'll be there in twenty minutes."

She lowers the phone, eyes blank as they stare at the snow-covered windshield. I clear my throat. "Gideon?"

She nods. "He's home."

I lean onto my heels, feet painfully frozen. "Too bad. We're in the middle of something a hell of a lot more important than him."

Her eyes snap to mine. "*We* are not in anything. But if what you're telling me about the animals is true, *you* are in something. Take it seriously. Call my brother. Mikey and Dani will help you."

She starts her engine and fear beats a course through my veins. I reach for her shawl, fingers twisting in the fabric and holding on for dear life. "You are the other half of me, so please don't go."

She plucks her clothing from my grip, eyes focused straight ahead once again. "What you feel isn't real. You're clearly the one in crisis so call my brother. And when you tell him about your car, don't mention the damage to mine. Just say yours was damaged because I don't want to deal with them poking around in my life too. They already do that enough."

She shifts her car into gear and tears slide from my eyes. "Since that night in my office, this has been real for me. Please stay. If you have one second of doubt about leaving me, any crumb of doubt that Gideon is right for you, then don't leave. Stay with me, Lily. Please?"

Lily's car disappears into the night, the lightly falling snow already covering her tracks. I run back into the house, stubbing my frozen toes against the wall as I swing one foot out toward a pair of sneakers, hands going in the opposite direction to snatch my keys from the floor.

Limping, I pull open the door of the small closet next to me and yank a jacket I haven't seen in a year from a hanger. I shove my arms into the sleeves and run back out the door with my feet stuffed into untied shoes.

Narrowly missing backing over my mailbox, I swing my car's back end around. The brake lights illuminate the open mailbox door. A long tail is spilled over the flap, fur matted and limp. I pull forward and turn around, shining my high beams on the box. Wedged inside the opening is a bloody mass of yellow fur, the faintest trace of steam rising from its still warm body. I lean over the steering wheel, staring into the eyes of the fully grown tabby. Its mouth is open, the tail pulled up through the severed head and lolling across the teeth in place of its tongue. My stomach flips. Someone is making sure I get their message this time, and they delivered it while Lily was right inside my door.

~

Lily

I've loved Darren Mansfield my whole life. When I was nine, I wrote in my journal that I was going to marry him. That stupid fantasy led me into his bed tonight, his evening of sweet words soothing years of heartache simply because I was predisposed to believe my childhood crush meant something.

I wipe my face, squinting as my headlights reflect off the snow. I pull into the driveway of Jill's house, stomach in knots. When I left earlier, I only made it to the car with one suitcase. I figured I would decide whether or not to come back for the rest after I talked to Darren. If he could calm the sisters down, keep Jill from hysterically crying and Emelia Alice from verbally assaulting me, I'd return and pack the rest. If not, I'd just leave it all here. This living situation was a trial run for me anyway, so I didn't bring much. And little of what I brought holds any value to me. If I had to leave it all behind, it wouldn't be the worst thing.

I don't see Gideon's vehicle. He must have taken a car service from the airport and come straight here instead of going to his apartment. I give my face one last wipe, hoping my tears have washed it clean. He'll know I've been crying. I only hope I'm a good enough liar to hide the reason why.

I approach the house, reflecting on every decision that brought me to this place. From saying yes to Gideon's date request when we reconnected last year, to the unexpected loneliness I felt when living at the Potomac Estate after Grandma died. I'm a solitary creature and the estate was always a favorite retreat, the grounds large enough that I could hide away with a book indoors or out and not see another soul all day. But I knew people were there, even if only Grandma. And I didn't realize being actually alone is different than self-isolation.

I didn't want to move back home with my parents and I'm still not sure if Gideon is the future I want. He's edgy and outgoing whereas I'm reserved and prefer staying home over going on the many adventures the world has to offer. The type of exciting escapades that light up

Gideon's face when he talks about them. He deserves a partner who will enjoy those things with him. A partner who doesn't cheat on him.

With a deep breath, I grip the door handle and enter the house.

~

Darren

My phone rings. I take one last long look at my mailbox, standing in the warmth of my house while the sun comes up, casting a glow over the blood-soaked snow beneath the silver metal box. I've been watching the woodline, the shadows, the flakes of snow that piled up to blot out any evidence of footsteps. If I call the police, have them dust the mailbox for prints, I'd be remiss not to tell them about the other cats. The mice. If I tell them and they dig up the one, they'll find the needle. A syringe I was dumb enough to consider being linked to Freddie's death and one I now can't explain to authorities without being suspect myself.

I drop the blind and trudge into my bedroom, sheets askew and pillows still tossed about in the aftermath of what was simultaneously the best and worst night of my life. I take the phone from the nightstand, not recognizing the number. "Darren Mansfield," I answer, not bothering to add doctor because that's a title I'm not deserving of anymore.

"This is Gideon," the rough voice on the line identifies.

Satisfaction beats a triumphant course through my veins. Lily told him about us. "This is a conversation we should have in person. Where are you?"

"I'm in the emergency room with Lily," he rumbles. "Get over here right now and tell me what in the hell is going on with her. They just took her to do some kind of brain scan and she's... Lily's not... She fell and cracked her head open. Now she's in some kind of daze. Jill said Lily's been sick a lot lately? And that you know what's wrong with her?"

I grab my keys and run for the door. "Is Jill with you now?" He grunts a confirmation. "Tell her to meet me at the E.R. entrance."

~

I park sideways, taking up three spots in Pemberton's lot. Jill races toward me and I run to meet her, gripping her shoulders. "What happened?"

Tears stream down her face, her hair sticking up in every direction. "I woke up to Gideon shouting. I didn't even know he was in the house. I didn't know *Lily* was there." She gulps in air. "I followed the shouting to her bathroom. Lily was on the floor, blood all around her..."

"Gideon was yelling at Lily?"

"No." Jill's trembling fingers curl around the hem of my t-shirt. "He was on the phone, calling for an ambulance and shouting at the operator."

I pull her toward the building, keeping my grip soft despite the rage billowing through my veins. "Where was the blood coming from? Did he hit Lily?"

Jill tucks into my side. "He said Lily passed out and hit her head on the corner of the sink. It's sharp, and Emelia Alice said there's skin and hair on it. She noticed it when she went to clean up the blood."

My jaw tenses. "Tell her to stop cleaning. It could be a crime scene." Jill looks up at me. I plant my feet. "*Gideon* could have bashed Lily's head into that sharp corner."

Jill jerks away. "Why would he do that?"

The muscles in my neck spasm. "Because she told him something he didn't want to hear. Which room is hers?"

Jill motions toward a cubicle in the corner with glass walls. The curtains of the room are pulled together so I can't see inside. She clears her throat. "Gideon doesn't strike me as the violent type, but he's not an ex-con for nothing."

I spin toward her. "What did you just say?"

She lowers her voice. "Gideon has a record. Lily says it's white-collar crime and not a big deal but..." She looks around, whispering so low that I have to practically press my ear to her mouth. "He works for the government by *force*, not by choice. It's that or go to prison. And I don't think the government is in the habit of *forcing* that kind of penalty on someone who isn't dangerous to them. If he's dangerous to a major world power, I guess him harming Lily isn't out of the realm of belief."

I stare into Jill's eyes. She's known all along what kind of man Lily had attached herself to and yet never breathed a word of this to me. That's odd, considering she's been all too willing to defame Lily at every other opportunity. But then again, Lily believes Jill outright lies for Jill's own gain. Or rather, *perceived* gain. An explanation as to why Jill has so easily misrepresented Lily in nearly every conversation I've had with her since Lily started working at Pemberton. If Jill had interest in me pre-Lily, she would have noticed *my* interest in Lily. Jeremy saw it plainly and he isn't trying to date me.

More disconcerting than Jill's finger-pointing is how Gideon ever got close to Lily in the first place. Her family isn't trusting, and if Jill knows Gideon's past, the Bellers most certainly do. So why haven't they put a stop to Lily's relationship? Or is she hiding him from her family and that's the real reason she moved into Jill's house? So Lily could basically live with Gideon without telling anyone she was.

"Has any member of Lily's family visited her at your house?"

Jill scratches the back of her neck. "Em was home once when Lily's brother came by. He had words with Gideon and Emelia Alice said it was scary, but that it didn't get physical. Why? You think Gideon has been violent with Lily before and that's why her brother didn't want him there?"

"I'm getting ready to find out." I move away from her and plow through the door of Lily's room, steps coming up short when I see her in the hospital bed. I didn't expect her to be back from the scan yet. I wanted to beat Gideon to a bloody pulp before she returned.

He's sitting by her bedside, cradling one of her hands in both of his, head bowed, and lips pressed against her fingers. I take my eyes from him and focus on Lily's face. It's swollen, the bruising along the left side already dark and tinged in yellow. There's a bandage covering the top of her head, running all the way down to the base of her brows. Her left eye is swollen shut.

"Doc," Gideon's scratchy voice breaks the silence. "What's wrong with her? Why did she pass out like that?"

I undo the bandage enough to see the gash for myself. There's a knot the size of a golf ball and in the very center, the skin is held together with stitches. I pull Lily's chart. I have to focus on being a doctor right now because otherwise, I'm going to rip this boy apart. "What happened, Gideon? I want every detail."

He rubs his thumbs over the delicate hand cradled in his, eyes trained on Lily's face. "She was in the shower. I got in with her and we were...being intimate. I could feel her shaking though, and she didn't look good. I could really see how pale she was in that lighting. So we got out and I wrapped her in a towel. I went to grab her robe from the hook on the back of the door but when I turned..." His voice cracks. He pulls their cupped hands to his lips and kisses her fingers as a tear slides down his cheek. "I should have just carried her straight to bed. I don't know why I didn't. That sound...there was a pop..." He presses his forehead to her hand. "She hit that sink full force on her way down."

I review the sedative she's been given and then recheck her head, trying to calm myself before I do something this kid might not deserve. "You said Lily was in a daze. Was that before or after she fell?"

He lifts his head from her hand. "After. She came to right about the time the ambulance arrived. They tried to keep her talking the whole way here, but she wasn't answering their questions right. Jill rode with us. She said Lily's been having these zoned-out moments lately so she didn't think it was entirely because of the fall. She said you know about it? That you know what's wrong with Lily?"

I rest my hand on Lily's shoulder, letting my fingers brush against her neck. I won't cry in front of *him*, but I'm not going to make it out of this hospital without breaking down. "I'm aware that Lily hasn't been feeling great. Did she vomit any when she was with you? Complain of headaches or pain?"

"No vomiting and she didn't complain about anything, but I hadn't been with her long before this happened."

Because she was with *me* before that, and she was fine. Well, after the IV she was fine. Until I caused her to cry again. "Were you two fighting? Arguing? Did you put your hands on her?"

Gideon stands, slowly stretching to his full height. "I haven't had an argument with Lily since I was eighteen and unintentionally embarrassing her at my graduation. And yeah, when I was reuniting with my girlfriend this morning, I put my hands all over her. In ways she *likes* them to be on her. So I'm going to pretend that you didn't just walk into this room and accuse me of hurting her because I just flew halfway around the world to check on her. I could *hear* in her voice that something was wrong, and I figured that out all the way from Tokyo. How about you take it from here? Think you can figure out how to get *my* girl healed?"

I study him, watching for any tic that might be a tell. "I am taking it from here, Gideon, so feel free to take yourself back to wherever you came from. And I'll contact her family for her, because I bet you've been too scared to notify them."

He drops back into his seat, hooded eyes trained on me as he lifts her hand and cups it in his. "I know the law. Lily is a legal adult and she hasn't been deemed not to be in control of her own faculties so until she says differently, *no one* is calling her family. Got it?"

I walk toward him. "Regardless of your relationship with her family, *they* are her next of kin. Not you."

He runs his lips over her knuckles. "I see the way you look at her. But no matter how much you eat your own heart out wishing you were me, you're not. You're her doctor, nothing more. So get her the help she needs and if this is some kind of ongoing illness, find out what's wrong with her and fix it. Do that, and we stay cool. Mess with *anything* else in her life, and I'll bankrupt your clinic, have your car repossessed, and drain your bank accounts before you can count to ten. *No one* calls Lily's family until the request comes out *her* mouth."

I crouch down beside him. "If I find out you did this to Lily, you won't have to come for me, I'll come for you. And I'll make it hurt in places you didn't know were capable of feeling pain. You get that straight in your head because I'm not some kid she went to high school with. Lily is my family. *Mine*. Not yours."

~31~

If Gideon didn't assault Lily, there's more going on with her than only exhaustion. If he did hurt her, I'm going to assault *him*.

"Dad." I burst through his office door. He doesn't even have his coat off yet. "I need you to hire me so I can use your privileges at Pemberton to order testing for Lily."

His face falls. "*For* Lily?"

I shove around his desk and grip his arms, steadying him as I deliver the news. "I just came from the hospital and she's stable, but she hit her head. It's pretty bad but not life-threatening. You're her doctor so you can treat her, but I need to be there. For once in my life, I need to actually be there for her."

He mirrors me, gripping my forearms. "Of course. I'll move my schedule around and be there with you, but you can take the primary position as long as Lily allows it. Have you talked to her about it?"

I release his arms and step backward, running both hands up through my hair. "She's sedated enough that I decided to get out of her room before I ripped that scrawny punk kid she's dating to shreds. Lily was with him when she *fell*, and he's trying to strongarm me into not calling her family." I nod toward Dad. "I figured I'd come here and get your okay before I call them anyway, and see if I can get my old job back long enough to treat her."

He takes his glasses out of his coat pocket. "We'll need to talk to Lily before we call her family. And hopefully, she'll allow it before any word spreads far enough to reach them. Or else they'll have both our heads for not calling them."

"Yeah, because she's in the *hospital*. And not with a sprained ankle. It's serious."

He nods. "I understand, and we'll head right over to see if she's awake and can tell us what to do in regard to them. But I'm not going to authorize the call or make it myself until I talk to her because she's been prickly about them knowing her every move. But it sounds like you don't believe she fell?"

I fold my arms. "I have reason to believe Gideon was angry right before Lily's supposed fall. It could be that his hands facilitated her head connecting with her sink."

"What reason do you have to think that?"

I look Dad in the eye. "Me."

Understanding crosses his features and I unfold my tightly bound arms. "Look, I know I drew a line in the sand where Lily was concerned and you stand firmly on Lily's side. I don't blame you. Her side is the one I always wanted to be on to begin with. And now I know that Lily isn't behind the worst of what's been happening, and she's probably not behind the least of it either. I feel like dirt for accusing her of the things I did. Especially after how I treated her. Last night, we talked about what happened *that* night when she was sixteen. The aftermath was worse for her than I realized. Because I didn't talk to her afterward. I left her alone not knowing what was going on and I won't abandon her like that again. I'm not a worthy doctor any more than I'm a worthy son, but I *need* this, Dad." Tears sting the back of my eyes. "I stayed away from her for *five* years. I let her be alone. Be harassed. Maybe become a victim of this boy. Last night, she told me that she came to my house on her eighteenth birthday. Because she cared about me. At eighteen Lily was braver than I am now. And I'm pretty sure I've screwed up so badly that she won't ever care about me again, but I'm not going to go another day denying my feelings for her. I love her and for once in my life I *am* going to be there for her."

He walks toward me, face long. "Despite the mistakes you've made, you *are* a good doctor. And you're a good son. So let's go to the hospital and let Lily decide what she wants from you because I think you finally grew up enough to be a good partner for her."

I drag my hands down my face to wipe the tears away. "She's my soulmate. My perfect person. If she doesn't choose me, that's fine. But there's a mutilated cat in my mailbox right now that has Gideon's name all over it, so she isn't choosing him either."

Dad gasps. "Mutilated cat?"

My fingers flex. "I don't think Gideon's been in Tokyo. I think when Lily started at Pemberton, he realized I was competition. The type that he can't beat unless he breaks me from the inside out, taking away my trust of Lily until I ran from her. But he didn't realize I'd already spent five years running. He miscalculated, and he took it out on her."

~

Dad doesn't understand my reluctance to call the police. He took one look at the beheaded and mangled cat, and swore to call them himself. I don't have time to exhume the needle though, so the cat has to wait. I placed a garbage bag over the whole mailbox, closing the opening with duct tape, and then placed a sheet over the bag, weighing it down with fallen branches so it doesn't blow off. Dad called the post office to have my mail forwarded to the clinic, so for the time being, I'm not going to worry about the cat in the box.

"Anything?" Jill asks, looking over my shoulder at the results of Lily's bloodwork.

I rub the heels of my hands against my eyes. "Her sodium level is elevated but that's all I'm seeing. I sent the CT scans to a neurologist, but I didn't see anything alarming and neither did the radiologist."

Jill leans against my chair. "That head wound looked bad. She's lucky it didn't do any damage."

I blow out a snort of air. "If you don't consider ripping a gash in her head *damage*."

Jill presses her hand to my shoulder. "I was there so I know it was bad on the outside. I was talking about skull fractures and internal swelling, things that would make it a whole lot worse."

I inhale deeply, willing myself not to take my frustrations out on Jill. "Lily's going to feel the effects of the impact for a while, but the swelling is within normal ranges and she's responding to questions with a seemingly clear head now."

Jill's hand moves from my shoulder. "Lily is young and strong, and according to this, not pregnant. Are you relieved?"

I clench my teeth. "Fishing for information to back up the lie you already told Angela?"

Jill swallows. "I didn't tell *anyone* that the baby was yours, though it's now evident to me that you wouldn't be surprised *or* disappointed if it was." She clasps her hands in front of her. "I care about Lily, but you know what she's been like, what I've had to live with and endure at work because of her. I called Angela with the pregnancy speculation because it would give us *all* a reasonable explanation for Lily's medication mix-up. I wasn't slandering her and I never mentioned your name. *Lily* did. And I was as shocked by that as I was by her being mad that I tried to salvage her reputation right along with my job. Plus, she has a boyfriend who basically lives with her, so I would've guessed *he* was the father, not you."

"There is no father because Lily isn't pregnant. And she knew that before you ran off blabbing about it."

Jill huffs. "Forgive me for not having a spare job in my pocket or loose change sitting around that's more than most people's yearly salary. I made *one* phone call about a *possible* pregnancy, and it wasn't entirely for my own benefit."

I look at her. "I bet you telling people I spent the night with you isn't for your own benefit either. Or is it? When you represent that night as something much more pleasant than it was?"

She sighs. "What did you want me to say? Everyone at the party saw us go into my room. They saw the *way* we entered my room. Jeremy and Lily both made comments about it where other staff could hear."

I turn my seat around and face her. "I understand that what happened is painful for you and that you'd rather put a spin on it. So go ahead, keep doing it. Tell people whatever you want about me, good or bad. But make sure you don't represent it like there is *still* something between us. And keep Lily's name out of your mouth. Because you might *think* you're doing the right things, but you're not. Lily isn't after your job. In fact, she turned it down."

Jill's face scrunches. "But Kassidy said——"

I stand, cutting off her words. "I don't care who told you what. *I'm* telling you that Lily isn't out to get you."

Emelia Alice tugs on Jill's arm. "Hey, sis. Everything okay?"

Jill gives a brisk nod, lips pinched into a tight line. "Darren was just letting me know what Lily's latest status is."

Em raises a brow. "She's still okay, right? I talked to Gideon an hour ago and he said she was fine."

I snort, irritation simmering under my skin. Jill glances at me and then to her sister. "*Fine* is subjective. Did you bring those flowers for Lily?"

Emelia Alice adjusts the card that's tucked into the yellow foliage. "Pretty, aren't they? I think she's going to love them."

I stare at the vase, wondering if Lily would accept flowers from me. "Before you deliver those, tell me what happened the day Lily's brother stopped by the house to see her. He had an argument with Gideon?"

Em's shoulders lift. "They were just messing around."

Jill's mouth falls open. "You said it was nearly a full-blown fistfight."

Emelia Alice throws her a look, frustration flashing across her features. "They were just busting each other's chops. It wasn't a real fight."

Tension rolls between the sisters in thick waves, blue eyes affixed as if they can read each other's thoughts. Jill breaks first. "I guess I didn't hear the part about it being a big joke."

I'm not buying Emelia Alice's new version. "What were they fighting about?"

A smile tugs at the corner of her lips. "Mikey acted all shocked to see Gideon with his sister. And I did think it was real at first, but Lily was unconcerned, so it was a pretend fight." She tilts her head to the side.

"Then again, she also didn't think it was a big deal to take you out of my sister's bed and put you into hers, so maybe the fight was real after all. You two decide. I have flowers to deliver."

$$\sim 32 \sim$$

Lily

I can't bear to look at Gideon. His eyes know I'm keeping something from him. They knew it the instant I walked into the twins' house, and I hate that he trusts me enough to never question me. He trusts me the way I trust him.

If it weren't for Darren, I would have remained true to Gideon.

Tears fill my eyes, the swollen one weepy already. Gideon dabs a cloth at the area with a touch so gentle I barely feel it. "Is that better, babe?"

I twine my fingers through his, holding him too tight as guilt chokes its way up my throat. He runs his nose along my ear, lips speaking softly. "You're going to be out of this bed soon, and then I'm going to take you home and hug the heck out of you. Right through all the bubble wrap I'm rolling you in."

I laugh out tears that don't know if they're happy or sad, the water display drying up when Emelia Alice darkens my door. "Knock, knock." She smiles, her face so innocent I nearly believe she is. "Am I interrupting?"

"Yep," Gideon answers, with a wink at me and grin thrown to her. "I'll run down to the cafeteria and grab a snack, but I missed her and I'm not done loving on her yet so don't plan on interrupting for too long, Em."

She places a round vase of bright yellow flowers on my tray table, fingers trailing over the mass of red ribbon tied around the vase. "You were missed too, Gideon. By one of the women in this room." She faces him, eyes scanning his entire body as he leans over me. "So please, do hurry back."

He pinches my chin between his thumb and forefinger, lips soft on mine. "I'm going to try to find you one of those chocolatey caramel bars you like, and I'll most definitely be quick about it."

I watch him go, wishing I could tell him not to, but the less time he spends around Emelia Alice, the better. She sits on the edge of my bed, giving the mattress a bounce. "He's too good to you. *Considering.*"

I fold down the top of my blanket and smooth the crease. "He's kind to a fault and goes out of his way to be sweet. Sort of like the way you were nice in the beginning, jovial to a fault. Only I've known Gideon for a long time and his mood never sours. He's what you would call *genuine.*"

She cackles. "What do you know about being genuine? You're the fakest person I know, Lily Beller, and the proof of that is in how you're letting one boyfriend go fetch you candy while the other is just down the hall waiting for his turn to come fan your poor little busted-up face."

I clench the blanket in my fists. "Darren is a grown man who is making his own choices. I'm sorry that he isn't choosing your sister, but I am *not* the reason why."

"Sure you are," Emelia Alice sings, reaching the card from the flowers out to me. "You're the cause of him breaking promises to my sister at every turn. He wants to be with her, but you're throwing yourself at him and he's drawn to your youthful beauty." She waves the card, impatient for me to take it. "Youth fades, and so does beauty. So read this. Because I did come here to check on you, to make sure you're okay after such a nasty fall. But I didn't buy these flowers. They were delivered to the hospital last night. For Jill." Her lips turn up in mockery. "When you were warming Darren's sheets last night, I bet you didn't know he was thinking about my sister."

"As if *you* have a clue as to where I was last night." I snatch the card from her, too curious not to. I peel open the envelope and slide pink perfumed paper from inside.

A spring bouquet to remind you, Jill, that winter will pass and when the seasons change, I'll still be loving you. With all of my heart, Darren.

Despair, anger, foolishness…it all whirls to my surface, pain writhing inside me as all the love I held for Darren seeps from the most sacred part of me and retreats into my darkest depths. He broke more than promises to Jill, he broke my heart. Again.

I close my eyes. "You made your point, Emelia Alice. Leave now, and take the flowers with you."

She slides closer, running her hand overtop where my legs are covered with the blanket, her voice sugary sweet. "Oh, honey, I don't mean to hurt you, but you deserve to know what kind of man Darren is. Jill is too good for him, and Gideon is too good for you. I would say that makes you and Darren perfect for one another, but sadly, he only wants you for what you gave him right before you also *gave* it to Gideon. Is that what happened to your head? Did Gideon find out about your cheating ways and attempt to knock some sense into you?"

I lift myself up onto my elbows. "While you're in the process of learning how to keep your opinions to yourself, stop eyeing Gideon like he's your next meal. You might be one shade shy of inviting him to your bed, but he barely knows you exist."

She pushes off the bed, a grin on her lips. "I guarantee you that your sexy ex-con boyfriend has had more than one dream about me. In fact, I just made a whole line of jewelry inspired by the convict's sexy tattoos and I'm going to offer to make more for him, but I've only seen his sleeve." She fluffs the pillow behind me, leaning close. "You don't mind sharing with your roommate, do you? I thought I'd take him home tonight and really dive into what else is on his body."

Gideon crosses the room, looking every bit the sexy convict with a hint of danger in his eyes. His lips tilt in a lopsided grin. "Found it." He holds up the candy bar. "But you're going to have to get rid of your friend because it might get a little messy when I start to feed this to you."

I twist around, unfluffing the pillow and putting it back the way I had it, swatting Gideon's hands away when he tries to help. "Remember how I said you shouldn't tell people about your record?"

He squints. "I'm not embarrassed that I got picked up for being awesome."

I plop back onto the pillow, biting down as pain courses through my scalp. "Emelia Alice here thinks it's *sexy* that you have a record. She's decided that she likes tattooed felons."

His gaze flits between us. "Sorry, Em. I don't have a lot of friends who are felons, and I don't know a single man as sexy as myself. And I'm taken." He looks at me. "How was I supposed to know the Pentagon would take getting hacked so seriously?"

His skills *are* to be admired, but what he's done with them is not. He's basically lost his ability to live as a free citizen, forced to work for the government when and how they tell him to. I'm surprised he was able to come back from Tokyo early. For all I know, he didn't get permission and some top-secret SWAT team is going to burst through the door any minute. "If you agreed to your current job *before* going to prison, we wouldn't even need to have this conversation."

He chuckles, because just about everything amuses Gideon. "Then I'd just be sexy instead of a sexy convict." He rips open the top of the candy bar in dramatic fashion. "Got to have that street cred, babe."

Emelia Alice pulls a box from her purse. "Sexy *and* smart. You're the total package, Gideon. And I missed your package so much that I made you a little something."

"A present for me?" He glances her way, breaking off a messy square of chocolate. "Let my lady open it for me. My hands are a little full right now."

Emelia Alice's lips flatten. "Fine."

She hands me the box and I give her a condescending smile, turning to Gideon with an open mouth, accepting the chocolate from his fingers. I pull the top off the box as I chew. Inside, there's a thick black leather band with copper plating running the length of it. Azaleas, Gideon's mom's favorite flower, are stamped into the copper. She knows those flowers mean something to him because he has them incorporated into the sleeve of tattoos covering his left arm.

He puts the candy bar down. "Whoa, that's amazing."

Emelia Alice returns my condescending smile and lifts the gift from the box, running her fingers over Gideon's wrist as she affixes it. "I've worked on the design the whole time you've been gone, always having you and your delicious coffee on my mind. I missed both, and was going to ship this to you to let you know, but here you are in the flesh."

He draws her in for a hug. "You're sweet. Thanks for this, it's really cool."

She smirks at me over his shoulder. I sift through what I'm feeling, it isn't jealousy. Possessiveness maybe, but it's overshadowed by guilt. Before I fell, I was in a hurry to strip off my buttonless jeans so Gideon wouldn't notice the damage. Then I rushed into the shower to wash away the evidence of my betrayal. When he joined me, giving me the whole view Emelia Alice is so spitefully determined to have, it wasn't Gideon's tattoos I saw. It was Darren's. Art I was finally able to study up close. The kraken covering most of his back, tentacles outstretched. He said it's a symbol of regeneration—growth and the ability to move past failures in order to rebuild and become stronger. That he put it on his back hoping he'd heal from the loss of his mom, and me.

I wonder if covering my entire body in a kraken could help me move past what I've done to Gideon. "The bracelet looks good on him, Em. But it's not hard to make Gideon look good."

He ends the hug and picks up the chocolate, breaking off the next messy square, eyes roaming over my face. "*You* look good on me. So if the boss man tries to send me away on a long job again, I'm going to go rogue and hold the Pentagon's entire network hostage until they understand *I'm* the one calling the shots." He places the chocolate in my mouth. "Or you can just start traveling with me. Your choice. I cause a crisis, or you sail into the sunset with me."

Gideon hasn't officially asked me to marry him. He hints at it, but I'm never certain if it's marriage or only the commitment of living together that he wants. If we live together in his apartment and I travel everywhere his job takes him, I think he'd be satisfied. I won't be happy, though. I like routine. Sameness. I'm not adventurous or daring, and a life of *excitement* doesn't appeal to me. I want simple. I want to wake up in my own bed each day, eat from my own bowls, drive my own car. I want to do a job that helps people, and until recently, I thought I was.

I meet Gideon's eyes. "When I get out of the hospital, we'll go to *our* apartment and talk about how to best keep you out of jail."

~33~

Darren

The hospital is busy today. It took some effort to get Lily moved into a private room, but her last name carries clout and I made sure everyone remembered who she is. She might be working like the rest of us, but Lily is out of all our leagues. Especially Gideon's.

"Emelia Alice!" I call her name when she exits Lily's room. I've been waiting for her so she can tell me what really happened between Gideon and Mikey.

She gives me a tight smile. "Already tired of my sister *and* her coworker?"

"I'm tired of your attitude so knock it off."

She stands unnecessarily close to me. "I'm not a child and I don't need to be coached in manners, I have them. Until some fool comes along leading my sister on while basically screwing another nurse right in front of her. Leave Jill alone."

I clamp down on the fury building in my stomach, not allowing it to billow up and out of my mouth. "Emelia Alice, I'm sorry for the way I treated your sister. I was wrong, and no amount of an apology can make

215

up for that—God knows I've apologized. But I *am* leaving her alone, and I'm not going to be continually berated by either of you. What's done is done."

Emelia Alice's shoulders lift. "Until Lily finds a new way to ruin my sister's life."

"Lily isn't out to get your sister so after you finish talking to me, go home and talk to Jill about how the two of you are going to stop bullying Lily."

"So sweet." Emelia Alice smirks. "We both know that if it weren't for Lily, my sister wouldn't be having any problems at all. Yet you protect Lily. Same as Gideon does. You remember him? Lily's boyfriend who she's moving in with? If he ran a clinic, I wonder which nurse he would choose? The cheating liar or the one who *hasn't* given a patient the wrong medication lately?"

Air sucks between my teeth but I smother the sound and school my features. "There's no reason to make snide remarks. One mistake with *one* patient doesn't make Lily a bad nurse, and the hospital didn't take any action against her so that tells you all you need to know."

Emelia Alice shifts away from me. "I implore you to remember who you were before you started spending time in Lily's bed because when she first made that *one* mistake, you were all up in arms over it. You also used to treat her like the black plague. And now that I've watched my sister's life fall apart from the moment Lily walked into it, I see why. But I suppose her bedroom skills have given you amnesia."

My jaw tics. "I don't appreciate your implications and Lily doesn't deserve them. I didn't about-face on how I feel about her. I turned away from how I was *treating* her. Not because of anything she did, but because of who she is. So get those facts straight in your head and then tell me if you witnessed Gideon having an issue with *any* of Lily's family members or not."

"Not." Emelia Alice folds her arms, matching my posture, eyes hardening with every word she speaks. "Why? Are you hoping they'll run Gideon off for you? Because he's young and you can't compete with him?"

I ignore her attempt to get a rise out of me. "Have you ever witnessed Gideon hurting Lily? Or did you hear anything this morning before she fell? Shouting or them arguing?"

"Ha," she blows out a satirical laugh. "Even Lily admits that Gideon is too good for her so if you think you're going to pin her accident on him, think again."

"Did it not strike you as odd that he didn't bother to wake up the nurse next door and instead made a big display of calling for an ambulance? So there would be a recorded call where he was shouting about how upset he was that Lily was bleeding out on the bathroom floor?"

Emelia Alice's head shakes. "Gideon has never so much as raised his voice to Lily, but she can't say the same. If either of them hit the other, it was *her* hitting him. And if I would have known what she was, I would have never let her inside my house. But she's good at fooling people." Emelia Alice drops her arms, the corner of her lip pulling upward. "Let Gideon know I'll be at home if he wants to drop by."

~

To my surprise, Gideon didn't put up a fight when he was told visiting hours were over. He stayed only thirty-nine seconds longer than he was told he could. I watched the clock like a hawk, listening to Dad telling me what he *wasn't* seeing in Lily's bloodwork results. I'm sure Dad came when he did only so he could keep me from physically removing Gideon.

I sit beside Lily's bed, holding her delicate hand and watching her sleep. I've tried to mostly stay out of her room, though I've not left the hospital since I came back from taking care of the cat issue. She's been friendly with Dad but has been cold to me. I understand why, but I still need this time with her. Time to be a man instead of a doctor.

"Hey," I whisper as her eyes flutter open, the swollen one still a narrow slit.

She licks her dry lips. "Hi."

I give her fingers a squeeze, my heart mimicking the motion. At least she's speaking to me. "Do you remember what happened?"

She looks around the room. "You've asked me that five times already and I've answered you. Where's Gideon?"

My muscles tense. "Gone home for the night. No one is here but the two of us. Okay? So you can say anything you weren't comfortable saying earlier."

Her eyes dip closed. "I don't have anything to say to you. Gideon was wrong to call you. Your dad is my doctor, not you."

My chest aches and I tighten my fingers, hoping she can feel how much I love her through this small bit of contact. "I'm not asking you to talk about us, Lily. About what our night together meant to you because I know what it meant to me and that's enough for now. While it's just the two of us here, I want you to walk me through how you hit your head."

Her chin moves down. "It isn't complicated. I fainted again. It was the same as before, a hollow feeling in my stomach and then the edges of my vision started going black. I reached for the sink, and the next thing I remember is Gideon yelling. I don't think I could understand him... Everything seemed so distant."

I rest my free hand along her cheek. "Before you got to the point of tunnel vision, what were you doing?" She looks away and a thousand scorpions spear me all at once. "I don't need details, Lily. I need to know if you and Gideon were okay? Or was he angry?"

She looks up at the ceiling, a tear sliding out of the corner of her eye. "I didn't tell him about us. And my betraying him is the farthest thing from his mind right now."

I wipe her tear, not sorry for being the other man but wishing I could take away the pain she's feeling. I move from the chair and settle beside her on the bed so I can see her whole face. "Do you swear to me that Gideon wasn't angry? He didn't hurt you? You fell because you passed out?"

She glares at me. "Glad to hear *I'm* not the only person you're determined to think the absolute worst of. I hate to have to pop your little fantasy all over again, but just like I didn't kill anyone, Gideon didn't hurt me."

I moisten my lips. "I understand your anger, but I have to ask these questions. Domestic abuse isn't uncommon and I have some concerns about what Gideon has been up to."

"Concerns that live only in your head, with no actual evidence of anything."

I run my thumb along the back of her hand. "Lily, prison hardens men."

Her eyes go wide, even the one that's swollen. "Gideon was in a tennis court prison for like a week! Then the government pulled him out and gave him a job. Other than that, he's a video game nerd, not a hardened criminal."

The way she's defending him makes my gut somersault. "Hardened or not, he could have still been angry that he flew around the world to find you not at home or work in the middle of the night."

"He wasn't," she grinds, yanking her hand free of mine. "You have nothing to gain by tearing Gideon down so just leave, Darren. Go home to Jill. And take your flowers with you."

I glance at the two flower arrangements on her tray table. One from Emelia Alice and the other I saw Gideon with. "I'm rusty at dating, Lily. I'm not sure I ever figured it out to begin with. When I was younger, I got more worked up over the latest scientific journal than I did girls. Until I fell for you, my idea of a good time was reading a book." I rest my hand on her wrist. "I thought seeing you be born was the most remarkable thing, and then we both grew up and now I know that moment was only remarkable because *you're* astonishing. And I'll fill this entire room with flowers for you. I haven't already brought you a bouquet because I didn't want to cause you any extra stress. But if you don't care that I write my love for you in flowers, then I'll do it. And I'll learn to be thoughtful and attentive in all the ways you want me to be. I just need to know that you do want me, Lily. Is there an *us*?"

Her throat bobs. "You kissed me after your dad told you that I might take over the clinic. Before that I was Satan incarnate to you. So you don't love me, I'm just a smart business decision for you. Your mom used to work the front desk in the clinic and I imagine you'd like to have a partner who works in the clinic with you too. But why not have her be a nurse?" She pulls her arm away and tucks it under the blanket so I can't touch her skin. "It's a good thing you have Jill now. She'll give you beautiful children."

"I don't want Jill, I want you. And I don't know why you're bringing up her name again. I went on *one* date with her, which ended in disaster because I saw you in the brewery and nearly smashed Gideon through the plate glass window. And the morning you saw me coming out of her room..." I rub my face. "You, Lily. I want *you*. No one else. Ever."

She huffs. "Then the next time you send Jill flowers, make sure her spiteful sister isn't going to steal them and rub my nose in the words on the card. You said you're going to love Jill in every season, so take your flowers back to her and get to doing that. Then never speak to me again."

A muscle spasms in my neck. I get off the bed and yank the vase from the table, petals scattering as I search them. "Where's the card?" She doesn't answer. "Where's the card, Lily? Because I didn't send these to *anyone* and if Emelia Alice told you I did, then I think she might be a sociopath."

Lily stares at me, vacant and hollow. I set the vase down. "I deserve your wrath, Lily. I've been slowly digging a hole for you to bury me in. But I wasn't doing it without cause. The problem is that all of my reasons weren't real. If you *haven't* been messing with me, then someone is messing with *us*. Does Emelia Alice have a cat?"

~34~

I'm already soaked in sweat and I imagine it's going to get worse before this conversation is over. I've detailed everything for Lily. Every cat, every mouse, how the smell of her was in my house directly after the hair on my neck told me someone was in the forest with me. I described the tool that busted my tire and the way my burrito went up in smoke. Now I'm leaning against her door, unease worming through my flesh. I asked the nurse not to disturb us tonight because as much as I don't want to add to Lily's stress, there's no turning back. We need to hash out the details of who is behind the dead animals because if it's Emelia Alice or Gideon, they're both too close to Lily.

I run my hands up my face and into my hair. "If not Emelia Alice, then who could it be, Lily?"

"I don't know, Darren," she nips. "Why don't you tell me since you seem to be so omniscient?"

Frustration tightens my muscles. "I'm not fabricating stories or pining to muddy up anyone's reputation. *Someone* is doing these things, though. And I can't go to the police yet because of that needle."

She tucks her hair behind her ear. "Yes, you can. Because I'm not the angel of death that you think I am. I didn't murder Freddie and then throw the evidence out my window. What you found is probably a needle from some drug user who got high there. I've seen people in the woods around the house, and we're tucked back away from the rest of the houses in the neighborhood, so drug users probably feel safe there."

"Exactly why I was concerned about your motives to be in that house. And upset when I found you out there wandering around in the middle of the night."

She glares at me. I run my hands down the dress slacks I'm still wearing, my undershirt tacky against my back as I shift forward and off the door. "Can you acknowledge the cloud of suspicion was valid? I mean, you even contacted Freddie's family to spout off about a theory before you had any way to know if it was true. That's way out of bounds."

"I called Freddie's brother to give the family my condolences. We discussed Freddie being diabetic and his carelessness with his medications. I suggested it could be insulin overdose and it was." Frustration rides her voice and a familiar pain shoots across my chest. "If you think the syringe has something to do with Freddie, then you should give it to the police when you call them. That's what normal people do when they suspect someone has been *murdered*."

I bite the inside of my cheek, nodding along with her because I deserve every bit of her rebuke. "The only thing worse than me believing you were capable of murder was my willingness to cover it up for you. At first, I told myself it was because you're a Beller. That even if you were guilty, your family would find a way to cover it up or have the charge reduced to something unfair. Then Freddie's family would have to live with knowing their loved one was ripped from them by someone who will never be properly punished. I imagine that would be more difficult than believing Freddie himself was responsible."

"Aw, you're such a saint," she derides.

I force myself to keep eye contact. "I'm a man, Lily. One capable of making mistakes and one who let his mind run amok instead of seeing that a *highly* trained nurse made an educated guess on a man's condition. It wasn't a leap I would have made so quickly, but that in no way should have led me to negate your level of intelligence on the matter. And it wouldn't have, without all the other strange occurrences. I still have no idea how matching damage was done to our vehicles without either of us hitting the other. Is there any way Emelia Alice could have driven your vehicle without you noticing?"

Lily turns her watery eyes from mine. "I don't sleep a lot so I doubt she would have chanced it."

I pace across the room, dreading her reaction to what needs to be asked. "Did Gideon have access?"

"Don't you dare," she hisses between clenched teeth. "You will *not* drag his name through the mud the way you insist on soiling mine."

I sit on the bed, stretching my hand out to rest on her leg. She recoils, a tremor underneath my palm when it finds its mark. I bring my hand back to my lap. "He was supposed to be gone longer, right?" She doesn't answer. I shift forward on the bed. "I'm not accusing anyone of anything, I'm only asking questions because you were right about this being serious. The cat in my mailbox is completely mutilated. Do you think there's any chance that Gideon never left? That he's been here spying on us the whole time? Or came back early?"

"No."

I swallow, holding back the hug I want to give her. She looks broken, and I'm the one who did this to her. "Are you hiding your relationship with him? Keeping it from your family?"

She laughs. Coldy. "You really do think I'm sinister, don't you?"

"I haven't seen your family anywhere near you and that's not the family I used to know. All of you were always in each other's business. Then Emelia Alice is saying Mikey stopped by and had an altercation with Gideon, but she's also saying it never happened because she's very likely out of her mind. But Gideon also basically threatened me when it came to notifying your family that you were in the hospital, so I can't pinpoint what the truth of the situation is. But you choosing to live in a questionable neighborhood would make better sense if it was only a place to be able to see Gideon without your family finding out."

She stares at the flowers. "I didn't create an elaborate scheme to hide him. Everyone knows I'm dating him, and they know it took him three months of calling me every day before I said yes to the first date." She looks at me. "Gideon is a good person, and that's why Mikey and Dani invited him to the party where Gideon and I reconnected to begin with.

He's their colleague of sorts, they call him when they need his particular set of skills, but his skills keep people on edge.

"Gideon did some things in high school that left a bad taste in Mikey's mouth, so he never fails to give Gideon a hard time. But there's no real hostility between them. And the choice to not tell my family I'm in the hospital is mine. Gideon is simply supporting my decisions. That's what a man who loves a woman does. He supports her. He doesn't tear her down and accuse her of murder."

My neck itches and my ears are hot, my mouth barely capable of forming words. "You're exactly right, and I'm sorry my suspicions have broken your heart. I can see on your face how badly I hurt you, and that's on top of the damage the fall did to you." I reach out and tuck that unruly strand of hair back behind her ear for her. "You deserve to have the galaxy prostrate at your feet and moving forward, I'm going to protect your heart and your body and the whole of you, Lily. I'm going to be here for you the way I always should have been."

Her eyes swim with tears. "You believed I killed Freddie. Not just for a fleeting second, Darren. You *believed* I murdered someone. And you think I intentionally administered the wrong medication to Mrs. Meadows. And that I mutilate cats."

I keep my voice low, hoping my tone will offer the comfort my words lack. "What I believed was that I couldn't reconcile the beautiful, smart, and soft-spoken Lily I love with the version that I felt like I was being forced to see. You know everything now, all of the crazy things that have been happening, and if you were behind any of it, then I figured my own heart was being used against me if I didn't suspect you. But deep down, I *knew* you didn't do it. That's why I was so willing to keep my mouth shut about it." Tears drip from her lashes and emotion clogs my throat. "Please forgive me, angel."

Her head shakes. "Stop calling me that. All we are to each other is two people who finally unleashed their pent-up lust. Now you can run off and call the cops, figure out who's stalking you, and I'll run off and move in with Gideon."

A bomb explodes in my chest. I slide down in the bed so that I'm face-to-face with her. "Our night together didn't unleash anything. It only got us started. Don't move in with him. Gideon isn't right for you, because *I* am."

Her eyes fill with tears. "Please stop saying that."

I rest my hand on her waist and she doesn't pull away, a small victory in a long line of suffering. "You have a concussion, so don't make any brash decisions right now. Because when you choose me over him, I don't want to have to go pick you up from his place."

She turns her face away but doesn't make me move. I gently lengthen my body alongside hers, stretching out on the bed and curling my arms around her. She settles against me with a choked sigh. I press a kiss to her shoulder; I don't need her to look at me, I only need her to hear me. "I wish I'd been smart enough to have faced your dad when you were sixteen, letting him know that I'd be waiting for you at midnight on your eighteenth birthday. He might have shot me or sent me to prison, but if I'd stood up for you then, I wouldn't be so close to losing you now." Heaviness builds in my chest. "I'm so sorry, Lily. For how I wasn't there for you today to keep you from falling, or from having to wonder where I stand because I'm too damn stupid to even bring you flowers. I'm sorry for all the days that have come before, when I was hiding from you instead of holding you. I shouldn't have ever let this chaos rage inside me for so long. I should have been figuring out how you feel and what you want, because you *are* my soulmate, Lily. And I think I somehow always knew that."

My heart thuds in time with hers, the quiet of the night settling thick around us.

"Darren," she whispers.

"Yes, angel?"

"What's wrong with me? Did you rerun the pregnancy test? Because this would be so much easier if I was pregnant with Gideon's baby."

~35~

Lily

Even though Gideon had tried, in my younger years I felt too awkward in my own skin to acknowledge anyone's romantic interest in me. The only time I ever felt comfortable in the presence of boys was when I was with Darren. But he wasn't a boy, he was a man. And maybe that's what comforted me. He wasn't immature and when he spoke to me, it wasn't to make silly jokes or quote lines from movies I'd never even heard of, let alone watched. When I was with Darren, I didn't feel like an outsider. I felt accepted.

Somehow, I twisted my comfort into a belief that Darren *liked* me. That's why I kissed him when I was sixteen. I let my stupid infatuation pluck up my nerve, sure the painful crush I had would bloom once I proved to him that I wasn't the child my years said I was. For a couple of minutes, I thought it worked. Then the horrified shock on his face crushed me.

Darren's actions in the years that followed were a knife in the chest. So it's ironic that he's now the one wanting me, and all I feel is horror. Horror that he actually believed me capable of killing people. That I slept with him. That his arms around me feel as good as they do. Is it because he's simply my childhood dream come true? Or because I really am his soulmate, the way my parents are soulmates, and Mikey and Dani, and my aunt Sheila and sweet uncle Avery.

"Good morning," Darren whispers into my hair. "How are you feeling?"

"Like it's time for you to get out of my bed. We've already created enough scandal and this is only fueling the fire. Jill and Gideon both are liable to hear about it."

Darren sits up on his elbow, looking down at me. I keep staring straight ahead. He traces the outline of my face. "Do you want me to call your parents? Your brother? They're the ones who are going to hear about you being in the hospital and go ballistic because no one called them."

"Don't call any of them, not even any of my cousins. When I get out of here, I'll explain to everyone what happened."

He checks my bandage. "Why don't you want to explain to them now?"

"Not because I'm hiding Gideon. Or trying to plot someone's murder."

Darren smiles. "Well, that's a relief."

I kick my heel into his leg. He chuckles. "You don't have to crack my shin, I'm just trying to make you smile because I feel like all we've done lately is argue. And yeah, most of it is my fault." He winces. "Okay, *all* of it is my fault."

I feign shock. "You're actually taking the blame for something?"

He grins. "I got to wake up next to you. Keep letting me do this and I'll take responsibility for every argument we have from this day forward."

I fight to keep the smile off my face, he sees it though. I point to the door. "Go. And do *not* call my family. They'll run back here in a panic for no reason, and ever since Grandma died last year, everyone's been really sad. They need this vacation and I don't want to ruin it." I swallow, lowering my hand. "If what's happening to you has anything at all to do with me, it will just remind them of how our family can't seem to get a break from all the bad things in life."

He cocks a brow. "Then let's hope Emelia Alice is only out to get me."

"Can you stop accusing people of crimes without having a single shred of evidence?"

He shrugs. "She's a liar, a manipulator, and she's being extremely mean to you. Unless you still think I sent those flowers to Jill?"

I let out my breath. "I don't know what to think about anything anymore, and I certainly can't condemn others when I'm lying to Gideon's face about what I was doing while he was gone."

Darren sits up and shifts his feet off the bed, cradling my hand in his and tracing over my knuckles. "I understand your confusion. I've been in a cloud of it, and because of the same reasons you're confused now. That's why us talking like this is so important. On my life, I'll *never* lie to you. You can search all my electronic devices, my house, access my financial records——anything you need to feel confident in me because you are rare, Lily. Beautiful. Delicate. *Strong*. Eaten up with intelligence and common sense alike. You're independent. And just the sort of woman who is put on this earth to bring all of mankind to their knees."

"Darren, stop..." I try to pull my hand away.

He holds it tighter. "I know I'm in the wrong here, angel. You have a boyfriend, and you're going through a lot of things between work and other relationships in your life. But I can't avoid what's going on between us."

He kisses my fingers and then releases them, standing and then turning to tuck the blanket around me. "I know you don't understand what's been going on inside my head because I don't understand it either. It's like I've been on edge and jumping off every cliff I come to just to see which fall was right. But once I realized that *if* you had actually murdered someone, I would still care about you to the point of covering up everything, it was like a weight lifted from my shoulders. Yeah, a different kind of weight settled on them then, because now I have to deal with the fact that I'd throw away my entire life and lose every drop of integrity I have just to ride through this life by your side, but at least I know that every leap I've ever taken has led me right back to you. I'll never spend another day denying that I love you. With you or not, in the same hemisphere as you or not, I love you, Lily Beller. You are my angel."

His lips brush mine and then he's gone, pausing at the table to take the flowers Emelia Alice brought. "I'll replace these for you. Maybe with a big bouquet of rare lilies."

"I don't want flowers."

He winks at me. "No flowers then, angel. I'll bring you something even better."

~

Darren

"What's got your lips all tied up to your cheeks?" Dad asks, brushing by me with a pat on the shoulder.

I give him a cheesy smile. "You, old man. It feels good to be working with you again. Even if it's here at Pemberton rather than the clinic."

"Uh-huh." He eyes my clothes. "Is that the same shirt you had on yesterday?"

I pull the collar up and dip my head, inhaling Lily's scent. Even though her wish to be pregnant with Gideon's baby left a thick coating on my skin, like I've been dipped in tar and rolled in thorns, she *isn't* pregnant. And if she really wanted to be, if she really wanted him over me, she wouldn't have let me hold her all night. "Lily slept pretty good, I stayed here with her to make sure."

Dad takes his glasses out of his pocket. "Does that mean you two have made amends?"

I shrug. "I'm not sure it's possible to make amends for the past, but I'm hopeful that she's going to let me try."

His smile widens. "Good. You'll need her as much as I have, so let's figure out what's going on with her."

I nod. "I'm hoping to have her scans back from the neurologist this afternoon, and I've already ordered more bloodwork and a kidney panel. I'd like to be able to give her some answers today because yesterday's results weren't helpful."

He looks over yesterday's bloodwork again. "Outside of her sodium being a little high, there's nothing standing out except the dehydration. One can lead to the other. I wonder why her sodium is spiked?"

"She drinks a lot of coffee. That could cause dehydration, and the caffeine could be the cause of the dizzy spells?"

He scratches his chin. "Could be. Especially coupled with the stress she's been under. The hollow feeling she described could be a blood pressure drop. Let's order some heart tests also, put her through the full workup so we don't miss anything."

I jot down the notes. "Nice to have a patient not restricted by an insurance company, isn't it?"

He chuckles. "Welcome back to my world, son. I can say I've thoroughly enjoyed not being restrained."

I swallow. "Would you really want me back at the clinic? After everything I've done and what's happening now with the dead cat that's *still* in my mailbox?"

He takes his glasses off. "Unless you killed that cat, it isn't your fault. Outside of that, I never wanted you to leave and I don't think Lily did either. Whether you two end up together or not, it would do my heart good to see you both working in the clinic again. I'll let the two of you decide if you want to share it, and if you do, I'll will half to each of you. Otherwise, it can go to one or the other of you." He tugs on the collar of my shirt. "You're going to have to talk to Daddy Beller, you know that, right?"

I pick up the books I bought for Lily in the gift shop. "I'm going to arrange a meeting with him just as soon as Lily tells me she wants to give us a shot. I'm also going to turn my old bedroom into a library for her, you know, to sweeten what I have to offer her because I can't figure out why else she likes me. She's smarter than me, prettier by far, and I can give her a comfortable life, but she can give herself a private island."

He chuckles. "Your mother was out of my league, too. But don't question the womenfolk, just do as they say and if Lily says she wants to be with you, son, thank all those gods you're convinced have cursed you, and say yes to that girl a thousand times over."

~

I stroll through Lily's door, keeping my eyes trained on her instead of Gideon in the chair pulled up right next to her. She looks my way and I meet her eyes. Green and sparkling, like pools of a tropical ocean set above high cheekbones and the most perfect button of a nose that's ever graced a face. I want to punish the sink that dared to not move out of the way of her fall. And the floor that was brazen enough to not be soft.

I lower the bed railing and sit next to her, holding out the books. "I have something better than flowers."

Her features still, the audible snort from Gideon followed by him shifting his weight on the chair. I place the books beside Lily. "These are the best of what the gift shop had to offer, but I'm going to run home in a little while and I'll bring you back some of my old medical school books."

"Good thing I cleaned off the bookshelves for you last night, babe." Gideon kicks his long legs out in front of him, hands tucked under his armpits. "Bring her all the books you like, Doc. If we end up not having room for them in our apartment, we'll just go ahead and upgrade to a house."

"The apartment will be fine," she responds.

I grow cold. "You've made your decision then?"

She places her hand atop the stack of books, sadness pulsing in the air around her. Or maybe that's my own sadness. Her frown deepens as she nods. "When I leave here, I'll go to Gideon's. I'll need to be discharged in the morning, too, before my family gets wind that I'm here."

Gideon leans forward, tucking his elbows onto his knees. "I'll send you Lily's new address for the house calls, but you might want to let your dad handle those."

~36~

Heart heavy, I walk through the halls of Pemberton. Gideon's been with Lily all day and after what happened in front of him this morning, I decided I couldn't have an audience the next time I spoke to her. I nearly cried, begged her to say she wasn't really going to choose him over me, but that would have only hurt her, and as badly as I hate that she could even consider moving in with him, I don't get to force her into telling Gideon she feels something for me.

Visiting hours are over and Gideon is gone now. Though I went home earlier, digging up the syringe and photographing the most recent cat's body before burying it like the others, I made sure to arrive back at the hospital in time to watch for Gideon's departure. I'm not sure what I'm going to do about the cats yet. If Lily isn't choosing me, now or at any point in the future, I welcome whatever malice the cat slayer is offering.

To know whether or not I need to sit out in the cold and wait for the darkness to come for me, I need to hear from Lily's own lips that there is no shred of hope for me.

Stepping into her dark room, I tread softly to the side of her bed and place two physiology books on the table. Her face is cast in shadows but I can still see the improvement. Her color is coming back and the swelling in her eye is down. Her EKG looks normal but because of the head injury, we have to wait for the stress test. If it proves to be like all the other testing we've done, the results are going to yield a whole lot of nothing.

I sit in the chair, leaning close to the bed so I can hear her breathing, letting the soft sound calm my anxiety. She's always been a night owl. I remember her parents talking to Dad about it because they were worried something was wrong with her. She couldn't have been more than seven at the time, and that I know of, she never outgrew a natural rhythm of being awake late into the night. At least I hope that's still the case, because I'd like to talk to her before she's discharged in the morning.

"What are you doing?" she whispers.

"Checking on you," I answer around the ball of emotion in my throat. "I didn't mean to wake you, but it's good to hear your voice."

She rolls onto her side, facing me. "I wasn't asleep. I was trying to decide if I wanted to acknowledge you."

I nod. "That's fair."

She sighs. "How did my last batch of bloodwork look?"

I move to the edge of the chair so I can see her eyes. "You're still not pregnant, your sodium level is back to normal, your kidneys are functioning normally, and everything looks good with your heart so far. I'm going to put you through some food allergy testing, and I'd like for you to stop drinking coffee altogether. There might be a mold or toxin in the beans that you're having a reaction to."

"Sleep more, and don't drink coffee. Two things it's hard to do."

I brush the hair from her cheek. "As best as we can tell right now, fatigue could be causing your problems. Especially when it's combined with the amount of stress you've been under lately. The studies on night shift laborers, many of them in the medical field, aren't good. Your health is impacted long term, and that could very well be what you're already seeing in your own body. And the caffeine consumption isn't helping the matter."

She frowns. "Gideon will be so upset if it's his fancy coffee making me faint."

"I think he's going to be a little more upset when you break up with him."

Silence spreads around us, my eyes on hers and hers on mine. I reach forward and place my hand overtop of hers, hoping the contact will remind her that she *does* feel something for me. "I don't have a right to say what I'm getting ready to say to you. And on my life, if you don't want me, I'll hear you and I'll leave you alone. But will you give me this one last chance to plead my case?"

Her eyes drop. "Darren..."

I slide a hand under her chin, my thumb caressing as I lift her eyes back to mine. "One of the things that made me hate having you at Pemberton was how, in all the noise of the hospital, I could always hear you. Like my ears were tuned to your channel above everyone else. You'd be two halls away and I swear I could hear you laugh. It made me angry, because someone else was making you happy. I don't want to sit on the sidelines anymore, Lily. I want to be the person who makes you laugh. The one who puts a smile on your face. Will you please give me a chance to be? A fair chance. If you have a boyfriend, that doesn't allow me to pursue you in any right way. And you moving in with him will outright stop all contact between us. Surely that isn't what you want."

Her lashes fall over her cheeks. "You knew I was with Gideon before you started all of this."

I slide my hand from her face and down to where I lace my fingers between hers. "I didn't know he existed when this all started for me, and from what you've said, you knew him but weren't interested. It was *me* you kissed back then. As much as I'm willing to go to prison for you, me giving in to any form of a relationship when you were sixteen would have been more harmful to you than us having that one gut-wrenching night. You deserved to be young, to grow up and enter adulthood without my shadow hanging over you. You deserved to have those moments with silly high school boys who ask you out in front of your brother's graduating class. It probably wouldn't have even been right for me to be on your doorstep at midnight on your eighteenth birthday." I rub my thumb along her skin. "I did wait too long, though. And the one thing it taught me is that running doesn't work. What's between us is here to stay, and now it's just a matter of us deciding how far and fast we want to take things. I'm all in. I'd marry you tonight if that's what you wanted. So if you said you'd move in with Gideon because you don't want to live with any of your family, you can stay with me. I can move into a guest room, move out... Dad would even let you stay with him. You have so many options, Lily, and all of them are better than moving in with Gideon."

Her chest rises and falls, a full breath passing before she answers. "In the morning, I'm going to Gideon's. I care about him, and he says all the same things you do. Only Gideon hasn't ever accused me of murder."

Waves of sorrow crash through my body, splintering bone. Tears slide down my cheeks. The things I can't take back are the ones that matter to her. I let go of her hand and lean back in the chair. "I understand. I do, Lily. I suck. But if you ever want to give me a chance to grow into a better man, I'll be here. No matter how many years pass, if you call me, I'll still be yours."

She sits up, tears in her own eyes. I hold up a hand. "I'm going to respect your choice, it just hurts like hell and I can't hold all this pain in anymore." I run my face over my sleeves, not even trying to stop crying now because I won't manage it tonight. "Before I go... The clinic is yours. You don't have to buy it, Dad will leave it to you in his will."

She moves to the edge of the bed. I stand in front of her, fingertips itching to touch her. "I'll stick around and work with Dad until you're better. And I can stay while you're in medical school if you want, and then I would probably have to go because whether it's Gideon or someone else, I can't watch you live your life with anyone else."

She presses a hand to my chest. I curl my palm over it and hold her tight one last time. "I'm sorry, Lily. I'm so sorry I didn't get this right, and I do hope someone else does. You deserve happiness."

She trembles, eyes filling with tears. I move closer and hold her against me, her tears soaking into the front of my shirt. She curls her fingers against my sides. "I don't want the clinic."

I bury my face in her hair. One last draw of the only air I want to breathe. "Don't give up on the dream you've always had, Lily. Take the clinic. It's where you belong. It's where you've always belonged."

Her face pulls from my chest and she pushes me back enough to look into my face. "Without you, I don't want the clinic."

I fist my hands in her hair. "Don't ask me to stay, angel. Because I will, and I don't know if I'll be able to remain professional." I press my lips to her forehead. "I can't separate the personal from the professional. How my heart feels about you is how it feels, no matter where we are. But don't hold that against Dad. He needs you now more than he ever did, and he'll never find a better nurse. A better *heir*. Take it, Lily. Take everything I've ever loved, including yourself, and live a life that will make the gods themselves jealous."

I step away but she tightens her hold on my shirt, the tails of it untucking from my slacks. Her chin lifts. "I love you, you idiot. And I don't know what to do about it because I care about Gideon, too. Every choice I make is wrong and..." Her chest heaves. "Stay, Darren. Tonight. At the clinic." She pulls me to her. "No matter what happens, don't ever disappear on me again."

I clench my teeth, fighting a battle I've already lost. Damned or blessed, I want this. I want her.

"Yes," she whispers. "The right answer is *yes*, Darren."

I lower my mouth to hers, the taste of her melting through my layers of sorrow. "Yes, Lily. *Yes*."

~37~

I lift off the chair beside Lily's bed and lean over her, placing a kiss against the corner of her mouth. I moved from her bed to the chair an hour ago, watching her sleep from here while I sorted through the many roads our future together can take. I don't want to be the man on the side, I want to be her man in a way that allows me to love her out in the open. But if the only option she ever gives me is this right here, stolen moments before she goes off to live her real life with someone else, I either choose to cope with it or lose her for good.

If she didn't want me, this would be an easy decision. I'd leave the state, maybe even the country, and let her live as happily as she can. But she said she loves me.

However I choose to handle this situation, I can't work out my frustrations in the gym. If I put on any more muscle, I'm not going to be able to move. I'm already outgrowing my clothes. The shoulder seam on my shirt ripped last night when I was lying beside Lily, her mouth on mine and her hand snaking up underneath my shirt, fingers working over each divot of my abs. It reminded me of how her lips had done the same thing when she was at my house. My muscles tensed with the memory, drawing a laugh from her when in the quiet, my shirt ripping sounded like the veil between worlds coming undone.

"Good morning," I whisper as Lily's eyes flutter open. "I'm going to take off before anyone finds me in here. I'll try to see you again before you leave."

She places her small hand in mine. "Don't. Gideon will be here and I can't stand seeing you two nip at each other."

A muscle in my neck spasms. "When will I get to see you again?"

She looks away and I take my hand from hers, letting it fall down my tired face. "I don't know what to do, but I do know that I can't share you, Lily. I might manage to for a little while, but I don't want to make you think I'll ever be okay with this."

She sits up. "I'm not asking you to share. I just need time with Gideon. When he left for Tokyo things were great between us, and as soon as he gets back I end up here. I need a chance to talk to him. And you need this time to talk to the police. No more putting it off. Go to the police. Today."

I trace the outline of her face. "I plan to. Then can I come to Gideon's to check on you?"

She ignores the question. "Before, when I was feeling sick for those couple of weeks, it felt different than any other illness I've had. Like something was seriously wrong. You're not hiding anything from me, are you? Am I dying?"

I grip her hands. "No. Absolutely not. We're going to figure this out *together*, and then you're going to have a long and wonderful life." I press my forehead to hers. "Preferably with me. Just say the word and I'll buy you a ring because I won't spend my life with anyone but you." I press my lips to hers, knowing that less is more in this situation. She needs time, and I need to get out of here before Gideon shows up. The image of them together is already burned into my retinas. "I love you, Lily. Now put on your grumpy face because it's morning and Gideon will be suspicious if you're happy." I give her another peck and leave, not meeting the eyes of anyone in the hall. If I'm going to keep from coming unhinged, I need to focus on something other than Lily leaving this hospital with Gideon.

~

I knock on Angela's office door. It's open so she sees me. "What can I do for you, Dr. Mansfield?"

I walk inside and close the door behind me. "The patient whose medication was mixed up, the one Lily Beller supposedly dosed wrong, has the hospital completed an investigation? I'm only asking because Lily says the medication was correct, and I believe her."

"Thank you for your opinion. Is that all?"

"No," I bristle. "The pregnancy allegation was false. Not that it should have any bearing on the situation even if it wasn't."

Angela leans back in her chair and folds her hands onto her stomach. "The hospital frowns on our staff moonlighting in other facilities the same as they frown on relationships between the staff. So Lily Beller being pregnant with your child while also being too tired to properly do her job here is absolutely relevant."

"Only if she made the mistake. Did she? Or was it Kassidy?"

Angela picks up her phone and sends a message, going back to whatever she was working on when I walked in. I lean onto the desk. "I was told that the pharmacy filled two orders for Mrs. Meadows and that somehow *both* were sent. That means Kassidy could have pulled the wrong one, and Lily the right one. Mrs. Meadows' reaction could have also been caused by something else, or maybe she's also allergic to Cipro and we're just finding out."

Keirstyn strolls in. "Mrs. Meadows isn't allergic to Cipro, and the reaction she had was caused by penicillin. Of *that* we're certain."

"Now are you satisfied?" Angela asks. "Or do you have more opinions you'd like us to hear?"

I massage the muscles at the base of my neck. "So the two of you think Lily administered the penicillin?"

"Neither of us said that," Keirstyn answers.

I wave a hand between them. "Angela calling you in here and the two of you closing ranks sure seems like you have a clear opinion." I meet Keirstyn's eyes. "And you knocked Lily out of the supervisory role so you hold a bias against her."

Keirstyn looks to Angela, who nods. "I heard that same rumor. It seems to have come from Kassidy. The nurse who says she *didn't* administer the wrong medication before Lily *didn't* administer it."

I pause. "You think Kassidy gave Mrs. Meadows the penicillin, and then said she didn't after Lily administered the Cipro."

Angela's shoulders lift. "No one knows where there's evidence either way. We only know that a mistake was made in pharmacy, both Cipro and penicillin being sent up."

Keirstyn frowns. "Kassidy accessed the med cabinet before Lily. Both of their codes are shown. So they both pulled something, and who got it wrong is anyone's guess at this point. The patient was asleep and her husband out of the room."

"That's convenient," I huff.

Angela nods. "We don't like to speculate, but if you have anything other than a...romantic reason to favor the word of one nurse over the other, please share it with Keirstyn. Otherwise, we remain dealing with the tale of two nurses. Or maybe there's a third party no one is looking at."

My teeth clench. "Any guess as to the identity of this speculative third party?"

She shrugs. "You're dating half of the staff, so I'd rather imagine you're more apt to have a guess."

Keirstyn waves me toward the door. "We don't need any more theories. What I've said, I'm certain of. And I wish Lily wasn't abandoning this ship because I could use a few more nurses like her."

I nod, reading between the lines to hear what she isn't saying. If she wants Lily to stay, Keirstyn believes Lily did her job correctly. "Lily Beller is remarkable. I'm glad to hear you acknowledge it."

I make it to the door. "Dr. Mansfield," Angela calls. "Lily is most certainly the better choice, but you may want to speak to Jill. She's as certain that Lily is in the wrong as Lily is certain that she checked the medication three times. Might Jill's contrary insistence have something to do with you?"

~

Bleary-eyed and still in yesterday's clothes, I approach Jill, cupping her elbow and pulling her away from the fishbowl. "What are you still doing here?"

She removes her elbow from my grip. "I'm covering a shift for someone because now that my roommate is bailing and you're not going to give me a job, I have to find different ways to come up with money."

"Lily isn't asking for her rent back so don't give me the *poor you doesn't have money* spiel. Why are you trying so hard to undermine Lily?"

Jill's cheeks flush. "Undermine her? I'm not the only person who has reservations about her."

"Who are these other people?" I question. "Kassidy? Emelia Alice? Neither of them are reliable sources."

Jill crosses her arms. "Have you forgotten your own words so quickly?"

"No," I growl. "I said things to you and you alone, when I thought you were actually scared of Lily. You intentionally spreading unfounded rumors isn't only careless and disrespectful to Lily, it's unprofessional. You keep telling me people are talking but I only hear *you* talking."

"Unprofessional?" She scoffs. "Have you looked in the mirror lately? Seriously, have you? You look like you haven't showered in days." She tugs on the sleeve that ripped last night. "Gideon doesn't even look this bad and that kid is downright devastated. Emelia Alice dropped Lily's car off at his apartment complex last night and he was in such bad shape, she ended up staying with him."

Rage coils through my veins. "Your sister spent the night with Gideon?"

Jill folds her arms. "It's no more sordid than you spending your night here. Emelia Alice was trying to help him. Isn't that what you're doing for Lily?"

"I have a feeling your sister doesn't do anything without the intention to help herself, and I suspect you're the same. So you heed my warning and pass it along to Emelia Alice. Tick off one Beller, and you go to war with all of them. And moving forward, you can consider me a Beller."

Jill's chin lifts. "I shouldn't be surprised. Isn't this how your dad built his business? Catering to the rich and kissing their tails? Like father, like son."

I give her a smile. "Thanks for the compliment. And remember, Lily might act like a passive ray of sunshine, but sun scorches. It sets wildfires that leave nothing but destruction in their wake."

~38~

True to his word, Gideon sent his address. I doubt he expected me to show up so soon after he arrived home with Lily, if ever at all. I didn't expect it myself. But Jill said something that I can't get out of my head. Emelia Alice *drove* Lily's car here.

I wait outside Gideon's door. He had to buzz me into the building so he knows I'm here. I knock again for good measure and try to not compare my dismal old house to the sleek newness of the building around me. The chrome and black accents are modern and I wouldn't be surprised if a secret panel opened up and a robotic maid stepped out.

Gideon opens the door and waves me inside, already walking away. "Lily's resting but I'm glad you're here, I need to ask you a few things."

I close the door and follow him to the curved bar on the left side of the enormous room. It's black leather with a dark wood top. "Can it wait until after I check on Lily?"

He thumps a tumbler on the bartop. "It's about Lily, so no. Want a drink?"

"No."

He fills his glass with amber liquid and throws it back, making a face as the liquor burns down his throat. "I don't normally drink, but this week I have a feeling I'm going to need to be plastered."

"Can't say I haven't been there myself."

He grunts. "You were sure drunk with Jill." He blows out his breath and puts the glass on the bar, extending his hands to grip the edges as he leans over it. "Look, I don't care what you do and who you do it with, as long as it isn't Lily. But that's not what I wanted to talk to you about. Since you're here, I guess you're Lily's doctor, and earlier, not long after we got home, she was sick again. And kind of talking out of her head."

I move to the bar. "Talking out of her head?"

His fingers drum over the bar. "It reminded me of just before I left for Tokyo. There was this day when Lily was doing weird stuff, like saying she was going to go wash the dishes when we'd just finished washing them together. And later that day she said she was going to make me something to eat because I had to be hungry, but I'd literally just eaten a sandwich right in front of her. She even watched me make it. At the time, it wasn't a red flag. She always has so much on her mind, trying to help everyone, so I just chalked it up to her being there physically but mentally somewhere else. That's part of who Lily is, you know, she's always processing something in that head of hers. But now I'm worried there's something seriously wrong." He straightens, rubbing a hand over his mouth. "I'm scared she's got a brain tumor. I've been doing some reading and her symptoms line up."

My jaw sets. "I had scans done and sent them to two different specialists. No tumors."

I fight the urge to scold him for using the internet as a doctor. "Did Lily have anything to eat or drink before she presented the confusion?"

He folds his arms over his chest and stares at a door that I assume is his bedroom. "She said she wasn't hungry, but she had some tea."

"Homebrewed?"

He nods. I scan the plants in the window behind the bar; I don't recognize any of them but something like belladonna could be used to make someone sick, and even cause mental impairment. "How'd you make the tea?"

He pulls a tin from below the bar and opens it, revealing an assortment of prepackaged teas. "Coffee I'm particular about, but I mainly have this tea because Lily drinks it. She brought most of this from her grandmother's place. You think it might be making her sick?"

I inspect a few of the packets. "Which one did she drink today?"

He bends back down and takes a pitcher out of an under-counter refrigerator. "Oolong is her favorite, but she likes it cold instead of hot, so I made this batch for her last night." He opens it and smells it. "I don't know, it all smells the same to me."

He slides it across the counter to me. I pick up the glass pitcher and scan the bottom. It's a little cloudy but that might be normal. I'm not asking him. "Mind if I take this and test it?"

He shrugs. "If you think the tea is poisoning Lily, then yeah, take it. I'm going back to Tokyo soon and I need her to be able to travel there with me, so throwing out bad tea is easy enough."

Addressing that comment will spark a storm no one is prepared for. I nod toward the door. "She's in that room?"

"Yeah, but..."

I ignore the rest of what he's saying and march to the door, slipping into the room and shutting the door behind me. He should take that hint and stay out.

Lily is sitting up in bed, shoulders slumped. "I thought I heard your voice out there."

"Right as always," I answer, eyes roaming over the large bed with the deep brown sheets. The clunky, dark wood furniture in the room screams man. Bachelor. Wealth. There isn't a takeout container or a sweaty gym sock anywhere. You'd think he was the doctor and I was the video game nerd turned government hacker.

"So?" Lily sighs. "Did something bad come up on one of my tests?"

"No, angel." I sit beside her even though I don't want to think about what they've done on this bed. "Everything I'm seeing looks fine, but Gideon said you had a bout of confusion earlier?"

She presses a hand to her stomach. "I haven't had much of an appetite today so that's probably all it is."

"You didn't say anything when I left you this morning."

The corner of her lip turns up. "I felt fine then. I didn't get nauseous until breakfast came. Gideon brought me some crackers and I've been sipping tea. They've both helped."

I pick up the cup from the nightstand. It still has the remnants of tea in the bottom. "Is today the first day you've had tea since being in the hospital?"

She thinks about it. "Maybe, I can't remember. Gideon will know for sure."

I set the mug down and shift my weight closer to her. "He knew you were having some sort of mental confusion but only just now told me the whole of it. Are you distracted, or do you feel like there's an issue? Be honest, Lily. It's important."

She wrings her hands together. "I don't know. Something feels wrong but I can't place what it is."

"Does it get worse after you drink the tea?"

Her eyes snap to mine, voice hushed. "Gideon is *not* poisoning me. What on earth is wrong with you, Darren?"

I tap my chest. "Lovesick. But that isn't what's wrong with you. Did you know Emelia Alice stayed here last night?"

Her face pales and I place my hand along her cheek. "That's not the worst of it. She drove your vehicle here. You didn't mention it so I assume she didn't ask?"

Lily swallows. "We're not exactly on speaking terms. I even asked Jill to leave when she stopped by my hospital room this morning. I want a clean break from both of them."

I slide my fingers from her cheek to her neck, fingers gliding underneath her hair. "I'm not sure about Jill's involvement, she seems unaware that anything is even happening, but Emelia Alice is behind at least some of what's been going on. If she helped herself to your vehicle this time, she might have done the same before. Maybe while you were sleeping. You don't sleep much but when you do, you fall out pretty hard."

She nods. "I've always been a heavy sleeper."

Luck favors the bold, so I ask what I came here to ask. "Would you consider staying with my dad until I have answers for you? Both about what's going on with you healthwise, and what's happening with the dead cats and Emelia Alice? I have a really bad feeling about you being here."

She rubs her arms, eyes tracking to the door. "My family is on their way. I called my parents right before I laid down so I'm sure they're scrambling jets and commandeering airspace as we speak. When they get here, I'll go home with them."

I lean closer. "Okay. But don't eat or drink anything unless you prepared it yourself. Or just order takeout."

"Darren——"

I press my lips to hers, cutting off her denial that Gideon is poisoning her. I don't think he is either, I think it's Emelia Alice. And she's using something that's flushing from Lily's system quickly enough that we're not finding markers that would lead us to theorize poison. And if we don't consider it as an option, we don't test for it. "On the chance that what's happening to your health is somehow connected to me, I need you to be extra vigilant. Once you're with your family, I won't worry so much but while you're here, watch what you eat and drink, keep your phone charged and next to you, and if Gideon lets Emelia Alice into this apartment, call the police."

Her head shakes. "Emelia Alice maybe stole my car and rammed into yours, but she wouldn't kill cats and there's no way she could stomach cutting one up. She gags over old coffee grounds, and there's a family of cats that she feeds..." Her voice trails off. "What did you say the dead cats looked like again?"

"Orange little tabby-colored things. The big one was a mother and had a white patch on her back that was almost in the shape of a dog."

Lily presses a hand to her mouth. "I forgot all about them. They've been staying in the woods behind the house."

Ice trickles through my veins. "Then we know it's Emelia Alice. I'll have the mailbox dusted and hopefully they'll find her fingerprints. Until then, stay away from her. And message me the instant your parents get here. I want to know you're safe." I press my lips to hers. "I love you."

~39~

Lily

Gideon sits on the edge of the bed, legs wide and shoulders slumped. "Do you want to tell me why Dr. Overstuffed thinks he can walk into my home and slam doors in my face?"

I slide forward. "Darren was wrong to do that. But he has some things going on right now and he isn't thinking clearly."

Gideon coughs out a breath. "I don't want to listen to you make excuses for him. I want to know what's going on between the two of you because ever since he showed up, you've been different. And he looks at you like he's starving and you're the buffet. Now he's acting like you're *his*, so just freaking tell me, Lily. Am I losing you?"

I clasp my hands together. "I don't know."

"You don't know?" He pushes off the bed and crosses the room, throwing open the lid of his suitcase. He digs through it, pulling out a ring box. He tosses it onto the bed. "I bought this for you before I left for Tokyo. Then I took a freaking helicopter out into the middle of the ocean so I could tell your dad I was going to ask you to marry me. Do you know what that was like for me? It was practically a tribunal. And the only reason your brother didn't tie me to the ship's anchor and let your uncle drown me was *you*. They knew that hurting me would hurt you, so we all aired our points of view and I left there feeling like I'd finally earned just a little bit of their respect. But you don't know if you even want to be with me? I should have just had them throw me overboard, Lily."

Tears well in my eyes. "Don't say that."

"Why not?" He scoffs. "You haven't even looked at the ring. I put so much thought into it and you don't care to even open the box."

"I do." I pick it up. "Gideon, I care so much about *you*. And I've thought so much about marrying you, what our life together would be like." Tears stream down my face. "I don't think I'll make you happy, though. I'll end up being a weight around your neck."

His eyes turn red with tears he's fighting. "I'm the judge of what makes me happy, and it's you, Lily. It's been *you*. All those times in high school when I'd work like heck just to get you to look up, and you'd reward me with a smile. Those were the best days, Lily. Of all the things I've done in life, the most satisfying is managing to make you smile."

"That's just it. You shouldn't have to work so hard to get my attention. But I'm not an engaging person, Gideon. I like to work and to read, and sometimes I take a walk but only when other people aren't around. I like being by myself. But you're outgoing and adventurous. You hang glide, drive fast, and never meet a stranger. I *love* your stories, all the things you find the time to do while you're out on a job, the mountains you've climbed, and the sights you've seen, but it's the *stories* I like. I don't want to experience those things myself. I'll listen to you talk about adventure, or I'll read about it, but I have no desire to do anything courageous. Sometimes I don't think I even have adrenalin. I just feel...plain. And I've always thought that once the excitement of being in our still fairly new relationship wore off, you'd find someone else because you're anything but plain."

He wipes his face. "So you thought you'd just soak up my time and manipulate my heart without ever telling me you weren't serious about me? You didn't think it was important to mention that you were just in this for a good time? For a short time?"

"I was serious. I *am* serious."

"No, I think you meant it the first way you said it. You *were* serious. Then Doc Muscles showed up and you decided you like him better so now you're spinning a story out of one of your books trying to act like you're my placeholder when really, while I've been falling in love and planning a life with you, you were just letting me keep his place warm."

He breaks for the door and I jump from the bed. He puts an arm out. "Don't. You need to be resting, and I need to go. I've got to get out of here, Lily. I can't be around you right now."

~

I haven't heard from Gideon in hours. He isn't answering his phone and the night is getting late. I take my keys from the nightstand, disappointed that Darren was right about my car being here. If Emelia Alice brought it, her motive was purely selfish.

I walk through the parking garage, hitting the lock button on my fob. The BMW's lights flash and I hurry across to where it's parked, sliding into the familiar seat and wondering where Gideon might be. There's an old arcade attached to a comic book store. It's closed at this hour, but he likes it there, and I have to look for him somewhere.

I turn out of the parking garage and drive slowly. I shouldn't be driving at all but I can't call anyone to have them help me look for the boyfriend whose heart I just broke. Or maybe I don't have a boyfriend anymore at all. My heart aches every time Darren walks away from me and steadies whenever he's near, but it beats for Gideon too and I don't want to lose having him in my life. If not as my partner, then as my friend.

Gideon isn't at the arcade and it's closed like I knew it would be. I travel past the building, swerving to the side of the road when my phone pings. It's a picture of Gideon lying in a bed, naked at least from the shoulders to the dip of his exposed hip. Even without the attached message, I know where he is. I recognize Emelia Alice's embroidered sheets. *I had so much fun searching for those hidden tattoos.*

~

"Gideon!" I barrel through the front door of Emelia Alice's house, Gideon's name ripping from my lips.

"Lily?" Jill gasps. She's standing in the kitchen wearing the oversized t-shirt she sleeps in, her hair a mess, and a spoon of peanut butter suspended halfway to her lips.

"Where's Gideon?"

She slowly lowers the spoon. "I don't know. I thought you moved out?"

I stomp toward the hallway that leads to the stairs. Jill moves around the island, reaching out as if she's going to touch me but falling short. "Are you okay? Do you need me to call someone for you?"

"I need you to keep your psychotic sister on a leash. She's taking advantage of Gideon and if Darren is right about her, she needs to be locked up."

This time Jill does grab me, her eyes moving up toward the ceiling as her voice lowers. "What has Emelia Alice done?"

I tug my arm free. "Right now, she's screwing my...Gideon."

I push past Jill but she grabs me again. "Wait, Lily. There's more, I can tell. What does Darren think Em has done? I need you to tell me because..." Her throat bobs. "Don't go up there, Lily. Emelia Alice has been violent in the past and if she's up there with Gideon, she's not going to like being interrupted."

"Isn't that what she did to you and Darren, though? Interrupted so he didn't have to make the mistake of sleeping with you." I clench my teeth. "Sorry, that was uncalled for. I'm mad at her and taking it out on you. But you've done plenty to me yourself, so let's call it even."

She removes her hand from my arm and moves aside. "Even."

I run up the stairs, through the jewelry studio, and into the bedroom. Gideon's body thrashes on the bed, the gag in his mouth muffling his shouts. I rush forward. "Hold on."

His eyes widen, screams becoming louder through the choking gag, his wrists bleeding as he yanks on the cuffs chaining him to the headboard. "Gideon!" I fumble with the strap that's holding the gag in place. He stretches his body forward as far as he can, red face screaming into mine. The wood he's cuffed to splinters. I yank on it, but it won't break further. I reach for the strap of the gag again. Pain slices through the back of my skull, teeth clanging together as my legs give out. I hit the floor.

Jill leans overtop of me, resting a baseball bat on her shoulder. "Now we're even. The rest is just for fun."

Jill holds a wide-bladed knife against Gideon's throat. "Get on the bed, Lily."

He bucks, tears running down his face. He wants me to run but the more he fights, the deeper the knife digs into his flesh. "Shh," I sob, climbing onto the bed next to him. "It's okay. Just stop fighting her."

"Aw." Jill walks around to where I'm kneeling, trying to find a way to comfort Gideon. She yanks my head back, my hair ripping from my scalp as she shoves me down into the sheets beside him. "It *will* be okay. For him. If you behave, little girl."

She zip ties my hands behind me and binds my feet with rope, flipping me over and ripping the bandage from my head. "This is going to hurt," she whispers, a wide smile on her face as she digs the end of her knife into my gash, splitting it wide open again.

Gideon kicks, choking on the gag, spit and vomit seeping from around it. Jill pushes the knife in deeper. I groan against the pain, trying to bite back my screams so Gideon doesn't have to hear the sound of my agony. "Close your eyes, Gideon," I plead. "Don't look. Just close your eyes."

He doesn't listen, fighting the restraints and watching every twitch of Jill's hand as she opens the wound wider. Deeper. The pain is too overwhelming. I can't bear it anymore. A scream rips from my throat. The headboard cracks, the force of Gideon's frenzy threatening to rip it apart.

"Stop it!" Jill yells at him, stomping around the bed and sticking a needle in his vein.

"Don't!" I scream.

Her eyes snap to mine. "Shut up. He's ruining everything with his stupid crying. Over *you*, the little tramp I should have killed weeks ago."

Gideon stops sobbing, face slowly going still as all the movement drains from his body. Even the rise of his chest. Jill presses the tip of her knife into his cheek. There's no response from Gideon. She smiles brightly. "That's better. Now I can work without him interrupting us. So sit tight, okay? I want to film this. For posterity." She walks toward the door and looks over her shoulder at me. "One day, Darren will get to watch you die. So practice screaming for me, Lily. He's going to love that part."

~

I turn my wrists, palms facing one another as I shimmy my thumb under the band of the zip tie just the way my sister-in-law showed me. Dani will be upset if I can't manage to get free of these, and if I can't, I won't even be around to hear about it.

The skin around my wrists is slick with blood. Gideon's are worse, raw and bleeding from his metal restraints. I don't know any tricks to get him out of the handcuffs. If he was awake, I could try to get him to do what I'm doing. "Gideon," I whisper, dislocating my thumb. I swallow the pain. It's not as bad as the knife wound, and there's no chance I'm giving Jill what she wants. I'm not going to scream for her.

I contort my thumb and drag it under the plastic band, freeing it first. My other fingers slide loose, skin scraping from my knuckles. I lunge across the bed, checking for Gideon's pulse. He has one. It's weak, but there. "Thank God."

I work the strap on his gag loose, pulling the ball from his mouth and wiping my fingers inside to clear his mouth of the vomit so he doesn't choke on it. I stuff a pillow behind his head to keep it tilted to the side then check the headboard. The wood is broken, but down below the crossbeam instead of along the thick post he's cuffed to. I can't free him. And I don't know what I'd do with him if I could. I can't carry his weight.

I press a kiss to his cheek. "Hang on, I'm going to get you help."

I drag my knees to my chest, willing my nerves to calm as I tug at the knot in the rope around my ankles. It loosens enough that I'm able to pull one foot free. That's good enough.

I search the room, Gideon's discarded clothing is in a pile in the corner. I check his pockets. He never goes anywhere without at least one phone and usually he has more than one, but there's nothing here. No phone, no tablet, no computer, nothing. The whole room has been cleared of anything I could use to call for help.

I check his pulse once more, kicking the remaining rope from my legs. "Please hold on, Gideon. I'm going to get you out of here."

I force my shaking legs forward, leaving him on the bed as I tiptoe to the stairs. Jill is whistling. I can't be fully sure, but I think she's in her bedroom. I wipe the thick blood from my brow and walk softly down each step. At the bottom, my weight lands on the last step and it squeaks. I freeze. Jill's merry tune doesn't change.

I ease off the step, my feet hitting the cool wood flooring. I walk softly. Quietly. Moving at a snail's pace as I round the corner and enter the kitchen. If Jill comes to her open door, she'll see me.

I search the kitchen for a phone. Any phone. Gideon must have come here with one in his pocket, but where would Jill hide it?

I slide open the catch-all drawer. There are bread ties, spare lids, pens, notepads, and two packets of yeast. I gently close the drawer, a smear of my blood left on the front of it. The door on the front of the house swings open. Emelia Alice pops around it, face draining of all its color when she sees me. "Lily! What happened to you?"

Jill's whistling stops. I don't wait to see if she's coming, I already know. I force my unsteady legs into a run, pressing my hand to the glass of the back door as I throw it open.

"Get her, Em!" Jill screeches. I keep running. Straight for the tree line.

The snow is cold on my feet but reflects the light of the moon so I can see where I'm going. That means the twins can see, too. I run for the darkness, praying the shadows will hide me.

"Lily!" Emelia Alice calls. "You can barely stand up! Come back to where it's warm!"

I fall to my knees, crawling around a thick log and shuffling up under the branches of a nearby pine. She's right. I can't outrun them. My feet are already numb and my tracks in the snow are clear. They'll lead the twins right to me. If I die out here, no one can help Gideon.

I press my knees into the soft blanket of pine needles and lift the boughs of the tree on the opposite side of where I entered. The night is deceivingly quiet. I know the twins are out there, tracking me. I can't make it to the houses on the other side of the wood. My only chance is to double back. To my car. My phone is there.

"Lily," Emelia Alice calls from behind me. I scramble out from under the tree and run, her voice growing distant. "Wait! Lily! Come back!"

Freddie's house is on my right. Still empty. The landlord hasn't found a new tenant yet and it's the only house closer than my car. I run toward it, sprinting to the back door. It's locked. And Emelia Alice is behind me again. "Stop right there, Lily!"

I dart left and run as hard as I can for the BMW. My head throbs, vision blurry. I scream out in anger, rage chasing the fear away as I force my legs to move. "This is for Gideon!" I shout, falling against my door, fingers working to get it open as the snow behind me crunches. I'm out of time.

I whip my face around. Jill's ice-blue eyes stare into mine. A smile curves her lips. "Boo."

$$\sim 41 \sim$$

"Wake up, little mouse," Jill sings, the sting of her palm sharp against my cheek.

"That's enough," Emelia Alice snaps. My eyes flutter open. I'm back in the room with Gideon. He's gagged again, still bound, and his eyes are closed though his chest is rising with a vigor it didn't have earlier. I look around. Emelia Alice is cowered against the wall behind her sister.

Jill slides her knife along the outline of my face, the tip carving a superficial wound until she jabs it deeper where my jawbones meet. I scream. Her eyes glitter. "I love that sound."

Emelia Alice moves forward. "Stop, Jill. You promised you wouldn't kill anyone ever again."

Jill shrugs. "That was before."

Emelia Alice throws up her hands. "Before what? I told you that if you wanted to punish Darren, I'd help you. But not like this. Look at what you're doing. This is insane!"

"But you drugging them isn't?" Jill snaps. "Why don't you ask Lily how she liked her tea. Or walk her through how you laced the studs on the earrings you gave her." Jill looks at me. "All that vomiting, you can thank my sister. She's a master with poison. Just ask our parents. Oops, you can't. They're dead."

"Because you used too much selenium," Emelia Alice defends. "You said you wanted to make them sick so we could go to that stupid concert while they were in bed, but instead you killed them!"

Jill rolls her eyes, talking to me while she waves her knife back and forth, as if she's checking my vision and expecting me to follow the knife. "Em has always been dramatic. We went to the concert *and* she lost her virginity that night. Instead of saying thank you, she cried for a month. Because of the dead parents, not because of the deadbeat boy who never called her after he got into her pants."

Emelia Alice sits on the bed, resting her hand on Gideon's bare leg. "Just because a male doesn't do what you want him to do, it doesn't mean he deserves to die. You can't kill everyone who makes you angry."

Jill throws her head back in laughter. "Says the twin who killed first! What was it that Abagail did to make you angry? Refused to share her doll?"

Em's face hardens. "I was seven, and I didn't realize when I pushed her that she'd lose her balance and fall out of the treehouse."

"But she did. And I was there to help her." Jill runs the knife down my arm and over my hand, smiling again when she goes deep enough to make me scream. "That's when I first knew I wanted to be a nurse. I watched the life drain out of Abagail's eyes and it was...beautiful. I'm going to make you beautiful, Lily."

"Stop!" Emelia Alice yanks Jill's knife-wielding hand away from me. "What do you think is going to happen when her family comes looking? You can't murder two people in *our* house. Lily's already bled too much, I'll never be able to explain this away." Tears fill her eyes. "You promised. This house was supposed to be our fresh start. Our new lives. But...did you kill Freddie?"

Jill places the knife on the dresser. "Of course I did. But Lily almost ruined it. Just thirty seconds more and she would have caught me leaving his house. But she's a good little mouse, she stayed in her hole until it was time."

"Why?" Emelia Alice sobs. "Why did you kill him? I liked him and he liked me. And after you got Darren we would have had what we always said. A house for the four of us."

Jill opens the top drawer of the dresser. "Freddie was always watching. So how could I do all of this with him next door?" She turns, a gun in her hand. "You're a good sister, Emelia Alice. So helpful. Loyal. And I don't want you to worry about me. I'm going to be fine. I've already started grooming Kassidy and she's going to be an excellent replacement for you." Jill's face scrunches. "I'm going to do this when the police get here. It's good, right? I've been practicing my faces, so the police will see Lily's blood everywhere and find me aghast at what you've done."

"What I've done?" Emelia Alice balks.

Jill nods. "Darren will be here by then, and we'll hold and comfort each other, thankful that we weren't part of your murder plot." A shimmer of a tear fills the corner of Jill's eye. "I'm never going to get over your suicide, Em. But I understand why you can't live with yourself after murdering this sweet couple." Jill pulls the trigger. Blood splatters across Gideon's body as Emelia Alice slumps over him. Jill turns the gun on me. "Your little run cost us precious time, but not to worry, after you and Gideon are dead, I'll continue to cut you into chunks until Darren arrives. And every time he makes love to me, I'll be thinking about you."

~

Darren

Jill insists that I meet her before Emelia Alice is out of bed for the day. I'm to pick up the rest of Lily's belongings because Emelia Alice is threatening to set fire to them and Jill is worried her sister really will. While the items are still in Lily's room.

I pull onto the street in front of the Tudor house because the driveway is already full. Lily and Gideon must have received the same message from Jill that I did, but I told Lily to stay away from Emelia Alice so I don't know why she's here. I don't know why she didn't ride with Gideon.

I walk by Lily's car on my way to the door. There are streaks on the driver's side glass. I scratch the frozen red lines with my thumbnail, eyes dropping to the muddy snow. There's more frozen red liquid, and the impression of bare feet. I run my hand over the glass, fitting the tips of my fingers at the top of the smear and dragging them downward. A perfect match for the swipe of a bloody hand.

I break for the house, hitting the door with my shoulder and working the locked knob. "Lily!" I shout. "Lily!"

The door doesn't budge. I slam my shoulder into it harder. The jamb around the deadbolt cracks. A scream comes from inside. I bite down and ram my shoulder into the door, splintering the jamb and shoving down the door. Jill runs around the corner, tears streaming down her face. "Help me! Help!"

I catch her, pulling her against me as I look around. "Where's Lily?"

"Upstairs," Jill sobs, pulling her face from my chest. "You weren't supposed to be here so soon."

My tongue trips over itself. "What? When did Lily get here? Is your sister upstairs?"

"I'm right here." Emelia Alice pulls herself to the corner of the hallway, leaning heavily on the wall, one foot dragging behind her. Her chest is an explosion of crimson, the crevices between her teeth washed in red. She sputters, blood bubbling out of her mouth. She raises her gun. I shove Jill behind me and hold up my hands. "Put the gun down, Emelia Alice. You need medical assistance and I can help you. So can your sister."

"No," Emelia Alice cries. "No!"

I feel the pain a split second before I hear the gunshot. A stab in my side. But the muscle is so thick the knife doesn't go deep, Jill isn't strong enough to sink the blade where she intends it to go. I spin away. Emelia Alice takes another shot, this one hitting its mark. Jill's body crashes to the floor at my feet. I whip my head toward Emelia Alice. She sinks to the floor, holding her chest. "Go. Lily is upstairs and she needs help." I walk toward her, eyes on the gun. Emelia Alice shakes her head. "Tell Lily I'm sorry."

Her words stoke my fear and I run for the stairs, jumping them three at a time and screaming Lily's name. Another gunshot rings out, followed closely by a second.

~42~

I was right about getting a pet. The cat Lily and I adopted from the shelter is a good addition to our home. So are the two dogs. The dogs are more for my peace of mind, like the added security system, but with Emelia Alice placing that second bullet directly into Jill's skull and then taking her own life, I'm hoping all of my security measures are unwarranted. Just like I hope Gideon is finding peace wherever he is. We've attempted to reach out to him over the years but he has no interest in speaking to Lily, and he hasn't acknowledged me since he was released from the hospital and realized that I wasn't a permanent fixture in Lily's hospital room simply because I love her, but because she loves me.

"What's got your lips all tied up to your cheeks, old man?" I ask as Dad approaches the new grill on the new deck Lily suggested we add to the house. I built it with a covered reading nook for us on one side, and she added a two-person hammock to the other.

"I'm just happy to see you finally fixing this old place up," Dad answers. "It looks nice."

I admire the work Lily and I have done. "It would've cost less and been easier to just build a new house, but I let Lily decide and this is what she wanted."

He grins. "Smart girl. And I see the in-laws are still talking to you after two years of marriage, so I guess my son is just as smart as his wife."

I scan the yard where a full family of Bellers are gathered. We invited everyone over for a housewarming of sorts. Lily moved in with me six months after the twins were buried. We married eight months after that, and I've thanked those gods in the sky for her every day since. I wipe a hand across my eyes. I get choked up watching the dream I always had play out before my eyes. "Life is good, Dad. Better than this man deserves."

He pats my shoulder. "You always deserved it, you just had to face it, son. That's the hard part."

He chuckles when one of the dogs steals a burger from the tray Lily just placed on the table. Instead of being angry, she laughs and gives the other dog a burger. "Those animals had me worried but they seem to be good additions to the family. That cat is pregnant, though."

"So is Lily."

I whisper the words, waiting for them to sink in. Dad's mouth falls open. I grin. "That's really why we invited everyone over. We're going to make the announcement today." His eyes fill with tears and I wipe my own again. "Don't start that or she'll be mad at me for blowing the surprise."

He looks up at the sky with a smile on his face and I know he's letting his heart communicate the news to Mom, the same way I did when Lily placed my old baby shoes on our bed and asked if I thought our baby's feet would be as big as mine.

I rest my hand on his old face. "What do you think, Dad, are you ready to deliver your first grandchild?"

A Note From The Author

"The end is never the end. It's always the beginning of something." ~ *Kate Lord Brown*

Thank you for reading *Marked By Forever* – the final book in the Beller Ties set. I hope you enjoyed the Beller family's journey to happily ever after. It was a complicated one, and I personally struggled with writing this last story. I didn't want to see it end. But what started with John and Mary all the way back in *Something So Beautiful*, truly has blossomed. You'll see these characters again, if only in passing——or in the whisper of a grandchild.

UP NEXT – Book 2 of the Hinton Thriller Series! ***Smother***, releases Halloween Day 2022. Start the series now with ***Descend*** ~ the thriller book readers are calling dark, disturbing, and **fantastic**!

https://leedawnabooks.com

For early release news on these and other future books, join my **newsletter** here:

https://mailchi.mp/c9aefdb4dab7/leedawna-books

Subscribe to my **YouTube** channel here:

https://www.youtube.com/channel/UCqtexMzJf8BZ0QsrxtZzrsQ

Connect with me on:
Instagram @LeeDawna_author
Twitter @LeeDawna_author
Facebook @LeeDawnaBooks

As always, I owe my deepest gratitude to my husband. His blind faith astonishes me every day, and his unwavering support is something I'm certain I don't deserve. I love you, handsome. Always.

My son is a continual source of inspiration and this year he made me a mother-in-law, a privilege I've been waiting for and a joy that's already filled my cup to overflowing. I love my son and new daughter, and I wish for their love story to be the greatest ever told.

Without my editor, nothing I write would make any sense. Thank you, Anita. If you read this section and there are grammatical mistakes, it's because I didn't send this part to Proof Positive. Mistakes within the manuscript are all mine, too. Sometimes I accidentally reject corrections instead of accepting them.

You, my dear reader, are appreciated. I'm honored that you took your time to read my book. May you be blessed with a lifetime of finding those gems that keep you up at night because turning the page becomes more important than sleeping.

About The Author

Lee Dawna is a thriller, suspense, and romance author living in the rolling mountains of West Virginia. An avid traveler and outdoorswoman, you may bump into her along a remote trail where a meandering stream whispers her next story.

https://leedawnabooks.com
leedawnabooks@gmail.com

www.ingramcontent.com/pod-product-compliance
Lightning Source LLC
Chambersburg PA
CBHW050832190726
48286CB00007B/2064